Once Removed

To Evelyn —
A memorable evening in Paris!
Best — D. Applefield
PARIS Oct. 99

Once Removed

by
David Applefield

Mosaic Press
Oakville, ON. — Buffalo, N.Y.

Canadian Cataloguing in Publication Data

Applefeild, David
Once removed
ISBN 0-88962-622-7 PB
ISBN 0-88962-623-5 HC
I. Title.
PS3551.P65063 1997 813'.54 C96-93076-5

Published by MOSAIC PRESS, P.O. Box 1032, Oakville, Ontario, L6J 5E9, Canada. Offices and warehouse at 1252 Speers Road, Units #1&2, Oakville, Ontario, L6L 5N9, Canada and Mosaic Press, 85 River Rock Drive, Suite 202, Buffalo, N.Y., 14207, USA.

MOSAIC PRESS, in Canada:	**MOSAIC PRESS**, in the USA:
1252 Speers Road, Units #1&2,	85 River Rock Drive, Suite 202,
Oakville, Ontario, L6L 5N9	Buffalo, N.Y., 14207
Phone / Fax: (905) 825-2130	Phone / Fax: 1-800-387-8992
E-mail:	E-mail:
cp507@freenet.toronto.on.ca	cp507@freenet.toronto.on.ca

Mosaic Press acknowledges the assistance of the Canada Council, the Ontario Arts Council and the Dept. of Canadian Heritage, Government of Canada, for their support of our publishing programme.

First Printing, 1996
Second Printing, 1997
Copyright © David Applefield, 1997
ISBN 0-88962-622-7 PB
ISBN 0-88962-623-5 HC
Cover Design by: Eric Walker
Book design by: Susan Parker
Printed and bound in Canada

for Alexander Singer
(1904-78)

Gustawa Krystyina Janet
Singer Applefield

&

all those who need to be remembered

What can I do to preserve my past?

— Young man, where were you born?

Elizabeth, New Jersey.

— Then your roots are in Elizabeth. Write about New Jersey; you can never know the *shtetl.*

from a conversation with Isaac Bachevis Singer, 1977

Prologue

Houston: Seventeen Days

There was something evil about his life ending in Houston — in the soothing tangle of mankind's best machines and research. The city air was still and the sunlight hung onto the petro-dust that floated above the grid of downtown. It wasn't difficult to imagine the barren landscape of cracked earth and chalky dust from which the skyscrapers and boulevards, modern factories and hospitals had sprouted. It seemed as if the entire place had been wheeled-in and setup like a moving carnival, plugged into some high-voltage power source, kicking up dust and fast food establishments, immigrant communities, campaign headquarters, and advanced medical institutions in the same geo-ethnic surge. Manned instantly with hoards of Chicanos, uprooted Asians, and packs of the new Americans, Russian heart surgeons were assembling Whoppers, East German gymnasts telemarketed New Age skin products, Cuban brick layers and sculptors were stocking the salad bars at the community college dining facilities.... And the rich, riotous grandeur of the outcrop tempted wealthy Kuwaitis and oil executives with its spanking new business hotels, special discounts, and prestigious cardiovascular clinics. Both oil and blood pumped through the shallow plumbing of the city. In time, it'd all be knocked down, disconnected and sent barreling down a sixteen-lane superhighway marked with a red flag reading CAUTION WIDE URBAN LOAD, only to be sold-off first as a tourist trap to a nation whose wealth and influence has yet to be suspected, and then to one of the new World Order Federation clusters as a ready-made gift-in-kind from the Old World. Remarkably obsolete, a whole city: Houston. The place had nothing to do with his life.

"No time to be sorry for roses
when the forests are burning."

- a Polish poet

1

Buried deep in the maze of the Medical Center, far from the dusty and sandy light of the afternoon, Jacob Simon lay half alive amidst a bank of machinery that monitored his vital organs. The air in there was cool and private like in the shady zones away from highlighted gaming tables in casinos, except drier and smokeless and less human. The hospital personnel in green and white wove busily amongst the network of equipment, strangely mimicking with their sheer movement the flow of fluids in the tangled tubes and wires. Up and out, back and around, they were functions. It was difficult imagining them stepping out from that rhythm at some designated break, joining the world for a tuna sandwich on thinly-sliced, high-fiber wheat bread and a diet cola, let alone finding at the end of the day a Mazda or Saturn several levels below, a route to an apartment, a bed — made or unmade — a tv movie on cable. They seemed as intricately woven into the design as the life-supporting paraphernalia and the patients. There was a persistent hum in the unit and a terrorizing smell of something overly efficient and clean. Somewhere someone was in charge with an impressive computer and a river of information and a lobbyist in Washington.

Dr. Fraser, the renal specialist, scanned with Visine-deficient eyes the monitor at the foot of Jacob's bed. There was only one set of numbers that he cared about; it alone made a difference to him. Behind it stood all those years of ferocious professional training. All the stress that rode in the flesh around his eyes rested on his knowledge of those numbers and the judgment they obliged him to make. "That's what I'm paid for," he told the audience at aconference in Aspen on Medical Ethics in the 21st Century. They weren't the ones the cardiologist watched. He spoke to Jacob's unconscious body in a loud voice as if it too made a difference. Even coma patients needed to hear you. It was a professional touch without any doubt, like the way a real chef singed the pin feathers off fowl or tested a sauce with the sweep of two fingers. But privately, over a few, limed Coronas in the presence of non-medical friends, Fraser would have chipped-in that not even he knew where patients like Jacob Simon really were, what was left of their humanity. "Shit, how are we supposed to know, and the god damn families press the hell out of us to know what's on the far side of Jupiter. No one really knows. This is tricky stuff." He wasn't wrong, but....

The numbers weren't good. Jacob's daughter, Jane, later implored Fraser for an indication. He translated science for her into, "He's a very sick man," replying with the look of regret bunched up around those baggy eyes. Fraser was thirty-eight and owned a sailboat. He had dropped LSD a half-dozen times as an undergraduate when college was relevant and it was fun to watch purple trees do cartwheels. At Med School he did a residence stint in rural Jamaica, nurtured his love of guacamole and swallowed oceans of Kenyan coffee. Now, in full competence, Fraser had no way of knowing that this wasn't the first time that Jacob

Simon's weight had plummeted to 110 pounds. Nor that the organs he was now treating had already been severely stressed once, and for a period of over four years, permanently weakened by the toxicity of extraordinary physiological and mental fatigue. It wasn't that he wasn't interested or lacked sensitivity; it just wasn't the sort of history they recorded on medical charts. "We can't do everything." He'd stress the initial diphthong, a little speech gizmo that he'd picked up unknowingly from some popular character on one of those sitcoms that even intellectuals watched to kill time or to unwind. It wasn't part of the equation. It didn't figure in the numbers to be examined, or calculated in the infamous success rate statistic, the win-loss column of laser-jet ink running up the perforated pages. He noted on the screen that he'd been to Jacob's side, activating automatically eleven sets of records, among other things a notation on the billing computer. He touched Jacob's bone-white foot as one would pet a quiet dog and glided in his silent, $400 — "why not, we're on our feet all day" — shoes back into the cool anonymity of the Intensive Care Unit. The Padres were playing that night at the Astrodome; an orthopedics intern had offered free tickets — box seats on the third base side — to a nurse he counted on sleeping with before Christmas. Juan Gomez, the young Astro pitcher who had signed for nine million, was home taking a nap in his sunken Jacuzzi, dreaming of the value of his own baseball card. Andso on.

Upstairs, somewhere on the expansive Bradford Wing, in his empty, windowed room, Jacob's suitcase rested shut, replete with the stickers from former vacations, including the three-week cruise on the SS. Shalom. His shaving kit sat at the edge of the polished sink, his slippers were neatly arranged at the edge of the bed. On the night stand, below the Living Section of the *Saturday Houston*

11

Post, the Arts and Leisure Section of *The New York Times,* and a month-old edition of *The Jewish News,* which he'd brought with him, his marble-covered ledger book rested. Sam Halberstam had been named New Jersey chapter president of the B'nai Brith. The cities of Frankfurt and Tel Aviv had signed a sisterhood pack, pledging cultural and economic exchange in the years to come. He'd left a ballpoint pen stuck in the page of his last entry, a lavender plastic give-away from a paint company. Although he had already spanned once the course of his life, skimming off the things that had first come to mind and the details that had never drifted far from the surface, there was more to be added. There seemed always to be more; memory could not be emptied out. It grew faster than it could be used up. "How do you write your autobiography?" he had asked his barber, a little guy named Vinnie who shrugged his shoulders and answered, "Why you ask me?" He had intended quite calmly to pick up where he'd left off and finish it in Houston. Recording one's lifetime memoirs hadn't been an easy matter, Jacob had learned privately night by night over the span of the hundred or so pages he had penned.

The hospital visit hadn't seemed to frighten him much, but then, who knew what frightened him? He approached it like a weekend trip to the Catskills or a trip across town for a gallon of paint. It was booked and it had to be done and so he'd do it. He'd been away from home many times and proceeded now as if this too were just another errand, not a severe cardiac procedure, open heart surgery, despite the fact that he hadn't been a hospital patient since early 1948 when Dr. Stern in Elizabeth General — where Benjamin, his first grandchild, Jane's son, would be born on a brilliant Sunday morning — removed the mangled bullet from his left cheekbone, "a souvenir," he called it, although he had never dreamed of keeping it like a model of the Empire State Building. An orderly had taken it home and stashed it in a drawer for years before finally throwing away the twisted little mass of metal, Darmstadt once engraved on the slim barrel. The fact that the operation was quite serious in a man his age didn't scarehim anymore than a television commercial for the American Heart and Lung Association scared chain smokers. It wasn't that he repressed his fear, his hormones simply didn't respond muchanymore when it came to his own well being. Should his grandson dart out across a busy street ducts would be secreting like a pump and his heart would race, but his own life, that was another story.

The night before they sawed open his chest, he replayed random details from his life as he watched vaguely the lights of a helicopter approach the hospital and disappear somewhere above his head. Live tissue had arrived via Harris Country Hospital from Muncie, Indiana.

Jane, his only child, the centerpiece of his life force, didn't understand his apparent nonchalance. "Wasn't he ever afraid?" she wondered, her own innards retching with fear. She held his thick, grainy, warm and gentle hand lightly where the tattooed number had long since faded, "a matter of fortune," as he explained in the diary. An acquaintance from Nowy Targ had administered the series of needles in a deliberately wrong way not breaking the last inner layer of skin — that would have made the stain permanent, and the purple ink had worn away by the early fifties. The number, 2222, matched the one on the armband in the shoe box in the closet. The proof was gone but the stain was internal. In return for what, he never explained; favors of that nature were almost always deals of need. Harriet, Jacob's second wife, sat restlessly on a straight back chair sucking nervously on a piece of sugarless hard candy. A gift from her dentist, Dr. Lakind, the first in Essex County to install a Sony TV over his chair.

Jacob told an anecdote about Grandfather Solomon, the one about the hernia operation that he had walked away from at the age of 101. The punch line came; Solomon lived to tell the story, but the doctor didn't. And then the other one about Grandpa not taking his medicine. When asked why he paid the doctor, he replied, "he has to live too." Why'd you pay the pharmacist? "He has to live too." Why didn't you take the medicine? "Because I want to live too!" Jacob smiled himself; the story warmed him. The others tried to release the tension of the moment. Under different circumstances mild laughter would have followed. They pushed smiles around their mouths. They had heard these sketches before and had them stocked neatly in their mental closets lovingly, but now any reference at all to mortality scared them like a jinx. The undying quality of Jacob's spirit, though, continued to amaze them, touch them with its selfless courage. "Didn't he know what he was about to face?" Jane wondered. Neither she nor Harriet could either laugh or choke-up with fear. Squeezing was about all that would pass. They both squeezed his hands and made inconsequential little remarks. To him, he had made his own choice and that was already a luxury. That was the definition of being free even if the decision were to kill him; it was his. That was all. Whereas the others felt trapped by the injustice of the predicament, Jacob knew in the deepness of his bones that anguish and anticipation brought nothing but deeper pain. To everyone except Jacob this crossroads had come on torturously fast. To Jacob it wasn't a crossroads. When the pinnacle on which life and death balanced wore itself flat and mundane the prospect of either outcome became real and bearable. Such was with Jacob. *Que sera, sera*, he sang in pre-op.

Jane held back her tears with a string of small muscles that ran along her face and neck and into her chest and back. It had been Jacob, this man right there in that tight bed, her father, who had brought her out of a tangled past, a childhood lost in eastern Europe, and delivered her to a new life of past-effacing positivism. George Washington had become her first president and Georgia O'Keeffe her favorite artist, "This Land is My Land,"the folk song she preferred singing around the campfire at the YWHA youth picnics. With Jacob gone perhaps everything would disappear. There'd be no "back" to not go back to. There'd be fiction and some unusual dreams and some incomplete knowledge and black and white snap shots marked *Krakow* in Old Venice type on the off-white backs. Abandoned in America. "We're survivors," her adult self asserted in a momentary rage of inner courage-gathering militancy. Surviving the Third Reich now meant a long life and a free ride to heaven. The worst was long behind them; there was the peace of adulthood to enjoy. And so she hated being destined to that Houston hospital room where in the presence of death the residue of abandonment and childhood gnawed cruelly beneath her thoughts and breath. She didn't know it. She wasn't ready for this; she'd never be. No. A tired voice muffled by low fidelity, trying to be gentle, invited all visitors to leave promptly. "Evening hours are over." Jane tried to smile encouragingly. It was time to leave her father again. To say good-bye, whatever that meant. To be deceived when she knew that it was she that was doing the deceiving, perhaps. But there were rules. She needed to believe in the sensibility of rules, of an orderly world, to show this time that she believed in the certainty of the outcome, of the future, of immortality, in trust itself. He was wiser: experience had imposed wisdom on him. He had learned not to believe; there was no pay off. He wasn't cynical or sour, just a non-believer. Grandiose spirituality was false belief and belief was the act of lying to yourself unknowingly. He trusted with humility the stance of benevolent and loving non-belief. "*Ve vill see,*" he would say in his permanent accent. This was his approach to the future. He smiled. He let her escape while she thought it was the opposite. It was their separation and re-unification played all over again unconsciously.

Harriet couldn't quite wipe the sickness of fear from the nervous stance of her mouth. The lines that creased her upper lip, reminiscent of the skin Dürer gave to women's faces, bulged like the sections of a caterpillar. Her bobby pins pulled at the roots of her hair that sat perched in a tight bun at the top of her head. They backed out of the pale room, waving desperately, hopefully. Smiling even. "Good luck" oozing from their silent mouths, too frightened of the triteness of the slogan. A thin veil of belief in the goodness of fate looked out from its trapped inner place.

"Um, hrumm," Jacob cleared his throat, and everyone hesitated as though he wanted to speak, fearing silently the pain of a poignant last remark. But instead, he raised his thick right hand, fingers rough, backs soft and veiny, "See you in church," he quipped in his Krakowian accent like a character out of Shalom Alechem. The heavy door gently swept shut. Shaking her head, Jane moved down the corridor, foggily. Harriet, in her corrective shoes, followed, her tight girdle ruffling against her slip. They were out. An innate sense of staging told them not to find a pretense to turn back. They hadn't forgotten anything, hadn't forgotten to tell Jacob anything, had nothing to check. "Just leave." Good-byes were indeed awful, Jane thought. It was better not to believe in them, Jacob knew better than anyone.

Then, alone in the quiet of his room, he watched the lights of the city come on in a crescendo. It was like watching the stars appear above the Tatras, or on a movie screen. He didn't especially like the movies, more like he hadn't really had time to spend in movie houses, except for those cheap matinees at The Bijou in downtown Newark in the late forties where he had built his vocabulary and took on colloquialisms. But this seemed like one he'd not go to, all the lights came on, with no real plot or story line. Boyishly, he thought about sneaking a glass of water but then abandoned the idea; the doctor had forbidden any solids or liquids till after it was over and Jacob was an obedient man, respectful. "Doctor's had reasons. If they know what they're doing or not, they at least know a bit more than us."

A team of doctors' attendants later came to prep him for the morning onslaught. David and Goliath, he thought of as they pulled and pushed and changed his linen armor. He was David, of course. It was a great story. It had given him strength as an asthmatic child at Hebrew School and afterwards at the wing position on the soccer team, all Jewish boys. He twiddled his thumbs for a moment. The team waddled out into the hall. The lights kept coming on, blenders in kitchens started turning, coins were floating from hands into wire baskets in toll plazas, the toll-free phone lines at U-Haul were all busy. Jacob sat motionless for a moment, remembered Serenka and those sad days in late 1939 in Lvov, gripped hisball-point like a soldering iron, and then reached for the marble-covered diary, tenderly.

2

Jane and Harriet took the shuttle bus back to the Hilton, and nudged their way through the mob of Shriners who'd just arrived for the annual convention. There was silence in the elevators and Jane watched the golden lights mount the row of numbers. At nineteen they slid out and moved along the dim, carpeted hall littered with the remains of room service. Room service was paramount to class. The shapes in the bit-into triangles of cold toast revealed both fine orthodontia and wicked cross-bites. The flame resistant corridor seemed morbid to Jane as did the thin luxury of the accommodations. They would have never stayed at the Hilton had they simply been on holiday, although if they had had to they could have afforded it. "A hundred sixty dollars a night to lay your head on a lousy pillow for six hours is criminal." Jane took the alienating plastic key-card from Harriet and stuck the perforated, coded edge into the veneered door. Jacob had over the years cut thousands of metal keys on the key grinder in the store; now keys had come to this.

They moped into the long room, dropped down their handbags, and with sighs of exhaustion embraced with the power of desperation. Beyond all the conflict, confusion, and hurt feelings, ultimately, there was comfort being with family, whoever they were. Jane snuggled her chin into the soft muscle behind Harriet's chronic collarbone and felt her age in the sweet loss of elasticity in the skin. The two women clutched each other, engulfed but yet untouched by the hideous visual explosion of floral patterns and synthetic fabrics that dominated the decor. Their hands pressed heavily on the backs of the other. "Oh God," Harriet whimpered.

To help dissolve the heaviness, Jane flipped on the Quasar. The Hilton bought American. A tattooed room number had been burned into the simulated wood siding, resembling an ugly scar. An indiscreet chain secured the color set to the hotel furniture, accompanied by an un-diplomatic sticker spelling out the jail sentence for larceny in the State of Texas. And this was The Hilton, not some flea-bitten drive-in motel along the state highway where you could pull your automobile right up to the screen door and you paid in cash upon registering. "What were things coming to?" Jane thought. The color was off; everything was slightly purple. The maid had dusted the set with reckless and rapid abandon and the controls were all maladjusted. The volume blared as electricity rushed through the set of micro chips. They jumped. Some commentator's mauve head appeared like an animated eggplant and the tail end of the local news was oozing from the face. "What a necktie!" A downtown Winn-Dixie had been held-up, a sixteen year old bag boy had been shot in the abdomen, had taken the bus to the Trauma Center, and was in stable condition. The cameraman pointed his lens at the stains on the linoleum below the advertisement for the latest State Lottery game, Wingo, and zoomed in for effect. Yes, it was the blood of the youth, right there next to a mountain of Purina and Pop Tarts. Jane thought of Benjamin alone at school and shuttered.

"It's the same everywhere. Isn't it terrible," Harriet said in a tone of massive disappointment.

"Mother, why don't you go first," Jane replied, getting up to draw Harriet's bath water. Moist heat gushed into the large salmon-tone acrylic tub, drowning the voice of the newscaster. Jane was exhausted, she realized, as her head hung over the splash of water and she tested the temperature with the back of her hand. Baths had always been a ritual under Harriet's domain. The temperature had to be just right, the tub had to scrubbed out and dried before the bath and after, the particles of dead skin that rubbed away from the ankles had to be rinsed off the sides of the tub where they would hang like barnacles, and every part of the body had to be thoroughly lathered, worked over with a wash cloth, rinsed...and then brutally dried, like in a car wash. She had dried Benjamin throughout his childhood, rubbing him so thoroughly with a terry cloth bath towel — dried stiff on the line in the breezeway, suspended by wooden clothespins — that his young skin would smart with healthy pinkness. With Harriet around germs didn't have a fighting chance. Towards dirt, she applied the intolerance of a fascist.

Harriet removed her cotton jacket and then stooped to undo the brown, peanut-shaped orthopedic shoes that were specially ordered from some outlet in lower Manhattan and gripped her feet. The room phone fluttered an inhuman sound and both Harriet and Jane jumped, startled. Harriet hurried to the receiver, not really wanting to answer, but not hesitating either, and caught the receiver before it could rattle a second time. It was the sound that jarred them. Jane felt the thumping of her heart and thought first of the kicking of a fetus, a sensation Harriet had never felt, and then of Jacob, who'd have his mitral valve replaced and three by-passes done in the morning. There wasn't yet any reason to have worried, but the ring startled them just the same.

"Hello," Harriet said, then listened, said a few words and replaced the orange plastic object back in its cradle. A white plastic guide masked the crown of numbers. Dial 8 for the hair dresser, 4 to reserve sauna time. It was a Shriner who'd reached the wrong room. "Mighty sorry mam."

"Jesus," Jane exclaimed. And then in another voice, "Mother, your bath must be ready."

Jane walked out past the two king size Posturepedic beds, those sewn-on serious labels that were illegal to remove hanging down from the frames like sick tongues, and poked her face behind the drawn floral drapes. Below, at the base of the deep interior courtyard the hotel's huge air conditioners whirled rapidly in their place. The sky above was boxed in by the rectangular building but Jane managed to see through the fine coat of window dust a piece of cloud gilded by rays of late sunlight. She let the drape drop back into place and crawled onto the polyester bedspread, letting the hem of her light fall dress rise up above the brown birthmark on her right thigh. There was nothing to do.

Then our younger daughter, Sarenka, which means "doe" in Polish, became very ill with diphtheria and at the age of two she passed away. We had a very hard time to bury her there in Lvov.

Several weeks later the major General of Winnicki received an order from the Gestapo that all Jews should gather in front of the City Hall from where they'd be assigned to a 'Special Work Force.' I started off with two of my other two brothers, Joseph and Lonek, but decided to go back home because my legs were hurting and I had a difficult time walking, and I didn't think I'd be able to work for a few days. I left them in front of the City Hall beside a beautiful magnolia tree, fragrant and in full bloom. Later, we were told by a Ukrainian militia man, who had accompanied them, that the entire group had been taken to a ravine outside of town and shot to death. My brothers, gone, just like that. To this day whenever I see in the spring time a blossoming magnolia tree I shudder.

Jacob looked out the dark pane into the darkening cityand let the distant flash of Pennzoil in neon dominate the life of his eyes. On off on off. Houston, Texas. Texas was where jokes about big, rich Americans took place. It had been forty years since he'd seen Joseph and Lonek.

My father escaped to Krakow the day before but somebody recognized him in the street and denounced him. He was arrested and later killed. We were told who the man who denounced him was. His name was <u>Rubin Ernst</u>.

Jacob underscored the name twice with his pen. It was his sole, tiny source of revenge, to get the name down on paper. To underline it. <u>Rubin Ernst</u>. The denunciation of the denouncer, in a diary, left in a hospital room four decades later in Texas.

At the same time, my brother Arthur who had secretly returned to Nowy Targ and was hiding in our sister-in-law, Sarah Zollman's parents' attic, was accidentally discovered by one of the Jewish spies, Turner, part of the Judenrat, who notified the Gestapo for a small reward. They came and shot Arthur on the spot.
Foolishly back from the Russian side, I sent my wife Amalja and our daughter to Krakow to stay at the house of a Polish friend of mine. Meanwhile, I hid for several days in Nowy Targ in different Polish homes, but most of them in

their friendly manner asked me to leave because there was a death sentence to anyone hiding a Jew. After running from place to place, one night I started walking for several hours towards Krakow all the time in fear of being recognized. As I approached Krakow I risked taking the train and in one station I saw a gallows on the platform with three naked, bearded bodies hanging (obviously Jews), and somebody hung on them a very funny sign 'Kosher meat.'

When I got to Krakow I found out that my wife and daughter had left for the neighboring town of Niepolomice, where my wife's relatives, the Finder's, lived in a big wooden farmhouse with their children. And so I went to join them.

We rented a small peasant house and stayed there without incident. After a few weeks, the town officials announced that all Jews had to gather on a certain day and time, a Thursday at ten in the morning, at the town sports stadium behind the grammar school. I rented a horse and buggy leaving a gold ring as a deposit, and after it got dark I loaded Amalja and Dzidzia, our seven year old daughter, into the buggy and quietly rode out of town, trying to escape to a destination I didn't even know. In the light of the full moon we trottedpeacefully in that wagon. Dzidzia sat between us, bundled in numerous layers of clothes. After about one hour we were stopped by the Polish police, pulled out of the buggy and dragged off the road where we were beaten up, kicked and punched — even Dzidzia, our baby, who refused to cry. Then they forced us with clubs to get back in the buggy and return to town where we had to wait for the morning evacuation. That was the last night we were together.

Jacob stopped, took inventory for an instant as his eyes swept the walls of the hospital room, the metal railing of the bed, the intravenous support stand, his own feet and the memory they housed. He didn't want to continue. He would have liked to have a piece of poppy seed cake with a scoop of Howard Johnson's coffee ice cream. The night had filled-in morosely. The window frame was black. Their last night together.

That night, a woman registered as a Volksdeutsche, *which meant she had certain privileges, had returned to the Finder's farmhouse. She had been the governess of the Finder children before the war and now had come back to try to help save them. She was given a quantity of money for this. Danek, the boy, now lives in London. His sister Marysia, I hear still lives in Krakow. Another Finder cousin became a very rich industrialist in Sao Paolo, South America. Their mother recently died at 95 in a hotel in Vienna. Amalja and I begged this woman to take with her, Dzidzia, since we knew that our future wasn't very promising. Finally, she agreed and I gave her the ring. The three of us slept the few hours that remained in one narrow bed on the top floor of the house, cramped and bruised but warm. A terrible look of understanding jumped back and forth Amalja and myself which we didn't dare share with our baby. In the morning, we dressed and parted with very heavy hearts not knowing if we'd see our child or each other again. But we knew we were fortunate to have had such a possibility. This was our only chance. We walked away hand in hand from that farmhouse, hiding our tears, Dzidzia waved at the window like we were going on vacation. Anyone who has one, knows the pain of deceiving an innocent child. We told her we'd come back; we promised. We didn't want to lie. We hoped.*

Like sheep we filed into lines at the gathering place and the Gestapo segregated us calmly into different groups. The elderly went to the cemetery to be shot, we later learned. Most went to the train station to be transported to the gas chambers — Auschwitz, Treblenka, and Belzec, we heard

— while some of us were selected for work. It wasn't until later thatI knew which group I was in, selected to work and sent to the Krakow-Plaszow ghetto near the Kablewerks factory, and then by simple deduction, the fate of my wife. We had anticipated our separation, willed it even, and at the time, although I remember the moment our hands broke away and our eyes followed each other into different lines, we viewed it as a victory. We hoped for our daughter's sake that if we were sent in different directions maybe one of us would be left alive to find her.

The door then began to swing open and Jacob closed his bulbous thumb into the marble-covered diary. He wasn't a writer; he didn't have the gestures of one. His sentences dashed across the page like items on an order form, on an inventory list. Yet, he liked filling-up the pages; it was satisfying, like whittling down a stick. As long as the unsheathing of details was gradual, he didn't worry about the ghosts that lurked at the core. Writing had been a casting-off, a lightening up, a hobby that filled part of the emptiness of retirement. "Write it down," Dzidzia had implored him, hungry to re-stitch the rags of her past. "It's therapeutic, father," she'd insist, stroking a cheek as an adult daughter. Now, he was tired, Niepolemice had been a bit too much. He hadn't planned going back. He wasn't masochistic, and although he wanted to put it all down he didn't relish the pain. He was ready to forget again. In the way one prayed to God, he wished Jane, and especially Benjamin, the first in the family to be born in America, would accept the wisdom of forgetting.

Just outside the door, half-in, half-out and invisible from Jacob's perspective, stood a nurse in her mid-to-late-twenties with long brown hair tied behind her head. Without seeing her, Jacob heard her as she spoke to another hospital staffer. It was her slight accent — European, eastern, possibly Germanic — that made him strain a bit harder to hear. He didn't know a soul in Texas and just at that moment he felt at home with that voice. Not exactly that one, but something about it, seemed to make his heart thud, like a truck downshifting. He thought of her, the voice, as something good-looking, shapely, dark. He still had attractions and even dreamed a bit of romance, although he never would have had said as much to anyone else, Rabbi Weissner included. Certainly not Harriet. Whatever desires he had as a man, he kept locked up and silent; the expression of sexual energy had grown superfluous during the war years, if those oddly inhuman times could be called "war years." And after the war, there was so much to recover that the vastly necessary and human drive to satisfy those luscious nags was covered over and smothered in fancy whipped cream. Yet there were times whenall that newness felt thin and all that it felt like he had had in the world just then was the paltry grasp of his own scrotum, privately beneath the thin wool covers. The loss of a young wife in the early stages of married life had undoubtedly played its share for spoiling sexual desire in him. There was guilt in all expressions of pleasure now. "Why do I have the right to this?" But the woman that stood on the other side of the opaque door — a mere suggestion of a form, a past, and a voice — nonetheless, held an attraction like a scent that never lets you forget, and returns in hints throughout your life.

"*Madame.* Good evening," Jacob offered to the slight presence in the door frame. His words sounded with the grace of a hardware man playing the role of baron at a fancy Hungarian ball at the Gellert in Buda, pronouncing *Madame* the French way, the word swaddled in his Polish accent. The woman standing in white beyond the door wore a moon-shaped hair clip and, on the front of her white uniform, a plastic name plate with the blue hospital logo: E. A. STADLER, RN. Had Jacob been introduced he would

27

have assumed what a shame it was she wasn't at home with her husband and children, ladling out piping and plentiful portions of beef stew with mashed potatoes. It would have been more like heating up those ready-made or previously frozen "helper" dishes that were so common and easy. He had no chance to spot the white metal wedding band that she so religiously wore. And he wouldn't have thought to ask where it came from and what it meant anyway. "It is for our children that we live, for our families." That she had divorced her husband, Andy, a retired Army Captain, now a sausage and smoked meats distributor in Denver who'd learned the business while part-timing for AAFES at the Rhine-Main commissary, and that their child, actually his child from his first marriage to an anorexic woman who did paste-up at a print shop in a college town, Kevin, a skinny and sensitive boy, age twelve, and who lived with his father's folks (by court order) in Beaumont, Texas, naturally never surfaced in the brief interchange between nurse and patient. Nor did the fact that the wedding band was an heirloom from her paternal grandfather, a valueless object that meant the world to her. He had made it as a prisoner-of-war in the Ukraine and later as an injured man — he'd received a head wound — gave it to his wife, who had lived out the war with the children in a small house on the Bergerstrasse in Frankfurt. Her grandfather,*Opa*, held a highly symbolic place in her heart, more significant than a father. It was he who pointed out the bees collecting pollen, the way goats were to be petted, how to stake tomato plants, the joys of dominos. It was *Opa* who had tucked the sweetest plum from his little field into her tiny palm, and whispered *Das bringt Gluck.*

"Doing a little reading?" she would have asked cheerily, noting the book in his lap, had she entered that room just then as she had intended before being side-tracked by a co-worker who needed help with a patient with a bedpan problem.

"I'm writing down some reminiscences of my life, inspired by my grandson, Benjamin, who just started college," he would have proudly offered had she or anyone else asked what he was doing, all that college meant to him reverberating triumphantly in his articulation of the word. He had put Jane through college after only seven years in America and had participated in monthly installments in Benjamin's college fund, chipping in the dividends from his shares of gas company stock and Continental Insurance. And when Macy's split 4 to 1 to Jacob's delight, he was able to up the ante. College was the kingpin of the American Dream; it was where the American and Jewish experiments held hands like a shy couple that liked each other and would eventually marry.

Jacob was proud. He sat there perched in his hospital bed in the dry heat of the American southwest on the eve of a brutal yet commonplace operation with poise and composure, patience and dignity. Nurse Stadler's voice rushed and retreated. It was mixed with the personal and the professional. He listened intensely, straining to bring her closer. She would have been taken instantly by his manner, his elegant calm, his erect posture with hands folded like a school boy. The way little boys and grandpas approached each other! "Adorable," she thought as she saw him, peeking in but not yet concentrated; she was one to go all soft in the presence of baby clothes, cute little outfits with smiley frogs and slices of pink watermelon, marked 18 months and designed for the body of a three-year-old. He wasn't one of those other cantankerous old and bitter patients who blamed their illnesses on the cruel world or the federal government or the doctor or weather or hospital administrators, the food, the Japs, the Jews or Amtrak. Not Hitler, nor Nixon, nor the Commies, Skinheads, or the Klan. Jacob was peaceful, generous in his acceptance of the state of things. And although she was tired, it wouldn't have been tedious standing there in front of the 73-year old man had she come fully into the room. She would have liked him wholly. Most people did.

"Pardon me," he called out finally. "Could you please give me a glass of cold water?" he lured the voice in from the far side of the door with the manipulative charm of a child too lazy to slip out of a warm bed. He wanted to see her. She peeked in with her whole head and smiled. She was young, brunette, with straight white teeth, soft. Like an apparition, she hung there, her torso wrapping into sight. He thought he had seen her in an ad or a dream.

"Oh gosh, I'd like to, you know, but I can't. Yourdoctor, you know, has marked your chart clearly: No solids or liquids. You have a big day ahead of you. If there is anything else I can get you...."

"No," he nodded. He had just wanted to see that voice, to not be alone, to be around pleasantness. He knew she was right. He certainly didn't want to get an innocent young lady in trouble. Obedience was part of instinctive logic in his world of second chances. What was there left to contradict? For what was important enough to dirty the air? What was the point? That the doctor's orders were for Jacob's own benefit, part of the standard pre-op precautions, didn't matter. Not getting the darling nurse in hot water was what was paramount now. "She was a very nice girl." Her voice told him. "Why aren't you married?" he'd want to ask. *Que sera*, echoed in his head.

"Try to get some sleep now," she suggested in her soothing, subdued voice. He agreed from his side of the room, privately admiring the tone of her sound, insistent yet soothing, foreign. He felt extremely comfortable — intimate wasn't the word, but close — with this virtual stranger.

"Okay, then, good night...," she hesitated awkwardly, not knowing and not wanting to have to look down again at the chart in front of her, and having ventured with her intonation too far to change her syntax with grace; it was to him that she was talking now, and she had to say his name, "Mister...".

"Jacob, is enough." He saved her.

"Why, thank you, Jacob." She emphasized the name. "Good night. Sleep well." And on a second thought she added, "You can call me..." Her name was Amy and the E — she'd pointed to her plastic badge — was for Eva. The A is for Amalika, "but people just call me Amy." She had the habit of telling patients that. Jacob smiled deeply to himself. He had thought of her. He never spoke of her. It was odd. He kept her thought far, far away from his life. It was too terrible letting the two touch. His wife, the one who hadn't exactly died, but just ceased to exist, and disappeared like smoke in the sky, had been called Amalja, with a *j*. He had never heard the same name since. This was Amalika, not the same, but he thought of Amalja nonetheless. Poor Harriet was back in the hotel worrying, and Jacob left the past in a hurry. Amalja came to him like that on that last of conscious nights.

And she left. The door settled back. She treaded away from the door she had barely entered. The white ripple soles of her shoes — the sort required of all floor staff — absorbed the sound of her walk. It was that something about her, he detected, that belonged to someone else. Elsewhere, Jacob followed the line of bright blue-white lights that illuminated Interstate 10 as it by-passed the dead center of downtown. Slightly beyond Jacob's view to the right, burned a short,tangerine-orange line of confident block letters: H I L T O N.

In room 1942 Jane had drifted away from the trappings of real time and her mouth fell open against the floral bedspread. Harriet soaked in the tub, easing away the pain of the blue-black bunions on both feet. Trucks of dental floss were rolling undisturbed across the state. Someone undoubtedly was belting back shots of Slivovitz in the Krakow dawn.

Jacob picked up the hospital menu and read the next day's lunch offering. Turkey and sweet peas, garden salad, low-calorie thousand island dressing and tapioca pudding. It was the pudding that sent him for the diary.

There was a time while being in the Kablewerks that the Germans received from the United Nations Relief Association a tremendous shipment of tapioca, and for several weeks we were fed nothing but this white gelatin. It was cooked without any salt or sugar and we were force-fed this stuff everyday for every meal. It was torture. Ever since, I cannot even look at tapioca, and I cringe when I hear the word. I'd sooner die than eat tapioca ever again.

Nurse Stadler continued on her rounds. In the nurses' station the weatherman on WHEN-FM 89.9 announced that tomorrow's air quality would be unsafe for breathing, a condition that people had become used to.

3

J ane no longer remembered much about the *Volksdeutsche*
governess who had taken her from Niepolemice to Krakow,
except that she was blond, around forty and had locked her
in a dark apartment when she went out at night. The Finder
children were hiding at her sister's across the Czech border, but Gustawa she kept herself. She'd not risk the others
for the sake of the new one. Nor could Jane now find the
thread of anger that grew from the incomprehensibility of
being given away to a stranger at age seven. She barely
even sensed the tight massiveness of the past that lay bound
like a mummy in some spooled inner chamber of her history. These recollections had been subjugated so
redundantly by time — and the protective paste of defense
that time secreted — that to be recalled to the forefront of
memory, even in part, would take six years of analysis and
a degree in psychiatric social work. Instead, Jane was left
with a collection of disconnected images of light and shade,
jarring sounds, unmistakable colors, all mixing oddly from
those weeks with the *Volksdeutsche* and blended-in over
the years with that revolutionary cousin Lala, to whom she
had been transferred through a fence in the Krakow ghetto

along with a rucksack of sugar, tea, powdered cocoa, two tins of fish, and a used pair of nylons. A dowry of sorts to ease the conscience of one and compensate the risk of the other. Lala grabbed the rucksack and yanked the girl by the wrist. There'd be a use for her; this was war. As an adult, Jane's dreams increasingly included moments from that scene in the frantic darkness of the inside of a locked closet. The racket of hangers banging around her head. The accumulation of splinters in hands pushing against the walnut panels. The redmess of a wartime, bedroom abortion — not hers — of being on her knees cleaning the pungent medallions of blood from between the soaked boards of oak parquet. "Strange how blood coagulates when exposed to air," she'd think later upon waking. The confused look and pained whelps of a sheep dog with a bullet ripping through his innocent flesh. The terrifying red fire and gray-black smoke of an airplane whistling crazily into an empty meadow. And then explode. The winter water of the Raba, a tributary of the Dunajec, rushing down her throat, a sort of primitive swimming lesson inflicted by Lala, who, aside from being resentful and slightly sadistic, she'd learn years later — already in America — had worked for the Russian underground with her lover, Victor, an atheist with a shoe factory. And together they lived in the little white-trimmed house by the river. "Swim or drown," it was Lala's way. For the next forty years, the whole of her adult life, Jane would insist of keeping her head above the surface of water even in the shallow end of a well-chlorinated municipal pool in Essex County New Jersey, and in the warm waves during those first summers at Bradley Beach with Harriet and her sisters. Even later in the stall shower in the master bathroom of her split level home, her head of stylishly-frosted hair stuffed in a shower cap, her eyes shut like the grip of dead shellfish, much tighter than necessary, her mouth scrunched up to make itself totally impermeable, she'd fight back the power of the pulsating shower head, never once suspecting that early trauma in the Raba could ever have intruded so far and for so long into her daily adult life. Jane began to snore. "Dzi?" Harriet called from her bath. "Dzi?" Silence. She was back on the cold stone steps of the Karmelicka Church where Cousin Lala insisted she should wait and then had never returned, herself rounded up and carried off in a Gestapo raid of the dissident bistro. "Your name is Krystyna Antoszkiewicz. Your name is Krystyna Antoszkiewicz. You were baptized in Warsaw. Your parents were killed." The cruel repetition of the name of the dead child she had to become: Krystyna Antoszkiewicz. And the possession of the real papers of the dead child whose identity she had to assume. The Quasar's green-gray screen looked on with the omnipresence of Mona Lisa's eyes as Jane's head floated on the pillow of hidden foam chips; there wasn't a feather pillow in the entire city.

"Dzi, wake, you haven't had your bath yet." Bill Cosby appeared laughing.

Jacob woke early, a quarter to six, and wound his watch like usual. Carefully, he shaved off the short stubble that had formed overnight on his chin and then lightly cleaned his brown leather shoes with a moistened paper towel. At home he'd always put on his socks and shoes first. Then underwear. Then make breakfast, traipsing about bare between the tops of hisstretch socks and the lower rims of his Jockey briefs. There was some movement along the highways below, but not much, a few heavy trucks rolling east towards New Orleans and west towards Tucson, places Jacob didn't know. Plastic mugs encased with emblems of the 28 teams in the NFL and filled with Taster's Choice rode shotgun in plastic holsters safety-stuck to the dashboards, the static of fuzz-busters humming. The pale Hilton sign had dissolved into the early Texan sun. Jacob craved breakfast. The bold lines of Hebrew in an ad for Fleischmann's on the back page of *The Jewish News* reminded him of the rough and smooth, golden and off-white texture of matzo, which then transported him like it was yesterday to the piping hot porcelain platter of his mother's scrumptious *matzo brai*. He reached for the diary.

The most wonderful woman in the whole world, Helena. There did not exist a person who knew her who did not love her. Good, charitable, always feeding poor people in our house and also sending cooked food in her containers out to people in need.

She used to buy before Pessach fifteen to twenty shooks of eggs (one shook equals five dozen). She'd send us to the bakery that baked for the entire Jewish population of Nowy Targ, and we'd pick up fifty to sixty kilos of matzo. She also had two or three wooden barrels of borscht on hand and she prepared this each day of the eight days in twenty-quart pots with thirty eggs, and we ate this cold with potatoes throughout the day. During the year on winter weekdays for breakfast, especially during the First World War, she would prepare caraway soup with broken pieces of old bread. When I think about this soup I can still taste it. And in the evenings she prepared the dough for homemade bread, which we let rise near the oven overnight. In the morning we took it to the bakery and they made six to eight large round loaves of rye bread, each about twelve inches in diameter, which lasted for eight to ten days. Sometimes I dream about this bread.

Jacob looked up blankly, the sight of the blood pressure apparatus hanging from the wall by his bed didn't register at all as a functional object. Jacob's mind was mixed with that rye bread. Then that thought, that taste, that world eased its grip and Jacob slid off the mechanical bed, tucked in the corners of the hospital sheets, smoothed out the coarse, green blanket, and then rested gingerly on the electrically-tilted mattress waiting for the doctor's team to take him downstairs to the OR, as everyone seemed to call it. From habit he read the bland articles in the *Post*, the columns on gardening, cooking, auto repair, licking like always his callused rightthumb before turning the page, gentle but not fine in his gestures. He was a hardware man, not an antiquarian although he intuitively knew "quality" but was bored by it. He shook his head as his finger and eye scanned Dear Abbey. He chuckled. "Signed Horny Dentist." He had once thought that he too would be a dentist, actually a *prosthodontist*. He liked repairing things, filling holes, cementing masonry, restoring real objects to their completed and entire state. He'd fix broken dishes or cracked cups in Jane's household. He scanned a filler about chicken at the bottom of a column, and spotted on the night table the blue and yellow glazed tie clasp Benjamin had made during arts and crafts hour at day camp for his 65th birthday, a yellowish 65 hanging there in the middle of the star-smattered deep blue background. Jacob paraded around B'nai Brith meetings and benefit dinners, clasped proudly by that tack and the 65. There were bells gonging here and there, up and down the hospital corridor and bodies bobbing past but no one yet had come for Jacob. A memory arrived like an unsolicited fax.

My father sent me on the night train from Nowy Targ to Biaty-Bielsko on the Silesian border, where I was supposed to enter the vocational Gymnasium. I climbed up into the upper bunk to sleep, with all my certificates and documents in my back pocket. These, I needed to register for the entrance examination. I'm not sure if they fell out on their own or were stolen, but in any case, they were gone in the morning and so my career ended right there. I returned home on the next train and began selling and loading carloads of cement, brick, and fertilizer in my father's store on the rynek, Number 28, just in front of where my grandmother's saloon was before the First War.

It was a small version of an American department store, consisting of hardware and houseware, farm equipment, building materials, fertilizer, plumbing supplies, sewing machines, and much more, including even some food items, confectioneries, and bread. Since the store grew so fast and my father could not help himself, he asked me to join him as a partner. I hesitated for awhile but later gave in. My brother Henek, or Hank, who now lives in Florida with his wife Lily, always said yes to my father, but was at the time in Italy studying to be a textile engineer. My youngest brother, Adek, on the other hand, left Poland for Palestine in 1935 and after a lot of suffering — malaria, mosquitoes, etc. — founded with a small group of others, Kibbutz Ein Hamifraz. Adek didn't get along with my father. Adek loved animals so he worked in the warehouse driving the horse and buggies into place for unloading the peasant farmer's merchandise. Whenever my father used to come out and scold him, Adek would go upstairs to our apartment and sit down and read a book. My father would yell even louder at him and Adek would say very calmly that as long as my father yelled he would not go back to work. As soon as he started talking nicely and humanely he would go back downstairs.

In 1938 we started to hear terrible things from Germany. And in the beginning of 1939 Hitler chased over the Polish border several thousand Polish Jews, Ostjuden, who had been living in Germany due to financial opportunities. Nowy Targ, like the other towns especially near the border, organized a committee to assimilate our share of these Ostjuden into the community. Like today's boat people.

Our prosperity, success in business, and good relations with our customers kept us, especially our father, from seeing and realized what was happening around us. When we did see, we tried to persuade our father to liquidate the business and emigrate to America, as did our Uncle Jacob, while there was still time. We knew of people who were transferring money to foreign countries, and emigrating, but it was not possible for him to believe what was happening in Germany and Czechoslovakia. Our father did not believe in anything but work. He opened the store at six o'clock in the morning, three hours before we arrived. Instead of being the boss he was a worker; instead of telling a stock boy to sweep up he did it himself. He was so engrossed with work that he thought that nothing bad in the world could happen to us. He wouldn't hear of it. And he scolded us if we spoke of anything gloomy. 'Not over my dead body.' His words became prophecy.

Quite often, I remember, clients came into our store and told us, or asked us if we knew, that there were people outside picketing, who were trying to persuade our customers to boycott Jewish merchants. We were so busy with supplies, selling brick and fertilizer by the ton, running the business and making our good living — that we did not have time even to go outside to see who was picketing.

I woke up on September the First 1939 at about five A.M. hearing explosions of bombs. I got dressed and ran to the store in the middle of town; there was total chaos and panic. No one knew what to do. I stared at the panic scene in the rynek and all I can say now is that our lives from that day on were condemned. My poor mother, Helena, kept preparing the matza brai all the same.

Jacob's door flung open; the team, learning as they went, had come for him with a bed that rolled. Jacob looked at his watch: shy of seven. He slipped it into the drawer of hismetal and clapboard night table along with the marble-covered diary, and the enameled tie clasp. The young men, clean-shaven and tired-eyed, covered in the same greens and whites, guided the stretcher into the room and held it flush against Jacob's bed, ready to shovel him out.

"Shall we go, gentlemen?" Jacob suggested rightfully as if it was he who led the procession. It was his life they had come for; why shouldn't he orchestrate the parade? They transferred his still robust and memory-filled body to the bed-on-wheels and evacuated the room, leaving behind the dead-still panorama of Houston and that whole outer world of future.

4

The wake-up call rang at ten to seven, five minutes later than what Harriet had ordered. She was annoyed, mostly out of nervousness.

"You don't expect this from the ritzy places."

By seven fifteen Harriet and Jane were already in the coffee shop, hurrying down coffee and commercial rye toast, the kind that looked like it should get stale in two or three days but just didn't. Though she suffered from anemia, Jane would have forgone the breakfast but Harriet needed something in her stomach. Harriet ordered her coffee "black and very hot." It was never hot enough for her. Somehow, she never burned her mouth. Jane's eyes were puffed and a general sense of strain rang through her body. The hot coffee came and all she took from the thick mug, still hot from the dishwasher, was the heat that radiated from its walls. "Jacob," she thought, "always ordered soup from the bottom of the pot, where it was hottest and the bits of meat and vegetable gathered." An unconscious habit he'd picked up in the camps where five extra calories made a difference. She slid out of the booth and paid the $3.12 bill at the cashier while Harriet finished her coffee and toast in the booth. There was a tax in Texas. "For the Governor," the cashier said, then keying-in on the imposing electronic NCR a series of codes — COF-CS — and then with a mechanical sweep spoon-fed the hulk of metal the perforated bill and skewered the serrated and slightly stained card on a nail. With a painted thumb nail she severed the bottom portion, marked in green script *Thank you, y'all come back,* and left it in on a plate with three quarters, a dime, three pennies and a mint in plastic. Harriet left the mint andthe stub and nodded; the cashier, engulfed among dispensers of Tums, candy bars, cigarettes, dental floss, and Slim Jims, smiled sweetly, her teeth held in line with a wire retainer. Jane hated America at that instant for the sticky, false pancake syrup stuck on each table. The bright glow of another hot day sickened her mildly.

The optimistic tone of AM radio filtered through the holes of the fireproof ceiling panels and hurt her like poison darts. She and Harriet moved through the lobby among small clusters of early bird Shriners and spun through the revolving door. Harriet hoisted her girdle.

"Yoo-hoo, mister, the hospital shuttle bus, when's the next one?" Harriet hurled blindly at the angular doorman who stood there, tall in a kelly green costume and top hat. Jane looked down at her flat shoes and the thin green indoor-outdoor carpet that embellished the hotel carport.

"Seven twenty seven. In two minutes. Right where you're standing, 'mam.'"

"Thank you, young man." Clearly, he was too old to be called a young man. Nonetheless, his colleagues called him "Chuckie."

The ICU waiting room was filled with alternating rifts of sadness and jubilance, sometimes contrived. On one side of the windowless chamber, an elderly Italian-American woman, standing not more than 4' 10", literally danced like a troll between the two facing rows of pale green and orange pre-formed plastic seats. With her energy she burned up the tension of waiting. Her 47-year old "baby" was having his heart remodeled: she'd have chosen *rococo* if the style of bi-pass sections could be ordered. Or else Italian Baroque with gold leaf. Meanwhile, the surrounding families and friends of other desperately ill patients were amused and relieved by this display of bravery and spirited optimism.

"What strength that woman has!" Harriet remarked with both marvel and envy, while tumbling a piece of dietetic hard candy discretely at the back of her throat.

"She's wonderful," Jane added sincerely although sounding trite.

In another corner sat a young couple fearfully still. Like wax. It must have been their child. Sickened each time they visualized what in fact doctors were having to do to their little one. To cut into perfect, fresh and young skin...

Next to Harriet, slouched a middle-aged woman with long, wavy blond hair. At her feet sat a straw basket from which a string of fuzzy blue wool stretched up towards her hands and onto the thick plastic needles. She pulled her long hair back to keep it from tangling with the wool. Jane remembered once having long flowing hair like that, and braids. But in 1947 atage twelve they weren't worn in America so they came off with a big pair of Wiss kitchen scissors. "What ever happened to them?" Out with the trash under the sink, a girl's braids carried from Europe and sacrificed in Newark.

Harriet admired the knitting, and the woman was quick to notice.

"Hi," she said with a drawl that sounded like she yawned when she spoke. "I'm Fanny. First time here?"

"Why...yes," Harriet replied with a nervous chuckle beneath her words. Fanny's gregarious way was touching, filled with kindness and sincerity, yet Harriet was uneasy sharing the moment with a stranger and, worse, was irked by the terrible implication of Fanny's question.

Fanny snuffed out her cigarette into the tray of cluttered sand and the smoke from the red ash was drowned in an instant. She shoved her knitting into the basket and quickly straightened a corner of her checked blouse which had pulled from the top of her faded Wranglers. As a girl she probably used a piece of clothesline as a belt. She looked Harriet straight in the eye, caressing the face she saw with her glance.

"Poor girl. It's your husband, I can tell. Open heart surgery, isn't it? Fanny asked frankly but with compassion that was reinforced by placing a strong bony hand on Harriet's shoulder. Harriet, who'd been brought up speaking Yiddish in New Jersey in a steamy apartment above her father's bakery, fought back her tears, as if Fanny's hand had broken through a tough wall of restraint. The honesty and directness of Fanny's gesture, which reached her from the cold anonymity of the unknown world of strangers, connected the moment with the reality of the place, and the realization of truth fell all over her at once and forced her to weep. It was healthy. And all of a sudden, in the wake of Fanny's gesture, the whole world seemed unfair; it was a total stranger who was cutting into Jacob's heart. Harriet was vexed if guests didn't remove their shoes before entering her house. But doctor's were different. They could do what they wanted, what was needed. "Oh, to have married a doctor! Or a lawyer! Henry Finkelstein or Nat Greenspan, oh the salaries they commanded, the cars they ended up with, the good seats they were assigned on the High Holy Days in the synagogue!" Actually, she hadn't a clue that Greenspan had opened a chain of furniture stores, specializing in wicker and gems from Asia, and went bankrupt. Finkelstein opened a breast-reduction center in

Teaneck and married a patient, who was also a cousin on his mother's side. Harriet had been nervous about marrying Jacob, who had reddish hair and didn't speak a word of English. But he was available and needy. She had three weeks to decide. He was helpless, plus, and this was the real selling point, he had a daughter which she could then have too. She'd get them both, a familyinstantly, a purpose, a position, a goal, a title. And on top of that the cousin who had introduced them had told each of them that the other had money. The wedding date was set. The party would be in the living room of Harriet's mother's house, above the bakery. The deserts would be sensational, bt on the heavy side; Jewish sweets had never been known for their delicacy. The weekends of knitting afghans and reading Booth Tarkington novels would be swept away as magically as dust beneath the brushes of one of those carpet sweepers. Now, loving him really, she thought that a stranger had his hands inside of him. Touching his warm and tired parts. She cried, squeaked almost like tiny mice in a wall.

Seeing an elderly woman sob was a terrible thing. Fanny threw her arms around Harriet's neck as if she had known her all her life. Jane gripped Harriet's hand, herself forcing back tears with her will.

"Oh mother. Everything'll be all right. Don't worry."

"This here is your daughter?" Fanny exclaimed excitedly. "You must be mighty proud, Harriet." There was a pause. "I can call you Harriet, can't I?" she asked, giving the name a long A. Harriet smiled slightly. Fanny had accomplished something, and Harriet composed herself instantly, reaching to assure the grip of those torturous bobby pins that held her long and swirly hair against the brown sausage shaped hair bun that Benjamin called a bagel, which made her laugh. "The *bandit*," she thought in Yiddish with the bluff of severity. "The darling."

"Yes, she is, and she is beautiful, isn't she. If only she'd watch her weight. I keep fighting with her." Harriet's s voice was riddled with pride. Fanny chuckled, finding Jane "cute." Jane would be 46 next June. Jane was embarrassed; Harriet would say anything, really, to anyone, like "Hasn't she a nice bosom? to a waitress or cab driver.

"Actually, I'm not her natural mother. I'm her stepmother, although she's legally mine. I was lucky to get her when she was twelve." She said this as if there was a larger accomplishment in adoption than in childbirth. Three months after the wedding, the papers were signed on Harriet's insistence and Jane legally had a new mother. This change of legal status, of course, to a child went unnoticed, like the changing of a passport. "It's my husband, Dzidzia's father, we're here for."

"Who's father? " Fanny asked, unused to foreign words other than "rendezvous" or "sayanara" which were often in the crosswords in the *County Weekly.*

"Mine, Dzidzia's my nickname in Polish. I was born in Poland," Jane explained. "It means 'baby'." Fanny knew it wasn't Poland, Texas, and repeated the word, which had a droll effect with the Southern drawl. Jane covered over the surpriseshe felt; she'd never heard Harriet repeat the private fact of her adoption in public. And somehow she'd never thought of the word "adopted" as one that applied to her. Harriet had done everything possible to convince herself — and Jane — and the world, that they were mother and daughter by blood. And whatever threads of contact with the world of Poland that managed to remain after the war and the migration to America, Harriet tried to block. Visits with the villagers from Nowy Targ, who were also growing into new lives in various neighborhoods in New York, were discouraged under the pretense that such encounters would traumatize Jacob and send him back into his hellish past. "Let's spend Sunday dinner with my family." Dinners and outings and shared leisure time, however, with Harriet's brothers and sisters and their respective nephews and nieces and circle of odd friends, on the other hand, was an obligation without recourse. And Jacob didn't protest; he polka-ed through it. What was the harm of an afternoon with a small crowd of silly relatives? A brother who was devoted to Plexiglas. An *artsy* nephew. Another brother who was addicted to the Golden Glove matches in Newark. Held up next to what he'd known not long before this was like dancing in the clouds. Who was he to say no, to battle for the right to another activity, to his choice? He was already awarded his choice, to have found his daughter alive and to live freely with her in good health. To be healthy, that was always the first wish. Health and happiness. Plus, Harriet's family were decent people and they deeply liked him and his daughter. For Harriet, this convincing of self, eased the pain of being childless in life and, at the same time, helped Jane obliterate or bury the black holes in her past, black holes that Jane as an adult had begun to shine light into. Now Fanny shared the secret, just like that, a stranger from a little town in Texas.

Jane diverted her underlying uneasiness into a question, "Who are you here for?"

"Bobby, my husband and Superstar. This is our third time back. Can you just believe it? He's had his poor tummy removed twice. It just keeps growing back. And now he has internal bleeding that they can't just seem to stop. He'll just die if they can't stop it."

There was silence. It was Fanny's turn.

Fanny lit another cigarette and sipped on a can of Dr. Pepper that had been standing open by her tennis shoes and surely must have been flat as well as warm. But as Jacob would have said had he'd been on that side of the wall, "it was wet." And the act of letting sips of this warm, sweet substance roll down her throat gave Fanny time to gain calm.

Harriet and Jane were reduced by the horrific story. Three returns. The thought of returning. The stomach that grewback. And death — Fanny had said the word "die" — a thought that they'd banished in a solid, American way, from their thinking, ashamed and blinded when its presence seemed to lurk behind a notion. Slowly, their eyes gazed around the room, singularly and yet somehow united, and their pain then seemed less private. They saw themselves severed from the rest of the world and cornered in a time-effacing chamber along with the other selected souls who knew something of the same hurt, were pressed by the impatience of emergency to deepen the well of strength or to perish.

The second hand of the clock above the nurses' station swept along with a steady nerve. Certainly, they thought, they'd have heard news by now; it was after two. It was all so strange and mysterious, waiting, trusting blindly some huge mechanism that was dealing the cards. In the belly of a 81-million dollar, state-of-the-arts medical complex there was nothing more rational to do than hope — and suppress the anger that hope, and not a series of empirical facts, was all that was available. People in white and green, people that Jane didn't want to see as people, but as perfect machines administering flawless technical salvation to Jacob, came and went carrying objects and folders and gizmos on wheels. Jane tried to mold the tension in her face muscles into a look of relief, rehearsing for the moment when the doctor's assistant came through those doors proclaiming, "He came through with flying colors." Or. "It's a boy!"

"I've been in this place two whole weeks tomorrow," Fanny added. "Morning till night. Have hardly seen the sun." She reached once more for her knitting while crumbling with the other hand her slim cigarette — the kind with the plastic filter planted in the tip — into the polluted heap of sand, a microcosm of Asbury Park beach on July 5th. A glow of inexhaustible patience radiated from her face. "Only faith, dear, can help us. Faith and hope and Him," she pointed up to the ceiling. Jane looked up and saw the perforated ceiling panels and the fluorescent bulbs of light.

Harriet and Jane settled deeper into the discomfort of the hard plastic seats. The armrests matched poorly with the form of a human triceps. They opened their magazines and prepared themselves for the wait. Everything would come with time. All they could do was wait.

By the time the sternum had been sawed in two and the chest cavity was split open and clamped, Jacob's thoughts had seeped into the dark distance, where past and present and the past's future mingled, regrouping elsewhere and in other ways with anesthesia and recurrent dreams and nightmares, the inventive chemistry of the imagination, the psychic constituents of one lifelong mind, the master lottery of genetic history.... The activities of his intelligence were now secretive even to his own conscious self. They would havebeen reduced to a wave of electrical impulses on a screen had they been monitored. Other than that, Jacob was unapproachably alone. No man's land. The possibility of self-expression had been exterminated. His thoughts rolled with the random terror of waves. Anyone else's attempt to know them was sheer romanticism and fantasy. Yet his mind undoubtedly expanded and retracted wildly as oxygen still reached it; Dr. Cavenaugh, the surgeon from Memphis, Tennessee, connected the messy end of the heart-lung machine to Jacob's body, and thus Jacob's own enlarged heart was relieved from its seven decades of relentless pumping. The heart pulsed still and quivered as a second surgeon routinely cut through the fatty tissue that encased it and prepared the scene for Cavenaugh's final solution.

Jane rose to her feet and felt the heat of blood rushing from her head. Harriet looked around in a lost panic. Their name had rung out in a garble over the waiting room loud speakers, hidden in the asbestos ceiling panels overhead. The syllables were absorbed in the insulation but the echo seemed to linger in Jane's inner ear. "This was it," they thought, "the news." Jane hurried to the ICU Nurses' Station and identified herself, her stomach churning.

"You have a phone call at the pay phone in the corridor. Next to the coffee machine," a Thursday volunteer told her, in a matter-of-fact tone. A current mixed with relief and aggravation surged through Jane's already frazzled nerves.

"Hello...oh, Benjamin sweetie, it's you. No, we're still waiting for the doctor...Not yet...I'll call as soon as we know." She paused to let her son express himself before speaking again. He had had that kind of upbringing. "Yeah honey, I know. And you might as well call Dad at work and tell him...Oh, he told you to call, okay...Tell...Tell him I'll call as soon as I know...No, no. I shouldn't tie up the phone any longer. There are a lot of people here. It's amazing...Okay. Bye *hon*. I love you. Bye...Okay, I'll hang up first. Bye." Jane placed the sky-blue receiver gently into its cradle, stared at the magenta monogram, ITT, and headed back to Harriet; the picture of her curly-headed boy was fixed in her mind.

Fanny had gone down two levels to get a reuben sandwich. Harriet sat on the edge of her chair, tense, with her red hands gripping her bluish knees. Jane stopped at the water cooler for a drink, hesitating whether to use the aluminum foot pedal or hand button, and observed teeth marks in the chewed piece of Dentine that had petrified on the stainless drain. Erie, PA. embossed around the edge.

Water splashed on her chin; she wasn't very good at drinking from a fountain, nor at using a straw. Or pronouncing "marshmallows." These were things that didn't belong to her childhood.

"It was Benjamin calling from his dorm. I told him we'd call when we knew something."

"The darling. How that boy loves his grandfather! And how Jacob lives for him! Did you ever know a better pair?" Harriet spoke with admiration, her gold fillings showing slightly; she'd only have gold in her mouth. Jane wondered if she also heard a tinge of envy, of insecurity in Harriet's voice as if she was less legitimate than Jacob and thus less loved. There was nothing though for Jane to say; she just nodded in agreement.

"Doesn't he have school,"

"Mother, he's a big guy. He knows when he has school or not."

Harriet marveled to herself how fast her life had passed. In her mind Jane still needed help dressing. She thought of those wonderful days when she was needed to hem a dress or brush Jane's hair. And how she surveyed the boys who called for her — Allan Finkelstein and Nat Greenspan — and asked a million questions and waited up and scolded her. And insisted that Jane practice the scales on the piano thirty minutes each evening. And corrected Jane's grammar: "they" not "them," "he" not "him." She'd been to the State Teacher's College in Trenton "a hundred years ago;" she knew her grammar. A distant stare glazed over Harriet's face, producing a pattern of soft wrinkles on hanging skin. Now Jane had her own child in college.

5

Amy had just come on. She tapped lightly at the door of Jacob's room and entered. Finding the bed empty, she walked back to the nurse's station and asked the shift coordinator, a middle aged woman with a Mickey Mouse watch fastened to the button hole of her blouse. Her Tegucigalpa Swatch was being repaired at the plant in Marietta, Georgia. "I shouldn't have worn it in the pool, even though it said 'water-resistant' on the back."

"Where's Mr. what's-his-name? Wasn't there an older man in 1604 who should have been back up from OR by now?"

Consulting a computerized chart the coordinator replied, "ICU." Amy's eyebrows arched like the stretched backs of two cats. She was disappointed, a bit saddened. Still in ICU wasn't good news, and Jacob had seemed like a nice man, with a good sense of humor, not crabby for an old person. She pictured her *Opa's* hexagonal thumb nails and heard his teasing voice and the way he wheezed when he said something funny and refused to show that he was amused by his own wit.

Later in the shift she stopped by the room once more. She entered silently and tiptoed to the window of the dark, lifeless space. There wasn't a flower to be seen, and she knew instantly that no one had been there to see him. Anyway, Jews didn't spend much on hospital flowers, carnations or tiger lilies which would wilt and go to pieces in a matter of days; they planted trees in Israel which would last an eternity and cast deep roots inspired by memory. Cut flowers with long stems, though, were okay at weddings, where life was supposed to be celebrated, flaunted even. Someone, nevertheless, alwayssnuck out with the center pieces pretending they thought they were free for the taking. Below, on the Interstate off to her left she spotted a sign that must have been very large, which hung over the center lanes near the East-West Exchange: Beaumont KEEP LEFT. How many travelers even knew that the name was French? Immediately, she thought of Kevin and felt guilty; it'd been over two months already since she'd last seen him, the July 4th long weekend. Although he hadn't come from her blood and genes, it had felt like it when the divorce was taking place. "You get attached to a child," she muttered to herself in German. She could see in her mind a hot-dog sticking out from the pre-slit bun as it protruded from his cute mouth. She'd give him anything in the world. It wasn't all her fault. Her in-laws wouldn't put the boy on the Trailways bus to Houston. "You want to see him," they told her on the phone, "then you come here. You're his step-mother." How the word "step" bothered her. She thought of the act of a shoe crunching an insect. She looked away from the road sign and hid her sadness in the bit of straightening she did to Jacob's room, stacking neatly the odd Get Well cards that had arrived that day, projecting her desire for redemption into the dignity she demonstrated in her treatment of Jacob's few things. She opened the drawer of the plain night table and spotted the marbled diary, and hovered over it for a momen. She saw his signature on the cover. It was the eastern European way of making capital Ss that hooked her. That was the way *Oma* wrote. She'd come from Mitterteich, an agricultural village deep in Bavaria on the Czech border, had left at the age of 18 because her cousin Gretl had heard there was a chance of work as a seamstress in the town of Sulzbach near Aschaffenburg. There, young, vulnerable, and filled with common dreams that would for the most part come true until the war, she had met Robert, *Opa*, who she'd said was unlike the other boys, darker, more exotic. There was some mystery about his origins on his mother's side. There was scuttlebutt, talk of a journeying Ethiopian or Somalian, possibly even a Jew — but that was rarely repeated — ravished by her simple beauty, and the ease of seduction. She took the man's identity, in any case, with her to her grave, but passed on the dominant genes forever.

Amy was the sort who couldn't walk past someone on the beach without turning her head to read the title of the paperback sitting on the beach towel. She hesitated, glanced at her Timex, the kind that survived the cliff-diving at Acapulco. She still had a few minutes. Carefully, she pulled the diary from the drawer. His wristwatch, an old Omega with a separate inset face that contained a sweep second hand that was still moving, slid to the side of the drawer, making a slight grating noise which startled her. How could she explainfumbling though a patient's personal belongings? She strained her eyes and made out the tiny radium-coated hand. She lifted out the diary and tilted it into the glow of artificial light that came from the city. In a low, almost faint, whisper she began to read the handwritten lines randomly from somewhere in the middle.

I was in bed, too weak even to stand up or walk, weighing about 110 pounds. A lot of our inmates who had enough strength went outside the gates into the town to welcome the Russians and to watch and sneer at the hundreds of German soldiers and officers who'd been taken prisoner, as they were led past. Some inmates attacked them, robbing anything valuable, and even killing them — grabbing a pistol and shooting — which was possible since nobody worried about protecting them. It was the only immediate way of trying to get back, but I wasn't really thinking about getting back. I knew that killing a German boy wouldn't undo what I had been through or place before me at that instant my wife and daughter whom I hadn't seen in over four years. No, I didn't have any real desire to harm anyone else, just to find my wife and Dzidzia.

Some of the inmates started to do business, buying and selling clothing, buying up the confiscated clothes of dead inmates and selling them in different parts of the country where there was a shortage. A group of inmates forced open the local bank, loaded up carloads of German marks and then wildly threw them away in the streets, believing that the German money had no value at the end of the war. Playing with the Third Reich's currency in a mocking manner, stomping on the swastika *and the face of the* Führer.

Amy pictured the scene of frail Jewish inmates in striped pajamas jumping into piles of bank notes and the repetition of Hitler's head. She held her jaw in her hands. He had been a camp prisoner!

Later, we found out that this money had full value, but who could have been rational under these circumstances? Who would have thought to load our pockets with Hitler's portrait?

The nurse held her finger in the pages and flipped back through the diary to find out where the start of this entry began. Where had all this madness taken place? She scanned the unlined paper for an indentation. Her varnished thumbnail rubbing along each line.

Finally, in the beginning of 1945 we were taken to Czechoslovakia to an old Austro-Hungarian army barracks calledthe Archduke Carl V Kaserne, formerly the Franz-Joseph Kaserne, which had been converted to a concentration camp. As a matter of fact, the whole town of Teresenstadt was being prepared for extinguishing the rest of the remaining Jews in the area, including Prague, which was only an hour and a half or so to the south. The whole town was encircled by electric high tension wires. The gas chambers, already built, were being installed when we arrived, but, fortunately, the Germans ran out of time before this work was completed.

Amy paused before reading further. There was something wickedly understated in the tone. The man had been nearly gassed and all he writes is "fortunately the Germans ran out of time." "I was angrier," she thought...," stopping in mid-thought, embarrassed by the banality of the comparison she was about to pronounce, bothered, nonetheless, by his simple, story-telling tone. It was the word *fortunately*; it just came too easy, as if had he been gassed it would have merely been "unfortunate." She understood it, the futility of aggression, but it gnawled at her nonetheless. A form of timidity. Her grandmother would pitch the other way, tears rolling out of her eyes and then laughter at her own foolishness as she rubbed the water away when speaking about the hard times around the *Krieg*. She read on.

After we arrived in Teresenstadt we were locked in specially prepared barracks and not permitted to move.

Gradually, we were taken in groups to special showers, and all of us, men and women, were ordered to undress to the nude. We tried not to look at each other, maintaining our dignity, although it was impossible not to invade the privacy of especially the women. Then two soldiers went down the rows of us, dipping long brushes, like the ones we used to sell for wall paper glue, in yellow-green disinfectant and smearing our genitals with them. Entlausung, they called it. We stood there with our genitals dripping with this cold green liquid.

Amy looked at the word *genitals* written in a sweeping manner in Jacob's hand and pictured the rows of sad hanks of drooping flesh and hidden, irritated lips hidden in bushes of brown curls. This wasn't sex, but genitals like the ones on animals in the zoo. She read on and the scene skipped to the May 1945 liberation. Amy approached the spot where she had begun to read. Her thumb was no longer needed to save the place.

When the Russians arrived we were checked by highly specialized personnel for lice and parasites with high-beamelectric lamps. After two days of inspection, photographing, and of documenting all that they had found, we were given clean underwear with blue elastic and cotton clothing and most of us were put in an infirmary established by the Russian Army doctors, mostly women. It was like we were in a museum and we, the inmates, were the living artifacts. After a few weeks I was taken to a real hospital since I was still too weak to even stand up or walk, and weighed still only 110 pounds.

Then, brusquely, she skipped ahead an inch of pages. How much does he have here? she wondered. Flipping quickly now through the blue-inked pages that crinkled and rolled. There was something remarkable about so much handwriting, far more moving than what typed print looked like. "Look at all of this." Both sides of page after page was filled with lines of Jacob's dancing script. There was something so touchingly human about all that ink marching in lines on paper, words rolling out of a brain.

I wanted to go back to Poland, that's all that I knew, because of my daughter, but one of the Russian women doctors, Jewish, started to yell at me, insisting that I go to Russia instead, that I'd be better off in Russia, that there was a future for me there. Hadn't I had enough? What did future mean anyway? I was too weak to resist and nearly gave in. But at the last minute I changed my mind and went to Krakow. I didn't really change my mind, I knew all along that there was only one thing for me to do, but I nearly didn't have the strength to insist on it. Imagine if I hadn't had gone back to Poland! I think of Dzi and I can't.

By seven forty-five the families of the intensive care patients were buzzing nervously. Each family was issued one pass per visit which could be used by one person and was relinquished at the door to the unit upon entry, like at a cinema or one of the New York playhouses that Harriet and Jacob loved to go on Sundays, usually on Broadway and starring one of those charismatic male leads like Zero Mostel or Yul Brenner. Although Jane wanted very much to go in first, she let Harriet take the pass. Harriet's nerves were more brittle, Jane reasoned. She *was* his wife, nonetheless. Fanny had returned from the ladies room with her long wavy blond hair brushed, shining, and pulled back, and tied with a ribbon.

"I want to look good for my guy. You know what I mean Harriet?" and she winked, youthful as a schoolgirl, while standing impatiently on the antsy line that had already formed by the unit's entrance. HOSPITAL PERSON-NEL ONLY, it said in black on the gray metal door, the gray worn away in the middlenear the word *Push* where all the hands and shoulders touched day in and day out, worn away like the lips of stairs in public buildings, like fossils. Harriet discretely hoisted her girdle and checked that her slip didn't surpass the hem of her skirt. Her hands and feet were like ice and she made small movements privately to warm herself and contain her riled nerves. Jane waited with her in line until one minute to eight and then sent her in like a Little League manager. All eyes had been on the clock, ready to scream if the door hadn't opened as soon as the second hand swept by the twelve, or if time had suddenly decided to stop altogether. A young Hispanic woman in a blue-green uniform ushered the crowd in and collected the numbered passes. They rushed by single-mindedly like shoppers heading to the check-out. Odd numbers to the right, even numbers to the left. Jane gave a final squeeze, (a motion not so much from encouragement but more from her own mounting tension). "Tell him I'll see him in the morning. Kiss him for me, mother," Jane said quickly, as Harriet bravely disappeared into the dimly-lit chamber.

6

In October of 1914 when I was ten years old, the same year the war broke out between Austria-Hungary and Russia, our house and store in Poronin burnt down to the ground and we had to move ten kilometers north to Nowy Targ, New Market in English. We found out later that it was arson, started by a former salesman of ours whom my father had fired several days earlier for stealing merchandise; the man's name I can't remember, but I do remember that he was killed two or three weeks later on the Russian front. Some revenge.

At this point I have to go back to the year before 1914 when a number of political prisoners had run away from Czarist Russia and lived in our village of Poronin. Among them was N. Lenin, known then as Vladimir Ilyich Ulyanov (1870-1924), and a lot of people who became members of his government after the revolution in November 1917. They all were customers in my father's store, buying candles, tools, canned foods. I remember Lenin himself once came in for a sheet of coarse sand paper. And this group was very friendly with us socially. After work my father would sometimes pour out shot glasses of schnapps.

He could pour them in one movement right up to the lip of the glass, even higher so that the whiskey would seem to hang over the sides. When the Austro-Hungarian war broke out in 1914 the whole Russian group was arrested and put in jail in Nowy Targ. My father organized a committee of the most respected citizens in town who convinced the officials to release the entire group. My father personally posted Lenin's bail. Released, they all fled Poland overnight for a foreign country. My father advanced Lenin several hundred Austrian kronen and in 1918 Mr. Lenin sent my father the money along with a thank you note from Copenhagen, Denmark.

Jacob would later travel himself to Copenhagen with his young bride, but Amy couldn't know it. It wasn't exactly a passionate beginning; their fathers had worked out the details, the mercantile trade-off, the red-headed son for the eldest daughter, but on the long train ride north across Poland, Northern Germany, and then on the briny deck of the ferry crossing the Baltic the young couple began to feel the excitement of their independence. The thrill of being away from family. They began to look more closely at the other's small features, the skin, the wrinkle in the bottom lip, the cute twirl of hair on top, the shape of their bodies, the quality of socks. There was a small hotel in an outer district of the city facing a canal, and it was there that Jacob and Amalja, in a small but quaint room with a bed that sagged and creaked, grew into their new role as husband and wife. It was there in that tiny Danish room that a new generation would begin, a generation that would ultimately save the family line from extinction, that would change the migratory pattern of a family. Who could think of such things at times like that. They ordered French champagne at dinner.

She read on. It was like eating beyond hunger.

While being a boy of eight or nine I remember sitting on Mr. Lenin's lap many times. Somewhere there's a photograph of me and Mr. Lenin. He died in January 1924 near Moscow.

The flow of Jacob's journal entry broke off there. He hadn't been sure whether to organize his pages by theme and location or to continue with the chronology of his life. And the act of writing forced him to confront the intricate way that memory worked and the dangerously difficult task of trying to write history. Of course, he had already skipped ahead and thus found that his memory wouldn't follow the time line that he had assumed it would. He resorted finally to a confused system of double-numbered pages and inserted directional instructions which confused Amy at times. In any case, he'd go back later and fix things up. There'd be time to edit; Benjamin at college would help him; it'd be a pleasure, he had thought. This temporary lack of order had at first been distressing to Jacob; he was a hardware man used to keeping careful books, exact inventory figures, clearly classified merchandise shipment statements. There'd be time to straighten it out later.

In 1920, after the fight was over and Lenin was in power and a Russian Embassy was established in Poland, the Russian Ambassador Karmieriew came to Poronin to pick up the hundreds of books and valuable papers that the group left behind and my father had safely stored when they were arrested in 1914, fortunately in a garage and not in our store which burned down. Karmieriew found out that we had moved to Nowy Targ and called my father there asking for a meeting the next day in Krakow. He said he had a very profitable business proposition to offer. Since Poland's relations with Russia at that time were not 100%

kosher, my father was afraid of this contact. He felt his reputation was at stake. The Russians weren't very popular with the townspeople, to say the least. At the advice of the President of the Krakow Chamber of Commerce, who warned my father that investigations by the Polish equivalent of the FBI and IRS were very real possibilities, my father decided not to attend the meeting. And that was that. It would have been very interesting to know what the Ambassador had to say to my father. Everything might have been very different. It was no small act; Emmanuel Simon had saved Lenin's life!

After buying a house in Nowy Targ (behind my grandmother's saloon), my father, having been a professional soldier before the War, was drafted into the Austro-Hungarian Army and was sent to Croatia and Albania as a Sergeant. He soon developed malaria and was confined to the Army Hospital in Dubrovnik, now part of Yugoslavia.

Meanwhile, my mother and I traveled by horse and buggy from village to village trying to collect the debts from our former customers. But since our record books were burned in the fire many refused to admit they owed us anything and we had a hard time collecting.

Jacob had paused for a long while there with his pen stalled on one spot. The sound of the heavy horse hooves clip-clopping along the country roads around Poronin came jumping out quite suddenly from some stored zone and he heard metal scraping stone like it was yesterday. Oh, and the thick stream of steamy pee that the horse let loose without even breaking gait. How funny it was.

In addition, the money from our fire insurance was transferred directly to our creditors in Vienna, so there wasn't very much for us to live on. Through a local military hospital we got my father transferred from Dubrovnik

to Nowy Targ. When he got better he was home quite often,
and on the side he earned some money importing sewing
machines from America.

Three hours into the operation the mitrol valve had
been successfully replaced and Cavenaugh began on the
first by-pass. These went more quickly. Inch-long arterial
sections had been grafted from Jacob's legs and were ready
to be reused in Jacob's left ventricle.

"Jesus H. Christ, I can't see a freakin' thing in here,"
Cavenaugh balked and a hand belonging to a moonlighting
OR grub, receiving a decent hourly wage, reached in with
a sponge. Then he remembered that he'd have to swing
home later to pick up his spikes for tomorrow's golf tour-
ney. He made a secure clamp, and backed off, stretched
slightly his lower back. This one was going to take about
two to three hours longer than he had thought originally. It
was a mess in there. The disease was advanced.

Fanny returned with two Hostess Fruit Pies for Jane
and Harriet, which they ate more out of gratitude than hunger. These specimens of food, urban Jewish people didn't
really consider edible; they were artificial and bad for your
health, items found in lunch pails on work sites or in the
Fred Flintstone lunch boxes of Christian kids in public
school cafeterias, the same lunch boxes that held thin sand-
wiches of Wonderbread, a wipe of Hellman's or Kraft Sandwich Spread, and a slice of chicken roll or bologna complete with the orange plastic skin, flopping around in a plastic zip lock Baggie, and a thermos of chocolate milk and a
Yoddle or Scooter Pie or Ring Ding or Devil Dog, and a
few coins for red Jello on the snack line. These were the
kids who belonged to people who drank Tang at breakfast
because it was better for you than fresh squeezed. And
bought Chocks Multiple Vitamins, the ones shaped into pre-
Speilberg characters. For Harriet, snack food was bread

and butter, thin-rye with or without seeds and a touch of margarine, or else an apple or a pear. Jane had grown up like that but the forces of modern American shopping and publicity practices had coaxed her away from such Spartan habits. The day-glo filling wasn't bad, she thought.

"Hi ladies," Fanny waved across the aisle, then stopped to admire a teenage girl's needlepoint, a bright pattern of a square house and a healthy tree and the word "Home". The girl's father was also having the by-pass procedure, as did forty each week at Methodist and sixty across the street or through the tunnel at the Southern Clinic. "Routine as having your teeth cleaned," was the way one of Harriet's brothers described the operation.

The clock said 4:01 at the nurses's station.

"Mr. McDougall," a tall nurse called out over the half-somber waiting room, startling everyone; Harriet admired, beneath her nervousness, the nurse's posture, breasts centered over the rib cage. That was how a young woman should carry herself, she said, smacking her lips together. "Could you please follow me." And a large man in Thom McCann imitation Wallabies whose waxed laces had bunches of interior knots sped towards the disappearing nurse.

"His wife had what your husband had, Harriet," Fanny whispered. I talked to him in the elevator. Nice fella. She teaches second grade in Topeka. Got a lot of cards. From her class I guess."

"That's not an easy job, Harriet replied in seriousness, having been a teacher's aide for eight years in a school for emotionally and mentally handicapped children. She'd been an absolute angel with those kids, remarkably sensitive and not even in her private thoughts even slightly repulsed by the sight of a deformed face or spastic movement.

Jane listened but failed to concentrate enough to have been able, if asked, to repeat what Fanny or Harriet had said. Words poured through her as pure sound. She could disconnect their power of association. Her thoughts were with Jacob. Fear rumbled within. What did this delay mean? Were there complications? Why hadn't the doctor come for them with the reassuring news? What was wrong? Surely something was wrong. But then again hospitals were like that. They made you wait. Things took time. Their internal logic was inaccessible to the outside, and even the patients were outsiders. There wasnothing wrong; she was sure. She could feel just then the plastic resilience of her anti-perspirant begin to falter.

The man in the Thom McCanns returned quickly bumbling around his seat to gather his shopping bag of magazines and crossword puzzles, an extra sweater for the evening and the strong air conditioning, and a thermos of Lipton.

"Going upstairs, George?" Fanny called out.

"Yes, mam," he hollered like a boy on the playground in a town made by Frank Capra. "Rhonda came through with flying colors and I'm just tickled. They're bringing her up to her room right now. Thank God."

"Amen. That's great news, George." Then Fanny faced Harriet and said, "You know, they like to get them back to their rooms as soon as possible. It's better for their morale. Plus, they need the room down here, bad." Harriet knew there should have been an "ly" on the end of "bad", it was an adverb of course, but held herself from saying anything. "Always more coming in. Y'all have seen MASH. It's like war."

It couldn't be, Jane mentally smirked, while it fixed Jacob's face on its screen.

The jovial Italian-American woman, just up from her nap, let the shawl drop from her shoulders and peeled an orange with a kitchen knife. She pushed several sections in front of the girl with the needlepoint. The girl hesitated — the instinct was not to take things from strangers, especially things that were to be eaten; even on Halloween, all the loot not securely sealed in its original manufactured wrapper went straight to the trash; anything homemade, cookies, candies, sugar apples, etc. was immediately tossed in the lemon-scented trash liner under the sink; too many sickos out there, her father used to say — but the woman insisted so the girl took the piece of orange and brought it to her lips. Jane was scared. She watched everything now as if in a cinema.

I told you before how, in a very risky move through the barbed wire fence at the edge of the Krakow ghetto, I transferred my daughter from the Volksdeutsche to my cousin's daughter Lala, who lived at the time outside of Krakow in Myslenice on Polish papers, with a man who owned a shoe factory. The rest I gathered from my daughter and my cousin Oscar after the war. Staying with Lala was not a life lined with roses. Bit by bit, I learned about the beatings, about being thrown in the Raba, being forced to work hard in the garden, turning over hard soil, and having to carry heavy packages to the post office several kilometers away. I must add here that when transferring my daughter to Lala I gave her a plan (sketch) of a cellar where I had a large fortune hidden underground and I knew that she got it, I believe.

Jane, watching Chicklets slide from a thin green box that kids used as a horn, and listening to the tinny rustle of magazine pages turning, unthinkingly pictured Lala, who now supposedly, was a woman approaching Harriet's age somewhere, perhaps in Australia. In her mind she saw the inside of Lala's little house. She saw her room, no it was a hallway, very narrow, just wide enough for a bed. And the other room, Lala's room. She kept it locked. Locked, because Victor used to come. I'd have to go to sleep even when I wasn't tired. They'd make me go to bed, Jane remembered and then choked with emotion, thinking of herself as a little girl, all alone in a house in a village during a war without her parents, the only people on earth that really loved her. I would have to go bed and then they would be in the bed," she whimpered privately. "The man's shoes would sit in the hallway, big and brown and looking like they were yawning, and worn socks balled up inside. And then the bed would begin to shake and the floorboards leading from the place beneath their bed would creak down the hall under the door and move in front of my eyes," she testified to herself, becoming seven. There was a key hole. I used to look through the keyhole while they were making out in bed. The covers would thump and I wondered if he was hurting her. I remember seeing them nude." Jane's mind was talking out loud. "And the abortion, huh." She paused. She just realized what it had been. "Incredible, I'm remembering all this stuff." She pulled it back from dead ends, sucking it out of tight spots. The abortion was also in that room. "I had to come in afterwards and clean it up. Blood all over the floor. The wooden floor, with those cracks, and blood soaking right through the wood. Cleaning it up. Lala wore glasses, sort of clear rimmed glasses. I wonder why, I don't know why. She beat me, beat me up one time really bad, with a fireplace poker. I had to lie down, with my face down. My nose flattened on the same wood that I had to scrub. The pain, I can eel it now, just now. I would put my hands on my rear end to block it out. But she bruised me so badly that all my nails came off. All my nails turned black. Black. Every one. Five on one hand and four or five on the other. I had to wear little booties on my fingers. Booties on my fingers with *ikviol*, a kind of salve that drew out the

69

infection. Yes, they got infected. All my nails fell off. I hate my nails. It hurt." Jane felt it; there was physical pain stocked in memory. Her eyes dropped to her nails. They'd grown back and were now chewed and ragged and pink, not black, and ugly. She had bought in the late sixties all sorts of products to inhibit nail biting, back in those days when her weight started to climb, varnish that tasted bitter, plastic coatings that were indestructible, hypnosis.... She was ashamed of her nervous habit, stunned by the pain she could still feel even there in that cool, remotewaiting room in Texas.

Dzidzia, my daughter, meaning 'baby' in Polish, and a nick-name we always used and still do because she was a beautiful baby and her mother dressed her like a Dresden doll, was loved and pampered by all the people in Nowy Targ, especially the gentile women, since she had blond hair and a Kosciushko-type nose and a typically Aryan look. Dzidzia didn't want to aggravate me by telling me these terrible stories about Lala. But I learned bit by bit.

Lala was only nineteen herself and I gather had little patience for a seven-year old girl during the war. (Minimizing the risk of keeping a Jewish child, Lala had Dzidzia officially baptized as Krystina Antoszkiewicz. Dzidzia remembers going to catechism in Krakow in the big church behind the Wistla. I still have the photograph of her communion class.)

Jacob didn't know that Lala had only been following Victor's instructions. It hadn't been little Dzidzia's safety they were considering, but the cause, and the easy movement of Russian-made guns and powder in the thick red wool linings of Victor's manufactured boots. Lala had been Underground too. Not Polish, Russian. The post office was two kilometers from the little house with the green shutters and whitewashed boulders in the front, like in that remaining snapshot that Jane kept among her things in the bottom drawer of her night table. Victor had taken it with the same Leica that he used to falsify documents. They had used the girl to lug the heavy parcels to the post; Jane had been a carrier for the Underground.

Amy remembered her communion and the mean nuns who ridiculed her in front of the others for wearing the red overalls that *Oma* had sewn.

Jacob's hand had dashed off the beginnings of a story that had always made his heart shutter; swish, the flow of blood coursed through the tired valves driven by its own harsh undertow.

One day Lala took Dzi to Krakow with her and told her to wait quietly inside the church at Karmelicka while she went inside a nearby bistro to meet some friends. After several hours, Dzi, being a small child, got tired of waiting and came out onto the sidewalk on Karmelicka. The whole area was encircled by German soldiers — not uncommon — who were checking the documents of all the local inhabitants and people in the bistro. Those without proper papers or those without proof of employment were arrested and shipped to work camps inGermany, or worse. And this is what happened to her cousin Lala.

Dzi didn't know what to do. She was scared and she started to cry there on the sidewalk. I can picture her although I wasn't there and I too started to cry. A woman who ran a grocery store across the street saw Dzi crying and went over to her to help. My daughter told the woman, whose name Dzi once wrote down on a piece of paper after coming to this country, but I can't find or remember it, but I think it was Golab, told her to go to the German officer standing in front of the bistro and asked him to let Lala go. Dzi did this but instead of getting an answer, the officer kicked her away and she ran back across the street to the

Polish grocery store woman, crying. The woman took her in and asked her name. Krystyna Antoszkiewicz, she replied, having learned to always say this name and no other, ever. The woman was a widow and unable to take care of a child so she transferred Dzi to her sister who had a small farm outside of Krakow in Male Bronowice. Dzi never knew what happened to Lala and never returned to her little house in Myslenice. The sister had two sons who were several years older than Dzi, and from what Dzidzia told me, they were very nice to her. There was enough to eat, chickens in the yard, and vegetables in the garden. Dzi says she remembers a round table in the kitchen and a goat tied to a tree.

When the sister and the two boys would ask Dzi questions about where she came from all she would repeat was the simple story that Lala had insisted she memorize, that accompanied her new Christian name, that her parents had been killed in the war by a bomb in Warsaw.

Meanwhile, my cousin Oscar Simon had set out to find his daughter (and mine) and found out about the raid on the Karmelika bistro. When he inquired at the grocery store he learned the rest and went out to Bronowice. Dzi was happy there and didn't want to go with him, he told me. I know that she hated his wife who was often nasty and bitchy. (I remember this too.) So Oscar let her stay and merely left his address in case he was needed. He lived on false papers in a borrowed flat in town.

Some months later when the Russians finally gained and occupied Krakow, the farm in Bronowice was expropriated and the sister with her two boys had to move into the small apartment above the grocery store on Karmelicka. My daughter was returned to Oscar. According to the story that he told me, he didn't have enough income to be able to take care of her and this is why he handed my daughter over to the Jewish Committee at the corner of Krakowska and Skawinska. Theyadmitted her into their overcrowded infirmary because she had developed jaundice.

Fortunately, she was recognized by her mother's cousin who was married to the President of this Committee, Dr. Stuhlback (who later immigrated to Sao Paolo, Brazil) and she was treated with extra care. After recuperating, she was sent to a children's sanitarium in Zakopane, where a wonderful woman, Mrs. Silberman, had gathered and nursed back to health a hundred Jewish orphans. I would be re-united with my Dzidzia, our promise kept.

Amy shut the diary and placed it in the drawer, her eyes wet. The world was filled with sadness. She felt like calling Kevin or walking in the Taunus with *Opa* looking for deer, but it was too late.

Jane pulled a cuticle and it began to bleed. Harriet scolded her.

"Why did you do that?"

Jane wasn't listening. She was silent, her eyes were fixed on a black athlete leaping on the cover of *Sports Illustrated*. Otherwise she was on a Krakow streetcar, a trolley car just for Germans, with Lala, forbidden to talk. Riding silently and listening to the strange voices and laughter. She didn't answer but left the cuticle alone. "A Leap for Excellence," it said.

7

Cavenaugh's eyelids were heavy and his gray-white eyebrows were wiry and confused, like the lines in a satirical cartoon. Harriet and Jane stood before him attentive as altar boys while he spoke. It was as much his tone as his words that mattered. Maybe more. He was used to these moments; they were part of the job, a part that doctors each treated differently. He had learned, like anyone who had to explain himself regularly, the art of manipulative tact the same way he'd learned how to operate: relentless practice. Sometimes you were good; sometimes you were slightly off. He knew the anguish that tortured his audiences so well that he could no longer feel it. Like nakedness to a prostitute, maybe. Routine. Of course they were feeling things. It had been many years already since he'd stopped feeling their pain. He knew it but didn't feel it. Cavenaugh didn't for a second feel remorse for this numbness. He didn't even think about it, for any thought about it was caught up in the numbness itself. He was confident beyond any doubt — to the point where the question didn't enter his head — that he was serving mankind in an exquisite way, just about the most admirable way one could think of. And even when lives weren't saved directly, the statistical reinforcement of theory was being built, the empire of medical knowledge advanced. That, he held in the confident pose of his eyebrows, an unshakable certainty and righteous intolerance for any inference, regardless how circuitous, of anything less than commendable practice. He was a pillar. The cardiologist. One of the big men of any hospital. There was no time to stumble emotionally over the rough edges of hurt and defeat. Hurt and defeat wereunnecessary elements in the larger plan of things. Individuals were only vital in that they, together, composed the whole. And it was the whole, the conclusive whole, not the rough data, that the journals celebrated. Not the individuals. The one-in-ten that died after open-heart surgery was someone's child or someone's father or mother too. The one-in-ten left clothes hanging in some closet, money in a savings account, photographs tacked to the wall by the mirror, a ledger of memoirs in a hospital room. Nobody really cared about the one-in-ten.

But Cavenaugh was human too and couldn't help every- one; yet individuals wanted magic from a mortal. The magic he offered was methodical and constant and human. Even mistakes belonged in the system, in that eyes grew tired, nerves bent, minds wandered. Statistics included margins of error. Each operation helped in some way the next, won or lost. Carefully, he suppressed his impatience with the small and desperate hopes of the families of those he cut into. Privately, he felt that they didn't realize their fortune in having him do the work. His voice was neither excited nor falsely calm. He spoke in a straight-forward manner, from the hip, reporting like a foreign, war-zone correspondent the events of the day, sequentially from most to least important. There was composure in his stance which obscured the tinge of boredom and the massive fatigue that ran below like a vein of ore. He'd just finished two big ones and there was more to do before he'd shuffle into his silver BMW in the garage below and roll out onto the smooth black tar into the anonymity of the Houston dusk, heading for his Guinness Stout. The radio tuned-in to WHUN giving sports updates every five minutes before the hour and classical favorites in between, Wagner to Leonard Bernstein. He was a surgeon, not a priest or diplomat. He tilted his silvered Aryan head as he deliberated. He owned cattle in Argentina and one-thirty-second of a famous race horse and one percent of a Broadway show.

"The operation lasted five hours and twenty five minutes, about two hours and ten minutes longer than we had expected. He took 28 units of blood and he's going to need more. So I suggest you contact your hometown blood bank to arrange a blood credit exchange." He inhaled and continued. Jane searched his blue clothing for signs of the Operating Room. A pack of some low tar cigarettes, True or Vantage, bulged slightly in his hospital coat pocket. "The valve replacement and by-passes went reasonably smooth." Harriet heard the faulty adverb. "But I won't kid you, I must say that aside from the enlarged heart situation, which we talked about before, the heart is severely diseased. Especially that right aorta." Cavenaugh wanted to say something crude, invent a graphic metaphor like they did in Med school, but held back. "I wouldn't have given him more than six months anyway. Maybeas little as three." Cavenaugh shook his head. "There's something wrong going on here," Jane was feeling. A photo of that aorta would make a fine little teaching specimen, Cavenaugh thought. Why not make use of it somehow. Cavenaugh was committed in that way; he cared how to keep other doctors, especially young ones, informed. "That sort of thing doesn't show up on the coronary angiogram. There still are things that the catheterization doesn't do. We couldn't know until we opened him up."

Jane sensed that this was a lead-up to something she instinctively didn't want to hear. There was a sense of order to his speech. The order served more to justify the actions taken than to cushion the information with tact. The little veins in Harriet's temples were pounding with blood. And the tiny piece of Carefree gum whose spearmint flavor had long been used up, Harriet held quietly beneath her tongue like a snitch.

"I had to insert what we call a cardio-balloon. Sort of a thin rubber ball which sustains the pumping action of the heart until the heart is ready to take over for itself." Cavenaugh mimed this function with his fist. He wore no rings. There was dark hair on his knuckles. "The balloon is snaked through the groin and up into the aorta, where it inflates and deflates at a prescribed beat." Harriet and Jane were still silent." His vital signs are stable though. I have him on the respirator to facilitate the breathing. We're watching him closely. The next twelve to eighteen hours will tell a lot. Very important." Jane's mind fought the lecture. Cavenaugh had given the guts of his talk; now he was chipping in the pep, the rhetoric that belonged to the military man in him. He'd been to Korea, and aside from a couple of rough details, had a ball. Although it did contribute to his first divorce. *Catch 22* was his favorite film; although he'd never read the novel or even heard of Heller. "He's a very strong man, that guy. He fought hard. He's been through a lot today. Five hours on the table is quite a shock." Cavenaugh tapped the tips of his right fingers against those of his left, almost forming the shape of a chapel. He was finished and now waited briefly for the sad and insipid questions that always followed. He hadn't talked "life or death" and he knew he wouldn't be released until he gave them different language and a few more statistics. Harriet wanted to know when Jacob could go to his room, what all this meant. What had happened to the confident talk, the 90% success rate stuff of a day earlier, even in a man of Jacob's age? It just as well might have been last year or a decade ago. Yesterday was a different world.

"This balloon," Jane started clumsily. She didn't want to talk about balloons; there was no choice. And she couldn't just let the doctor walk away. "Is it normal, a standardprocedure." That was an easy one for Cavenaugh. He didn't mind it. He could talk medical, turn on automatic pilot, like the speed control in his car, a feature he absolutely loved, like the FM scanner on his radio.

"I don't have to use it in most cases, but in cases of severe heart disease, like with your father, it's virtually a necessity in preventing heart failure in the immediate postoperative period. Is there a risk?" Cavenaugh asked himself rhetorically. "Yes, most certainly. Of rejection, infection, dependency. Is there a choice? No, not really. That's why the next day, as I already said, is crucial. Because we can't leave it in more than 36 hours, 48 at the most." A wave of nervous fear rippled through Harriet as she mistook the doctor's word "crucial" for "critical", the label of a condition she'd lived dreading. Her father had been "critical" before he died. So had her brother. And Golda Meier too. Jacob had a framed picture of Golda on his hi-fi along with a heavy bronze, modern Menorah that he liked.

What could Jane say back. Deny? Disagree? These were the words of undeniable reality batting against her life. If she refused to believe them she'd also know that she was deluding herself. This man that stood before her had cut into her father with his hands and sharp instruments; he knew things she couldn't say "no" to, even if she wanted to.

"Can we see him?" Harriet managed to ask.

"Briefly. At eight tonight, during ICU visiting hours. Talk to him. Encourage him. Try to orient him. Tell him what day it is, what's new, things like that. He's not up but don't worry, he can hear you. He's got to help out now. It's up to him; he has got to want it." With that, the tail end of his "one for the Gipper" speech, the doctor fled down a narrow corridor that he knew quite well, and disappeared through a door, thinking of nicotine.

Harriet sent a loud, slightly obsequious "thank you, doctor" after him, subconsciously hoping that her politeness would make Cavenaugh like her and thus attain special treatment for Jacob, save his life. Her tone, though, could have easily been taken for sarcastic but Cavenaugh barely even heard Harriet's voice jumping out after him.

Jane and Harriet stood there battling to be pleased. At least the cutting was finished, the stitches were in place, the chest cavity closed.

"His vital signs are steady, mother. That's a good sign," Jane remarked in a tone meant to comfort, grasping with her voice a world of filtered air. Secretly, the part about the balloon terrified her. It returned to her thought each time she twisted it away. She pictured a red helium balloon like the ones at Olympic Park in Irvington and felt the deep disappointment when one once got out of her hand and flew up rapidly out of reach until it disappeared. Harriet just stoodthere on the tiled floor, half alive, biting her bottom lip. She had gold in her mouth; she'd hear of nothing less than gold.

"Come on mother, let's get a bite to eat. There's nothing more we can do here. We'll come back at eight. Come." And Jane led her stepmother into the brighter corridor where doctors and nurses and visitors and orderlies with carts of hospital supplies and beds on wheels passed by in a whir. They walked as if they saw both everything and nothing, stiff and disbelieving. "Yes, this is my life," Jane admitted. Fanny was back at her spot in the waiting room playing Go-Fish with a child neither Jane nor Harriet had spotted before. Another operation.

The quality of light and the unique smell of hospital, sickened Jane, and she longed at once to be in a country meadow running naked through a paean of wild flowers, Tatra flowers like the ones that dotted the fields on the outskirts of Nowy Targ. Running naked, it was a recurrent dream, but she hadn't an idea where it came from or what it really meant. In real life she was rather shy, modest. At a beach on the French Riviera she'd not remove her top like the other women. The elevator didn't open at G as programmed, but instead sunk another floor into one of the underground levels where Burton wanted to get in with a cart of laundry, his name stenciled into his work whites. Labs, parking, garbage, morgue, laundry...the whole gamut of hospital underground possibilities ravaged...rats, abortion aftermaths, amputations...Janes's racing mind. The Houston safety inspector had been to the elevator that summer; it said so on the certificate behind the Plexiglas holder. Jane closed her eyes and momentarily relaxed her will to mold the future. It'd come on its own. When the elevator opened on the Ground Floor the moment eased, and they squeezed out, turned right, and passed the fluorescently-lit gift shop. Then they passed the bulbous US mailboxes with their squeaky yawning lids, the local newspaper boxes with the bent-up grillwork and coin box, three spanking bright dispensers for *USA Today*, the Nation's Newspaper, with the weather patterns swirling in tones of Van Gogh offset, Fed Ex and DHL drop boxes and then the bank of Southern Bell telephones. They spun through the revolving doors and into the hot and steamy evening air of Houston. The first waft of air felt like standing by the ventilator shaft outside a laundromat. Jane remembered Benjamin as a kid, had chased a chipmunk around the back of the house. Instead of plummeting down the drainpipe as usual, the critter popped into the exhaust vent of the Maytag dryer. A week later the repairman, wearing a belt of tools, had to come to remove the dead animal. With a brush he freed the striped thing from the filter and swept him out from under the machine, dry,flattened and linty along with a lost and forgotten bed slipper and a few coins.

The day had dissolved. They had missed it. A trail of taxis, late-model Chryslers mostly, part of the recovery personally guaranteed by author and political aspirant Lee Iaocca himself, queued up along the hospital's circular drive. There was a flagpole in the tiny island of lawn. Two, elongated, black and chrome limos — with diplomatic plates embossed in Arabic, were parked in a tow-away zone near the electric eye-beam doors.

Jane couldn't manage the lively array of parking lights; she wanted the world to stop and wait for Jacob to rejoin it. Technology seemed to have advanced even further since early morning when she and Harriet entered through the electric doors. It grew faster than bamboo. She felt foolish. The downtown lights seemed to be winking now at her vulnerability in the fading purple glow of day. Mocking her punishment. On off on off, the circuitry of the town didn't feel; it didn't care. It laughed and laughed in a humorless pitch. The senselessness of everything, she thought, picturing on the billboards Aunt Jamima pancake batter, the new Sony Interactive, Eyewitness News at Seven, the Sushi bar that was opening on the 29th.

"Let's walk a bit," Harriet suggested strongly. "I have to walk." She had poor circulation in her legs. In the heat of the American south in early autumn her feet were cold and streaked with blue. The two women, alone and tentative, chilled in the heated air, followed the sidewalk blindly. They were prepared, almost, to take it wherever it led them. Jane half-consciously avoided the cracks in the sidewalk. They crossed Fannin Street and moved briskly towards Outer Belt Drive. No one walked in Houston. It was like LA without the reputation.

Without passion, they waited for a uniformed hostess to seat them in a quiet booth at Denny's, a family restaurant started by a baseball pitcher who had gained short fame by winning 31 games one season in Detroit, and to place plastic-coated menus with clipped-on specials in their hands. Jane was tired of uniforms. The water, with giant convex lens of ice cubes, landed on the litho-protected table top. Jane couldn't eat, but felt the need to go through the motions.

"Order for me, mother. Platter number Three. No onions. I'm going to call home." Jane slid out and followed the arrow towards the rest rooms where the phones were loyally found.

Jane punched in her number and coded tones squeaked like Martian mice. Computers were busy gathering up bits of information and were singing their way through the job, gaining for her Frequent Flyer miles with a leading domestic carrier. As the phone rang on the other end Jane imagined her voice rushing through the wires across Texas and Louisiana andGeorgia and up the Eastern seaboard to her state and town, and then into the neighborhood, up the hill, across the street, to the pole by the mailbox, over the crab-apple tree and into her house. And then, simultaneously, into the touch-tone units in the kitchen and den, the cordless in the hall, and princess model with the illuminated dial — $4.00 extra each month — on her night table in the bedroom. She pictured the framed school portrait of young Benjamin in fifth grade with the V-neck she'd knitted him, and the ragged, old-model Polaroid snapshot of Benjamin on the shoulders of Jacob, in the summertime, in the backyard of a small, former house, and the chemical fixative (that was now built into the film) streaking the priceless black and white photo, both guys shirtless.

"It's me..."

8

I arrived in Krakow on Dzidzia's tenth birthday in June 1945 and began immediately to search for my sweetheart. I remember vividly the day I became a father; Amalja was in the hospital in this same city. Dzidzia was so beautiful and blonde cradledin her arms, the white sheets bunched up around them both. It was her birthday and I didn't even know if she knew that it was! How do you start looking for a child in a city of over 300,000 people after you haven't seen her for almost four years? I didn't even know then that she'd been given a new name. Nor did I then know about the transfer to Lala, Oscar's daughter, or her arrest. I didn't even know who, if anyone, I had ever known in the world, was still living.

I walked and walked, visiting every house at every address at which I remembered somebody that I had even vaguely known had lived — but without results. No one was where they had been before. The telephone book did not help. The city was in an organizational nightmare. No one knew where anyone was. Everything was in disorder; nothing worked and no one dared trust anyone. But the buildings were all standing and the rynek strangely was a beautiful site. I cried seeing it. It had been a common site, and now it was so rare. I was frantic and miserable on top of being terribly weak and undernourished. There was nothing to do but search. I walked feverishly, trapped in the anonymity of my exhaustion and freedom. Krakow was a city of walking skeletons and dubious charlatans. Everyone seemed lost and everybody had lost someone.

Amy began to whimper. At least she knew she could always get Kevin on the phone. Just ten digits on a push-button. At worst, she could get into her Cutlass and drive for four hours and five minutes down the Interstate, exit at Beaumont-East and be in front of the house in no time, where his mountain bike was always crash-landed in the driveway. She was surprised by her emotions. And there was something else behind these tears. Someone else. She cried at movies sometimes but she couldn't remember ever crying over a book, and this wasn't even a book, and she had only read a dozen pages. It wasn't the story that got her, she figured, although the image of a lost child and a lost and lonely man wandering the streets of a city in a maze of disbelief, pieces torn from the past — she could hear the book jacket proclaiming — was all it took to dampen her eyes. She held everything back, cautious of the mascara and the gummed lashes. She didn't want to be detected. And there was nothing to explain; her father wasn't dying of cancer; her boyfriend wasn't seeing another woman. She didn't even have a boyfriend at the time. It was the handwriting that caught her off guard. The dignity of having written this all down and then leaving it here alone while he was downstairs in a coma. The humility, the matter-of-factness. The absence of anger or meanness got the tears flowing. He just stated the story of his experience, like if he had been reading out loudthe operating instructions for an electric sander. The repression that the tone had grown out from, a covered-over well of diffused emotion, Amy was unable to know. All she saw was the plain and quiet sentences on the page and the effect they had on her. Neither Jacob nor his reader knew how the words would work, that less would have meant more, that the inability to render deep feeling could produce more powerful results. Amy let her eyes go out of focus. The handwritten paragraphs quivered like liquid, like underwater photography. She thought again of her grandparents in Frankfurt. "Why am I here?" she thought and checked the minute hand of her Timex.

Her mind wandered. It had been more than thirty years since the war. *Opa* had been in it. Russia and the Ukraine. And Jacob, only just now, was writing this down. All that stuff filtered through a thick gauze, time. His "sweetheart" was now a grown woman, fit snugly into a size-14 dress, a mother herself, anxiously waiting somewhere at that moment in Houston, maybe downstairs. She felt close to her but she didn't know why. She didn't want to meet her, just him. And, then she felt herself feeling proud to be a nurse, a member of the "helping profession." It was true that the crazy and irregular hours had spoiled (or at least helped spoil) her marriage, and had caused the split up or at least favored her husband's chances of *boffing* that dancer. "If she'd been around more... "That was how, in any case, her husband explained it but despite all that loss there was something vital that she protected by staying-on at the hospital, holding to the course. Beneath that layer of sadness, even regret, she felt affirmed that she had followed a deeper conviction. Kevin, one day, hopefully not too far off, would not only understand this but love her for it. Poor Dzidzia, she thought, not picturing the slightly overweight suburbanite from New Jersey, obviously, but the lost ten-year old on her birthday in Krakow. "How on earth did he ever find her?"

At twenty past eight a child's naïve joy spread over Harriet's face.

"He squeezed my hand. He heard me, pray tell," she squealed with excitement. "I asked him to squeeze my hand if he could hear me and he *did*!" Harriet beamed. Her voice filled with increasing exuberance until it thinned like a bugle note and cracked, suggesting behind it the possibility of false hope. She spread her fingers over her chest like panels of a Chinese fan, as if they might re-amplify her voice. Jane's eyes showed a readiness to believe in her stepmother's bright pitch, yet lodged serenely in her most secret knowledge a mass of dark suspicion lurked.

Then, they caught sight of Fanny. It took a lot to deflate her, and yet her eyes were already pink from the strain of holding back. She shook off the signs of her own anguish and centered her concern on Harriet, a selflessness she'd learned from the Lord Our Savior and all those Sunday School sessions. She manifested His mission and gleamed with delight at Harriet's perception of her husband's condition. There was always joy to be found in the world.

"And how's Bobby? Jane was quick to reciprocate, feeling the instant possibility of guilt should Jacob be better and Bobby be worse. The gleam passed from Fanny's eyes. The Lord was testing her now.

"He's bad." She couldn't pretend. "They can't stop the bleeding. He's up all right, talking and all that, but that don't mean anything. It's inside of him that's not right." She bit with her white front tooth into her pink bottom lip. A strange and cruel sense of justice hung over the encounter; the three women at once felt the unfairness of it all. And just how little appearances meant. It was as if there was only a limited, fixed quantity of good news to go around and when it graced one soul it abandoned another. One lousy game of sharing the covers. A dim siren from the street raced towards a hit-and-run case on Summer Street.

88

From the hospital lobby Jane called home using her AT&T card, hating the mechanically polite quip about 'how can we help you?' She wanted to crucify the bilbo operator in Lincoln, Nebraska, who was just doing her job. And then she tried Benjamin at college. Harriet called her sister from the next booth. The foliage, they learned over the wire, had peaked that weekend in New England. There was no foliage in Houston; there was no autumn like the one Jane or Harriet knew. Houston was neutered like a casino.

Amy, having medicine to dispense, closed Jacob's diary and headed back onto the floor thinking about the private world she'd just violated. Nosing into the private effects of patients wasn't something that she was used to doing. But since there wasn't greed or malice in her intentions she didn't feel remorse. In fact, she felt honored, honored to have shared Jacob's story, although she was the one who helped herself to the diary. Down the empty hospital corridor she walked, unconscious of the underlying hum of the florescent tubes, turning over in her mind some of the details of the writing along with the tiny call of a day-old mosquito bite on her left calf.

After three or four weeks of solid searching, by chance, pure luck, I found my father-in-law's family. They had spent eighteen months hidden in the attic of the Krakow Gestapo Headquarters, of all places. Imagine twenty people, including small children, hiding in the most dangerous spot in the city. The superintendent of the building, an old friend of the family, who continued to wash the floors and polish the banisters right throughout the whole German occupation, secretly delivered parcels of food when he could, every few days. They survived. But they didn't have any information about my Dzidzia. It was a relief though to find a familiar face and to know that there were others who came out of this whole nightmare alive.

*Three times a day for the next three months I visited
the mobbed and makeshift offices of the Jewish Committee,
the Kongregacja, on the corner of Skawinska and
Krakowska. This was the group, organized by Dr. Stuhlbach,
my father-in-law's nephew who now lives in Brazil, who
issued an appeal in the Krakow newspaper for Poles to
register with the Committee all Jewish children (or those
believed to be) that had been left with them or abandoned
or found.*

Counting out capsules and dropping them into tiny
Dixie cups, Amy thought of the time they'd lost Sounder,
their golden retriever, and searched day and night for him
all over Harris County, even got the local radio station to
put an announcement on the air. The false hope, the leads
that didn't materialize, the dogs that looked just like him.
The thoughts of Sounder run over by a truck, or starving to
death in the woods, or stolen for medical experiments.
Imagine losing a child.

*One day in mid-September, I went to ask my usual
questions to the secretary of the Committee —any news of
my child? A lady overhead me. The lady had large, working hands, facial skin that was thin as the wax paper used
to wrap smoked fish and had prematurely wrinkled, and a
long blue and brown kerchief, which she tied under her
chin. My mother had one like this, I remember. In a rush
she assaulted me with questions. I was so used to bored,
negative responses that I didn't realize right away what
she was getting at.*
*"What does your daughter look like? The color of
her eyes? Her hair? Short? Long? Blonde? Black? Her
name? Give me some details!" I was in a flutter and even
started to cry. I no longer knew my daughter. I couldn't*

describe her in that I was sure she had changed since I had last seen her. How big was she now? I didn't know.

"Any birth defects? Does she have any birthmarks?"

I gathered my nerves and felt adrenaline flowing once again. 'Yes.' I got excited. 'Yes, she has a beauty mark on her thigh, her left thigh, round and copper-colored, little like a zloty *coin.' I told her yes. The lady in the kerchief cut me short, and just like that, with certainty, blurted, 'You're saved. I have her. She's safe, in a children's home in Zakopane. She's safe. Do you hear me?' She was almost yellingto make me understand. I almost blacked out and started to cry. I didn't believe it. It couldn't be true. This was a cruel joke. More sadistic humor.*

Her review of the evening clipboards was mostly mechanical; she heard Jacob's voice. Miss Washington needed her medication at eleven. There was an IV to change in 1654. She heard his words, though, thirty years after they were spoken, weeks or days after they were reconstructed and recorded, twenty minutes after she had read them.

The next day I went by train to Zakopane. The train passed through Nowy Targ and I remembered the funny sign I had seen on the chest of a naked Jewish man who'd been hung from the station rafters: kosher meat. I just stayed on the train, motionless, until we pulled away from the town.

Benjamin didn't know what to make of his mother's voice over the phone. He meditated, repeating his mantra, hoping to himself that if he did in fact have any mental powers as he suspected especially after having taken that course in Buddhist thought and the weekend seminar in Mind Control, he could transfer these into his grandfather, whose medical condition, when cramped into words, became abstract and unknowable. He hid under his covers in bed that night in his clothes wondering about God. Metaphysics was a new language for Benjamin. Although he had thought about spiritual questions before he didn't know there was specific language and methodology for such pursuits. He read the assigned chapters in his philosophy text and tried to answer each week the questions at the end of each chapter. His books for the morning classes were stacked neatly on his desk along with his room key and his meal card.

There were sounds outside his dorm window, drunken students rambling back from a mid-week mixer at a fraternity. It angered him and yet instantly he knew he was being ridiculous. "On another night, it'd be me out there babbling happily across campus with a head spinning from stale, tapped beer, stopping to pee under a tree, intoxicated with both alcohol and the feeling of being free from being accountable, never thinking for an instant that some kid was lying sadly on his bed in one of those dorm rooms because his grandfather or someone else for that matter was dying."

God had lost a lot of esteem in Jacob's eyes by the time the war had ended. Benjamin knew it. What God could have ever sanctioned such a thing? How could one still thank God for the world? And yet, there were things that were miraculous and holy and required constant thanks. Like the re-unification of Benjamin's mother and grandfather, and thus his ownpossibility to be a part of the world. Or to others, the State of Israel. In the dwindling moments of Jacob's life Benjamin sensed the strangest affinity with Jacob, as if their separate missions touched, as if there were really missions.

Everyone — Jacob, Benjamin, Jane, Harriet, Amy, Dr. Cavenaugh, Fanny — was breathing alone at that moment. Sounder though was never found.

9

The next afternoon at two, it was Jane who went in. Harriet
sat cross-legged in the half-abandoned waiting room telling herself stories, planning trips with Jacob that would
never materialize, peeling apples and slicing orange peels
into her celebrated apple sauce, a recipe and tradition that
came from "mother." She spoke adoringly of "mother" as
if there was only one in the world, and everyone knew her,
the one she nursed till the very end and buried in the family
plot.

"We could go back to Australia," she offered to a
lively and amicable man in her mind. She was really talking to him. And he answered her. She replied, asked him a
question. It wasn't the Australia that Lala lived somewhere
in, a woman approaching sixty, with a mind and name and
memory of her own. Those details from the past, from Poland, she just sort of swallowed with a tssskk and a shake
of her head and an over-bite that depressed her lower lip.
She, not wanting to comprehend things deeper than the
abstract adjective "terrible." She loved "family" but was
frightened by what she loved. "Or else Arizona. The des-
sert is just divine. The dryness is good for us. And the el-

evation is right for your condition. Yes, Arizona," she remarked like the matter was settled; they'd return. They'd been there once and Jacob particularly liked the climate and the open spaces and the feeling of freedom.

Meanwhile, Jane stood with rounded shoulders between the respirator, whose pumping coil inflated and deflated like a prototype shock absorber in a Monroe waiting room, pushing and pulling air in and out of Jacob's chest, and another machine that she knew was "working" only by the red illuminated dotsthat ran across its chrome and gray face. She held her hand in Jacob's and spoke loudly in a voice burdened with the task of having to sound calm and pedestrian.

"It's Tuesday, Father. Everything is going well. Soon you'll be back in your room." She stopped, wanting to choke. She was a terrible liar. This was not how things would end, like in movies made for tv. Or, for every movie that ended like that there were two hundred real cases with ugly and inelegant endings. Two thousand, probably. She could mislead by omission but she could never articulate convincingly a full-blown fabrication. At home she was a horrendous card player, unable to bluff at the dining room table in a family game of "I Doubt It". And not very convincing in covering the receiver and then telling clients who'd called at home for her husband that he wasn't in at the moment when in fact he was sitting three feet away. As a child, her lies were true. As an adult she either laughed in the guise of her own falsity or choked mentally. Now, her words sounded so thin and alien, detached from their meaning like the way lines came from the mouths of student actors in junior high school plays. "I spoke to Benjamin last night. He sends his love." She paused. What to say? "He's at school." She was slightly better now that she veered into the sphere of fact. But now in the one-sidedness of the exchange something else halted her. The dead echo of words. What did a word mean anyway? Alone, nothing. A lie was like a truth. Paint on a canvas. Because of the moral dilemma of lying, the truth became clearer, even painful. She extinguished her voice, exaggerating the silence that filled in around her. She squeezed the hand in hers, hard, too hard perhaps. "Can you hear me, father? Squeeze my hand if you can." She resorted to Harriet's method, hoping to reach the same euphoria of hope. The loneliness of no reply was intolerable — the silence echoed with the ultimate hollowness of existence, of language, the fact that we are always talking to no one — and without knowing so herself, she began then to understand what Jacob's silence meant. She concentrated then so hard, straining her ability to sense beyond the boundaries of normal perception, groping for a sign of life, so hard that she felt (or invented), finally, the tiniest pulse in his hand and sensed the frailest widening of his nearly-glued eyes. The most modest suggestions of life — perhaps nothing more than the movements of the life in a flower or fruit — and yet she felt them and used them as enough to feel revived with promise. This was a glimpse of his will to live, she was certain. He was giving her that much, or were these the nearly imperceptible jitters of the most minuscule involuntary nerves that continued-on even past, technically, the last moment. There isn't a child that doesn't know that a severed worm continues to wiggle and a beheaded chicken can flutter and dance, even fly, for a short time beyond its own demise.

And then a cough, mean and dangerous, rumbled through him, and his head went deep red and his feeble legs kicked. And the machines flashed and sounded for an instant and then settled back to their old pattern as did Jacob, before Jane could even run for help or know what had happened. Actually, nothing had happened and although Jane feared that this was the dramatic way people died, it wasn't at all, and no staffer on the floor would have been alarmed a bit. Machines were always sounding. He was alive. She knew that better now. Somewhere beyond all the tubes and wires and nasty incisions and roughly stapled stitches, there was still meaning to his existence. Because he still existed.

Jane rubbed Jacob's thick fingers, and the faint layer of blood beneath his white skin returned sluggishly each time to where her hand had pressed. She watched the colors change with a crude fascination as if just then she gained access to Dr. William Harvey's 1628 discovery of the human circulatory system. And then felt guilty or perverse in being fascinated.

"Good afternoon Mr. Simon, I'm just going to change your IV, okay? Won't take a second." A nurse's assistant budded-in between the two banks of equipment and announced loudly as if she worked in the geriatrics ward — and Jacob was merely hard of hearing — or rather a chamber maid at a motel, coming in to hastily change the sheets and empty the ashtrays, put out new soap, turning her head, conditioned to see nothing in the presence of all the great perversity of dailiness and traces of the night before. She had a sticker pasted to the back of her hospital shoe. I LOVE ROY ROGERS. To think of it! The word love was replaced by that little red heart, that un-protected trademark that everyone from the local pizza shack, to the city of Singapore had used and over-used in publicity campaigns. Jane was put off by the intrusion. The visiting periods were like fixed prayers, private seances with God, sacred audiences with the Buddha's tooth. "Plus, who's she kidding? Who does she think she's talking to?" The nurse's firm and direct tone, amplified and condescending, seemed farcical and insincere. "She might as well be a waitress," Jane thought, as she stood-by, agitated and aghast. Why should I have to share my time; this could have waited. It wasn't medical. I'd understand if it was medical. The nurse moved off to do the next chore on her long list. It was that staged, high-energy indifference or optimism couched in revved-up friendliness that got Jane's goat. But then she quickly retreated like usual. "She's just doing her job," she reasoned, and returned quickly to Jacob.

Bubbles of air were moving faster now through the clear plastic sack of glucose, or whatever they fed into the perforated veins of their intensively cared for patients. The thick clear substance passed through the plastic tube and ran into the vein above Jacob's thumb. Few people knew that onecould actually drown to death if too much fluid rolled into you. She watched the needle slide around in the blue black hole in the vein and she witnessed Jacob's teeth grind against each other like those of an injured horse. The fresh flow of fluid must have burned his flesh as it entered his hand. His teeth grated; they were stained and coated like a mare's. "We put horses to sleep," she caught herself thinking. "We spare them this."

It pained her to look at him and yet she hadn't the strength to look away. Or leave. The nurse had tried slightly to hide Jane from the sight of Jacob's body while she changed the needle and shifted the wretched hospital sheet that was bunched up beneath Jacob's mass and matted, oily head. It wasn't pretty. But Jane had resisted. "I have a right," she told herself, and held her vision firm, frightened to abdicate that right. And now she was stuck with more horrid images to stalk her dreams. The line of gruesome, industrial staples that reached to the base of Jacob's neck and disappeared below the line of the sheet, stained with crusts of blood and greenish leakage. Tracks.

Jane cushioned her voice and spoke to her father's body, "Good-bye, Father. Mother'll be here tonight at eight." She hesitated. The silence was back. "Bye. I have to go now." She stopped. "Today's Tuesday." She stopped. It meant nothing. She reached over the tangle of tubes and placed, carefully, a small kiss on the side of his damp and waxy head. There was a queer odor, half chemical, half human, that encased his person. Embalmed him almost. She'd never sensed it before and imagined that she'd never again. It was like a taste. She backed out of the dim, cool cave, a dismal place, a forgotten place, too dismal for the importance it was supposedly carrying, and moved towards the exit. Jacob's smell lingering in her nostrils. It wouldn't go away; even when the essence faded its memory would not. She composed herself quickly for her stepmother, who, now at twenty past two, hung by the swinging gray door, tip-toeing inside her corrective shoes. Her hands going all blue and cold. Jane, in a matter of seconds, stepped boldly into the uniformly lit corridor and rejoined the real day, where people were talking, chattering like birds, and eager, where things still seemed to matter, and the price of a meal or the color of a scarf had importance. Where she'd been was like underwater. To those standing on shore, few things mattered underwater.

There was good news for the Italian-American couple; their baby, a supermarket chain vice-president, in charge of produce acquisition — he'd started out as a bag boy; his father started out in the street — was checking out of the ICU, heading upstairs. He was already walking on his own, couldn't stand being idle, was furious at the drop in the price of sugar while he was under. In a week he'd be home, resting on his porch in Connecticut with a checkered blanket on his lap. Three daily papers delivered to the door. Plus *Shelf Life News* and *Produce Weekly Report*. A frisky setter tied to his Chinese maple out front. His cordless phone perched on the painted wrought iron garden furniture. Bird feeder with suet in the gentrified woods at the back of the property. In three weeks he'd be back at his metal desk with the new price lists from General Foods and Libbys. Jacob, though, needed a bit more time, another day or so. It was normal, he was older. That was all, Harriet told herself. Everyone's different. Plus Jacob had that balloon. Another day or two would do it.

Amy found a few minutes that night to return to Jacob's diary. He still wasn't back on the floor. That was a bad sign. She knew the heart balloon meant complications. It usually did. She also knew to doubt her knowledge. When it came to the human body and the medical profession absolutes were unreliable; there were always exceptions. Unexpected recoveries and unexpected deaths. Both turned heads. Everything imaginable, travesties to miracles, she'd seen happen over the eight years she'd spent in hospitals. It was just like that on the outside too, she thought, but in hospitals the process of living and dying was speeded up and intensified, and somehow, the rules changed in the expectations of the public. Hospitals were sort of non-secular churches, the science of being saved. She found her spot in the marble-covered diary, pulled her hair back and fixed her eyes. The slight coat of oil on her left fingers slid minutely along the cover. "Don't assume a bloody thing; just wait."

Our meeting took place in the office of the children's home. I sat at the desk frightened and excited. Then I heard feet coming down the hallway. I braced myself in my chair. This seemed more terrible than all the tension I had in the last four years. But wonderful. All of a sudden, they brought Dzidzia into the room. I was so terrified. And then there was tremendous emotion, crying, and hugging, and kissing. I was so overwhelmed that I didn't even think to slow down and observe her reactions. She recognized me immediately even though I looked like a skeleton. I kissed the top of her head and I remember the scent of her clean and braided hair. I wept. There was nothing more miraculous in the whole world. She was so beautiful. I was so embarrassed.

Amy turned the page.

Jane was no longer sure what it was she remembered from that day, and what she had been told afterwards. The two were sort of hopelessly muddled into one vague recollection. That day continued to gain meaning each time she revisited it as anadult. She remembered crying, she could even picture herself crying, but she couldn't recapture the feelings behind the image. It was the dress rehearsal for a wedding, all motions, no emotions. And she found herself wanting with increasing intensity to turn on the sound, to flush out the experience, to add the sentimental engagement that now as an adult she had learned was missing from her responses. Once when her mind took her back to that little office in the sanitarium in Zakopane after the war where she reunited with her withered father she tried to see him. Images of a gaunt and pale man with pinkish eyes, wailing and throwing his bony arms around her haunted the inner scene. She didn't feel anything other than slight repulsion which she masked like all other feelings. Even the guilt of not really feeling the joy that this man, this half stranger seemed to need from her, she denied any expression. She saw herself smothered in his arms, neutral and safe, numb to all and any emotional mauling. Any tears that her eyes produced were there because some mechanism that had grown into place knew that that was appropriate. "This is my father, this is my father, this is my father," she repeated in her mind four decades later as a girl of ten, wishing like Dorothy of Oz, to make it seem real. "What is a father?"

That night in the loud lobby of the Hilton, Jane felt lost. The actual moment of existence, then and there in Houston, Texas, could in no way penetrate the complex inner cloak of her mind. She was re-experiencing. A sensation of reversed metamorphosis rolled inside her life just then causing the anxiety of confusion. Her memory's direct link with the past and its subsequent regrouping based on what had been later added, had overlapped and grown together like the mend of a fractured bone. In some cases the bone gained new strength, in others the pain grew chronic. In a comfortable polyester-covered, flame-resistant armchair Jane felt for the dark inner mend. The mend had naturally taken on sediments of reinforced matter, becoming thicker than the fragments it had joined, and her original memory had covered over with layers and layers of protective padding. Although these layers gave her the confidence to carry on, a diffused but persistent discomfort, a leak or fissure, gnawed from the inaccessible, shielded innerness like some last bleeding finger still scratching on the walls of the showers that were really tombs and were then to be covered over in mud and rhetoric and forgotten. For years the knowledge of that nearly imperceptible inner ache had been suppressible, blocked out in numerous facile ways in Jane's busy life in America, from tennis lessons to Weight Watchers, TM to psychotherapy. Covered over like make-up on dry skin. But it wouldn't become extinct. It wouldn't ever cease totally to be. It would eventransform and grow into other forms and sensations in her children. Benjamin would have it. And the ache would be even more remote and unreachable. Like genes, she had passed it from one life to the next, generation to generation, Europe to America, automatically, without volition, in the deep and terse channels where the subtlest transactions of culture and history took place. It would seep out and follow dark and unhealthy tunnels if she didn't help it break out from all the reinforced, well-cast, new and improved bone. And even then...."we can't wholly control the transmissible," she'd read somewhere.

"Didn't the past always remain in the present? Wasn't there only the present?" she asked herself while making static electricity with her Lord & Taylor shoes on the half-mile of carpet. But how to find her way back to it while maintaining some mental order, a minimum of good posture. Stand up straight and salute the flag and pay your bills and bake cup cakes on Martin Luther King Day. Her eyes blurred the activities of the hotel lobby; it was this very faint but terrible pulse or cry from beneath the mend that possessed the collective soul of an entire people. She was sure of it. A people who were perpetually losing and finding themselves: the Jewish people. And just then she wondered, "maybe we should live in Israel." And this moment of personal existential awareness, this pull — not far from the one that asked 'Who am I?' ' What am I doing in this world?' degraded into a sentimental battle cry. An inspirational pulse of slogans, a kitchy zeitgeist for survival and the new Masada took over. Keep your eye on the prize. We shall overcome. We've existed this long! Four more years!

At two o'clock, it was this that had begun to haunt Jane as she hung at Jacob's side and stared at the ripples of tension that were being carried across his wet, waxy forehead. His now poor testicles slid from the cover of the wrinkled hospital robe. There was nothing private there, no longer anything attached to the man's ego, sense of self, pride, or personality. Nothing sexual. Just a smallish pair of glands protected by a creased sack of skin below a hank of circumcised limpid muscle. Not even the potency of sperm. In from that groin a rubber balloon had been snaked up the arteries to the heart and Jane tried to envision the path and the objects and the force of blood of anonymous donors into tired organs, organs that were running on borrowed time, who'd been shocked too often and for too long to continue to resist. The same organs that were responding so vibrantly, marvelously in that sanitarium office in a skeletal but still potentially robust body. Thinking back to the afternoon she began to understand that it wasn't him anymore. It wasn't Jacob. And without him, her definition of self clouded over even further. If it wasn't Jacob, it wasn't Jane. It was someone else. In that glaze of unknowing, locking in the hum of those dead machines from her comfortable seat in Houston's most expensive hotel, she was lost again in the floating puzzle of who she was and who she would now be. An undertow of anxiety pulled at her. The more she resisted, trying to hang onto her notions of a safe world, insisting on controlling a body of water that was now moving tumultuously, the more frightened she grew, feeling and fearing the fragile outer lip of control crumbling in like a sand castle weakened and erased by a rising surf. She reached for and grabbed a car rental brochure that shone there on the lobby end table. There was an attractive weekend rate with unlimited mileage. And free upgrades. There was a toll free number. There was a spanking red model with a girl with red lips on the cover. She felt like driving away fas and forever in a flashy red sports car.

A Shriner with two-tone shoes and leather tassles and skin-tone elastic socks mashed the end of his cigarette into the glass tray to her right, and smiled cordially. Jade cufflinks studded with initials that she noted but forgot instantly anchored the sleeves of his heavily starched shirt. He looked like he was wearing loud aftershave, a Mennen product. In the gap between his two front teeth, Jane spotted a bit of lunch, some beef or a raspberry seed, perhaps, and without knowing it felt envy.

10

They ordered Sanka in the hotel lobby and it came on a shiny silver-metal tray that was filled with nicks. Harriet sent hers back, claiming it wasn't hot enough. The room service waiter, first generation American descendant of Vietnamese boat people who'd spent their first three years below groundfolding towels and sheets on a rolling machine, didn't show the slightest bit of displeasure. He knew how tips worked, and at the back of his mind there was always that one destination: enough money to start up for his father the sandal factory like the one the family had outside of Saigon. It would come, but not this year. He hurried off to the kitchen in his tight-fitting uniform, the fabric between his legs, piling and wearing thin. In his spare time he wrote sentimental short stories in English. A literary quarterly in Amarillo called *Green Sand* had been promising to publish his story "Shrimp Man" if he agreed to change the last line.

Jane drank hers uncaringly. What did temperature matter? She looked out at the faces of the Shriners and the hotel personnel, the boys who cleared the ashtrays, mostly Hispanic, the porters, the clean-shaven gentlemen at Reception in preppy clothes, ambition perking behind those blue-green eyes, lurking in the way they slid the credit card machine over the embossed plastic money, avoiding contact with the dirty carbon backs. The rows of baggage in formation, marked with tour stickers. Places to go, places to come from. Planes to catch, to meet. People to see. Jobs to get back to. New trips to plan. She let the voices fuse into one confused noise, and the whole scene backwashed into a pastiche of swirling color. "This is the world we live in." Colors, lights, sounds, movement. Life seemed stupid. Pointless. Harriet didn't detect any of this, and carried on with her talk of little things, panty hose, her sister on Union Avenue, the house repair they were considering, her sweet tooth, distractions, the importance of brushing your hair before you go out into public, a new diet that was supposed to work in three days, based on two ripe pineapples and eight glasses of water a day.

I rented a room with board in Zakopane close to the children's home, and tried to regain my strength. I spent most of the days with Dzidzia and the other children, watching them in their activities, playing with them. It had been a long time since I had seen children play, even smile and laugh a bit. For the first time in God knows when I had the time to see a bird fly across the sky and head towards a green tree with a worm in its mouth.

Almost everyday someone's father or mother or guardian showed up, as I had, looking for their children. Most of them went away sad and desperate or else sternfaced like they knew in advance that it was a hopeless search and getting angrier and angrier by the minute. But some of them, a very few, found their children at the home, as I had. This was wonderful to see, but hard to believe, like a dream that comes true in another dream. We wanted to tell everyone, but most people hadtheir own problems and didn't care about hearing our joys. And the ones who went away looked at us with hate, or more like the absence of feeling, a deadness in their eyes. Although I wanted to feel sorry or thought I should feel guilty, I was simply pleased when they left.

When the Partisan groups of anti-Semitic Poles organized and began attacking the Jewish children's home in different ways, even shooting at the windows, Mrs. Silberman, the woman in the blue and brown kerchief, began pleading with the authorities for permission to take the children out of the country, to Palestine. There was no other choice in the world for her. Palestine. She got a lot of resistance and had many problems trying to make the arrangements, but she decided to go in any case, with or without the help of the authorities. There was no future for Jewish children in Poland. This was after the war and the Jews were still the victims, blamed now for the misery that the Poles had endured throughout the war, but mostly because those who stole from the Jews in their absence didn't want to give up new wealth. I wasn't fully ready or prepared to leave. Now that I found my sweetheart, I had affairs I wanted to clear up. I had to return to Nowy Targ. Think of the things you have to take care of just for leaving on a vacation trip. I had to prepare to leave my country, although I wasn't sure if I thought of it as my country any more. So I decided to take Dzidzia and move to my parents' old house in Nowy Targ and to try to live there. In Nowy Targ I was thrilled to find a few friends of mine who came back from the camps — Morris Trepper, Emek Langer, and his girlfriend, Hanya, and together we stayed in our house, which had been virtually gutted of everything of value.

Soon after the beginning of the war, my father had sold fictitiously the store and warehouse, filled to capacity with merchandise, to a "very nice" and "cooperative" Pole by the name of Jan Jaskierski. There was no money exchange involved. This was because we'd heard of cases of property being confiscated from Jewish merchants and my father finally decided we must protect ourselves.

When I got back to Nowy Targ in 1945 I of course went to find this nice guy who had done us the favor of buying our store for nothing and found that he had moved to another location. He'd taken apart our warehouse and had used our materials to build himself a new house and warehouse of his own on his new location on the other side of the rynek. This way in the unlikely case that anybody from our family would return, he'd be exonerated from any responsibility of returning or really paying for the business. There'd be nothing that we could do and no way to prove anything.

Several days after coming back I went to visit the self-elected heir of our family's life-work possessions. He was unpleasantly taken back to see me, and it wasn't because I was ghost-like, weighing 110 pounds. Talking with him was unsuccessful. He tried to assure me that he had paid for the business in full. I knew this was a lie because in 1943, during the war, when I came back to Nowy Targ from Lvow, my father, being under the impression that the war would be over in a few months, gave me a complete resumé of the verbal agreement he had with Jaskierski. No money was ever exchanged.

Finally, we agreed to meet at his lawyer's office, Antoni Celewicz, who was also occasionally our notary before the war, and he now being on Jaskierski's side of course, and I being weak and disgusted, alone and powerless, coming right from concentration camp and not having any strength to fight, with no papers and my parents, bothers and wife dead, settled this transaction for peanuts. I knew the second I laid eyes on him what had happened. He had become a big shot in town, a rich and respectable citizen. I heard later, being already in Krakow, that through *jealousy of local informers, he was arrested by the Russian Secret Service and shipped to Siberia as a collaborator with the Nazis, where he was shot. So I guess justice was served in the end.*

The slant of the handwriting changed then, as did the color of the ink.

After months of planning, Mrs. Silberman took it upon herself to emigrate to Palestine with her one hundred orphaned children. She rented trucks and drivers, bribed border guards and slipped through the nearby Czech frontier at night with her new extended family. Of course it is easy to describe a pilgrimage in words but it was a very hard thing to accomplish. Mrs. Silberman did not have any passports or papers permitting her or her children to pass through all those borders. And traveling for days and days with small children in trucks posed many difficulties, which I don't have to explain.

Amy closed the diary softly and went back to work. At her next break she'd return, ignited by the secrecy of her act, the obsession maybe, and the passion of the story. This was like a movie, she thought.

The house in Nowy Targ was completely empty, robbed of everything, including the plumbing and electric fixtures, not just the fixtures but the boxes and toggle switches and copperwiring too. We made the place livable by bringing together some necessary furniture and by heating and cooking on an old wood stove. I didn't have time to think of all that was ours that was now missing. It was hard enough getting the local police to let us stay in my own house.

*A few more boys came back to live in town and to-
gether we started to manufacture candy and sell it to re-
tailers who sold it on market days in Nowy Targ and the
surrounding towns. Emek and Hanya, who now have a small
chicken farm and orange orchard near Tel Aviv, got married in our house and I witnessed the civic wedding. Hanya
had flowers from the fields near town and, of course, we
had candy. So we made do with the best we could find. She
was a very nice girl and she took very good care of Dzidzia,
braided her hair, etc. and cooked our meals. I remember
one day Dzidzia developed in her mouth a mushroom from
drinking raw milk that had come directly from a cow. Dr.
Mech prescribed a medicine which Hanya gave to Dzidzia
three times a day and it helped her.*

"A mushroom?" Amy thought, and read for another
five or ten minutes in the subdued light; then, upon hearing
the buzzer of a patient summoning assistance, dashed the
book back into the drawer and stepped out of Jacob's room.

The next morning Cavenaugh withdrew the balloon
from Jacob's heart and cut off all sedatives from Jacob's
treatment. Pain killers slowed down the natural process of
healing, increasing the chance of dependency, and so mini-
mized the chance of recovery. If the balloon remained in
place any longer the chance of infection would have been
great. That was a known fact. The balloon had to come out
at all risk.

Harriet went in at two and came out before the full
twenty minutes had elapsed, sickened by the tortured grimace on Jacob's face. Now, without the sedatives, the pain
hit like acid on a open wound. It spread over his face. Pure
misery. He trembled and wretched, and the tubes in the
mouth and nose brought up ugly fluid from his lungs and
chest. The corners of his mouth were red and sore and

cracked from the friction of plastic on skin and the dehy-
dration of the mucous membrane. His tongue and lips were
drying out like salted cod. This had happened once before,
but Jacob was graced now with the inability to make conscious connections. To Harriet, it didn't matter that this
new measure was ultimately necessary from a medical point
of view; the outward expression of pain that possessed her
husband's body was more than she could tolerate. The look
of peace was more comforting than the war that was being
waged in Jacob, the offensive that could bring victory, even
though the look of peace might have meant
terminalsurrender. Knowledge of that other time when
Jacob's physical endurance was pushed beyond human ex-
pectation, was wholly vacant from Harriet's hysterical state.
That other life was a black cloud that hung over her own
legitimacy. Her task in the second half of her life was to
convert Poland into an esoteric word, sixty points in advanced Scrabble, and Jacob into a normal American man
whose trauma would become untraceably covered-over in
nice new rayon, Orlon, banlon, dralon, nylon, polyester,
rhodia, and tergal menswear. And Howard Johnson's ice
cream. In short, a citizen of Newark of the fifties. Although
more liberal than the retired General, and not necessarily
Republican, he'd ultimately have to cast his vote for Ike.

He had seemed to motion something ever so slightly.
It was just a small shift of the eyes and a pull of the hand.
The pain had jolted him closer to consciousness. He wanted
water, moisture. That was all, no message, no words, no
desire to communicate, just the need to satisfy excruciat-
ing dryness, parched to the point where each pore on his
tongue puffed and spread like a ripe seed. Each pore to
Jacob, if he could have realized what his tongue was still
capable of perceiving in its own strange way of understanding scale, was its own inflated wound. Water marked the
purest drive for survival, and yet water, in his state, would

have filled his lungs and drown him in ten to twelve minutes. Water, he, or some mechanism within him, wanted. In his kitchen back home in their modest apartment above the store he kept in the refrigerator at all times a jar of fresh tap water, iron-tasting Newark city water in a thick bottle once used for Acme brand grapefruit juice, with plastic food wrap under the metal cap to facilitate opening and prevent rust, a bottle used over and over, the thin, oversized flask with curved shoulders and roundish concave frosted indentations on the sides where the thumbs and index fingers could grab nicely, a jar that'd one day command a quarter or half a dollar in a garage sale somewhere. Jacob loved water; it was his favorite drink. He had learned to appreciate its simple greatness, having been without it for long, long periods. Privately, it bothered him to watch people with fingers banefully posed under the tap let gush those fast, modern inox faucets in American kitchens, waiting simply for a cooler temperature.

Harriet cried for a nurse. Not really articulating any words, just making a fearful, disruptive sound, and moving about to gain attention, wriggling her toes like a disturbed person.

"Give him water," she pleaded in a nasty, sickened tone. "Can't you see he needs to drink."

"He can't have fluids," an attendant replied not impatiently but firmly, slightly annoyed that this woman had cried wolf. A dry tongue, that's all it was. "No fluids, youdon't want him to get pneumonia now do you?"

"Nnnnn."

"What I can do is moisten his tongue with a swab."

"Anything," and Harriet nodded in consonance. Just do it, she thought.

Jacob hacked cruelly and a cruel lump of green-black phlegm slid up the thin clear tube and disappeared into the tank of the aspirator. His frail chest, white and bluish-pink, pale and bruised like a singed turkey, heaved and settled, collapsing on itself, deprived of the structural support of the sternum and pectorals which had been sawed in two and stitched closed, the tugged-on stitches now widening their own holes. And Harriet, half-looking, half-fleeing, feared that all the new work inside Jacob would rupture and fail. She'd learned the hardware business well, too well, and now, although wanting to maintain a romantic image of life, pictured the workings of the body as plumbing or electric circuitry. One avoided putting stress on the pipes or overloading circuits. This couldn't be that different. She couldn't stay and watch; it would have been masochistic to stay and watch him be tortured. It was the torture in his life, that she'd always negated, eradicated from the possibility of her thoughts, every day since at least that sunny June Sunday in her mother's house in Carteret in 1948 when it became evident that life would in fact take a fresh turn. An unlikely spinster, abandoned by the well known cycle of courtship, marriage, children, would swiftly catch up, and she'd let in no sour-tasting details that might remind her or anyone else of the unreal circumstances of its root.

Harriet found the exit and whimpered faintly, squeaking almost like a mouse trapped on a glue pad, advancing her cold bluish legs, harnessed in support stockings and an impossible girdle, in small lifeless steps led by the weight of her corrective shoes, which were ordered specially from New York and took six weeks to arrive by United Parcel Service, that bulky green truck double parked outside the store with its yellow blinkers flashing, its clean-cut driver with green cap skipping off from the then always opened sliding door with clipboard in hand. Out through the swinging door she emerged, limp and defeated but alive.

Jane instantly counterbalanced Harriet's weakness with a new burst of courage. Strength came when weakness grew too dangerous. Survive, that was the game. Jane could suppress anything, play ventriloquist with her own emotions so well that no one — not even her own distant self — ever noticed, except perhaps a specialized psychiatrist fifteen years later with a video camera at three hundred dollars a session. And then... To Jane, strength of this type came as a natural mechanism. "Don't be devastated by Harriet's heaviness." Death, destruction, abandonment, disease, torture — they canbe tolerated, held off, unfelt. People sometimes thought that Jane came across as cold and ungracious upon first meeting her, an observation that surprised her because she wasn't really that way; it was this protective mechanism that left its trace, she came to realize. Jane held her step-mother like a child, not feeling, but manufacturing naturally the gestures and strokes of authenticity. This woman she called mother because that was the only choice given her, hung for a moment, whimpering in her arms. For a moment, a flash flood of the worst fluids, enzymes or hormones, chemicals and electricity, scourged Jane's body, heart to cellulite and back in a millionth of a second: 'Jacob had died' was the thought that whipped her. She fused with Harriet. Two sets of pains, two humans, possessing two sets of bones, enmeshed as one mass in the tangle of limbs and whimpers, and yet very much apart and private. This was no mother and child, this was the common law affection of illusion, deception, and hope that had grown in place over thirty years. But the slightest mention of any of that — as improbable as it might have been (in that repression wore away a facility for words) — would have been overwhelming to both of them just then, cruel or perverse even. And there was no place nor need for any of this fact to find its way into either recognizable thought or spoken words. Fanny, yards away, knew to hold still, leaving Harriet to the private dignity of her own tears. Fanny possessed that kind of innate wisdom.

Loud as a choir leader, but discrete as a nun when necessary.

Jane thought of the silly task of having to face a platter of dinner preparations a little later, a salt and pepper shaker, labeled respectively S and P. An outcrop of Heinz 57, French's New Recipe Spicy, A-1 Steak Sauce, packets of Domino sugar and Lo-Cal Sugar substitute and maybe a coated card with some new thing on Special, chicken fingers or a color photo of Billy Fernandez: Employee of the Month, in uniform. Harriet would insist on dinner at precisely six; six-thirty was already too late and her meatloaf would be ruined. This was her plumb line, her psychic metronome, centering her hold on both the material and spiritual worlds. With a waitress she knew how to steer. Jane pictured the cherry Jello at the end of a cafeteria line, singing its artificiality, cut in Bauhaus cubes and piled in a saucer, lined up on aluminum bars. Age eleven and a half, having had a new first name for only a week and a half, not a word of English, except "Jello" and "Indian Rubber," the term for eraser in her new primary school, Molly Pitcher, in Rahway, New Jersey, her first school, ever. It was there that she saw, touched and finally tasted Jello; it wiggled and wriggled and kind of coolly melted or disappeared in her mouth. *Amerika* to Jane was red Jello. It was marvelous, so frivolous. The basicswere reinvented. Frigidair. Kleenex...Eskimo pies...Heinz 57. The moment dissolved like that. He hadn't died.

In the evening, Jane went in, prepared for the worst. She looked curiously and almost perversely into the other dark corners of the ward, trying to guess the severity of each patient's condition by the quantity of machines that encased them and the density of wires and tubes that embroidered their limbs. A black man with bristled, salt and pepper hair sat silently slouched in a special formless chair sort of an upright hammock zipped into an oxygen tent that was sewn to the edges of the frame. No one was there to visit him. It was five past eight. No one was coming. Jane fixed her eyes on the plastic patch that covered his head and face. It was eerier than the body bags used by "Homicide" and the military in tv police series. The life inside that plastic sack appeared to her instantaneously as dead as the turtle they'd thrown away in the kitchen trash. Then she recognized him. He was the one Jacob had met in pre-op on that first night in the hospital. Jacob had never heard of Kozad, Nebraska and the man who introduced himself as Sticks, son of a cotton-picker, well, "Poeland" was to him the town of just shy three thousand halfway to Odessa, where Jamis, his half-brother, installed swimming pools for H.H. Thomas and Sons. The two of them, Jacob and Sticks, out of nowhere, started to sing at full volume, in their African-American Texan and Polish Jewish 'Joisey' accents, "Que Será, Será" from *Man of La Mancha*, and then bursting into a masacred rendition of Sinatra's "New York, New York," harmonizing at moments completely by chance, and then melodically scattering like chased beetles at the next score. Two humans about to be sacrificed, singing their guts out. Now, there he was zipped into a plastic oxygen tank, stunned as a beached sand shark.

Jane approached her father and clenched the muscles in her own arms, squeezing herself aggressively for no good reason. She had to get tough and manufacture a bright tone, a positive disposition. If not, she too would crumble and break as Harriet had. The smell of the previous day recurred in a flash and she battled to remain stronger than it. She wasn't sure if it was in her nose or her memory that she smelled it, but it tantalized her and she fought to make it go away.

"Father, you're doing just fine," she asserted right off the bat. He was perched higher on his pillow than he had been the day before and she liked this small change because it proved to her that her father was not just a forgotten carcass. She assumed the new position was to help him drain his fluids. Doctors almost always seemed to talk about fluids. What we do with our fluids determined the degree of our problem. They either pumped them into you or drained them out of you, she thought. Surely, it had to do with fluids. But the idea of moving him, a bag of hurting bones, literally made her quiver. He'd been shifted, that was certain and whatever pain he felt in the process was now immaterial. Did responsibility hinge on what we're aware of; Jane had this slightly philosophical, moral pitch to her outlook.

His tongue was swollen and gray like the tongue of a larger mammal. And his legs and arms, thin and weak, assumed force only when each cough rumbled through him, a subway beneath the streets of a city that each time weakened the supportive layers of concrete and thus slowly like erosion edged the center towards disaster. Then, they contracted and fought as if hit with a bolt of electro-shock. Pain, she focused on it close-up. Seeing it hurt but not being able to feel it. It was like witnessing volcanic lava from a safe distance eat people alive. The guilt, but there was no way to either participate or flee. She watched, stalled in her own uselessness. Was pain as painful to the unconscious? What did he feel? "He's expressing it." What was he thinking? She'd read once in the *National Geographic* at the dentist's office that shellfish didn't feel pain. But lobsters revolted in seeming agony when lowered into boiling water! Wasn't that pain? Jane couldn't remember any pain other than childbirth, not the beatings with the fireplace poker or tossing in a damp bed with scarlet fever. But that was long ago, just scar tissue. As a father, Jacob had never raised a finger to her, he was incapable. She could have done anything under the sun without fear of punishment, but, perhaps unhealthily, she never did. It was Harriet in those early days who wielded a sternness that didn't exactly frighten, but most certainly intimidated. She herself was terrified of losing *Dzidzia* and, although incapable of more than a violent hand or facial gesture, she imposed lovingly the parental discipline that Dzidzia's narcissistic self needed least. What was Jacob feeling right now? Was it possible to block out the pain by imagining, by creating and inhabiting an invented world? Or a past life? An adolescent on an outing in the Tatras with other boys and girls eating roast potatoes and playing post office? Or were at this point thoughts merely raw impulses like the lobster's in the pot? Jane thought of the story of her grandfather, *Dziadzu*, Jacob's father-in-law, a pious Orthodox Jew, a hay trussler from Wadowice, the Pope's village, who had escaped to Russia, spent the war in a work camp in Siberia before finally making it to Montreal on a boat and later to New York by road, where he lived-out his life displaced, cranky, and sad. He had kept loaves of honey cake — which permanently housed pilgrimages of tiny red ants — and musty yarmulkes from Bar Mitzvahs that he had never attended in his dingy nursing room closet at the Daughters of Abraham in the Bronx for years and years, and had staged a hunger strike atthe age of 96. When the nurses had tried to force feed him, he lashed out, struck them with his bony forearms, pushed them away by their breasts. Having grown very weak in several days, he had lost consciousness; the home administrator, a Puerto Rican woman with a hyphenated Hungarian last name and red hair and freckles, opted to call Jane in New Jersey, collect, afraid that he'd die before the family had been notified and then there'd be complaints and professional inquiry, and the promotion would be even slower to come. Plus, the family had the right to be notified in time. Not that the care was inadequate, although four times they had stolen Dziadzu's woolen overcoats. Each time the official explanation was "He forgot it someplace. They forget. They're old." *Dziadzu*, the word meaning grandfather in Polish, fell into a deep dream; he was on his way to Heaven, as the story went. He was walking and walking day and night following the cobblestone road to Heaven, but Heaven was very far away, very far, "and I was getting very tired and weak and very hungry, very very hungry. So hungry." His false teeth clacked like the keys of an abused piano left in the teen room at a Catskills resort hotel. So in his dream he decided that he had better start eating again to gain enough strength to complete the journey. Heaven, you know, isn't like Miami. "I had to make it to Heaven, didn't I?" So he accepted the idea of eating, first just broth, but later a pureed mixture of carrots and rice, and within a day or two re-gained his strength. Consciousness bolted back and he got wheeled back to his room, where his overcoat was missing again. He had not only lived to tell the story but hung around for another three and a half years, finally succumbing at 99 and a half, falling short of the required 100 to get the President's letter, and was buried in a pine box decked with an artificial geranium in the Jersey Meadowlands in a narrow plot next to his daughter, Jane's aunt, Amalja's sister, who had died at 62 in New York of leukemia, overlooking the new Giants Stadium and a hundred chemical smokestacks with a view of the rusty Pulasky Skyway and Allen Ginsberg's *pays natal,* Patterson.

Lobsters.

"Father, Benjamin is coming to see you. He'll be here tomorrow. He's flying down on Delta Air Lines," she told him. What did the airline matter? It felt stupid mentioning it, but the doctor had told her to tell him details, to orient him, give him the time, the date, the weather, the baseball results. It seemed like a farce. The king was naked. It was her, she suspected, not him. She continued though; there was nothing else to do.

"It's hot today. In the nineties. You have lots of cards waiting for you in your room. I didn't want to bring them down here. I thought it was best to leave them on your night tableupstairs. You can..." she stopped short. Jacob lay there in front of her, his involuntary muscles reacting to pain. "Why am I telling him these stupid things?" The cards would never be read, opened weeks later in defeatism by Harriet. Polite notes of acknowledgment and thanks would be sent back in small ivory envelopes. She heard her own voice as if she was speaking into a tape-recorder; it was directed to someone else but that someone was not hearing it. Like most people, she hated the sound of her own voice, didn't think it sounded like her, didn't like the person it was. It didn't congeal to the image she had of herself. The choppy disconnected phrases embarrassed her. For a brief instant she even thought she'd detected the slight accent that strangers had told her lingered on certain words. She never heard it nor did those who were close to her, but the others heard her stretch out the short vowels. Fanny did. Her voice enunciated her uselessness and she wondered in the same thought-frame if language made any difference anyway, if words meant anything in the long run. She took her eyes from her father and sprayed the unit with a mean, cynical pan, like a slow sweeping camera shot manipulated by a director with a deeply ironic, European, as opposed to American view of life. Slowing and growing tender as she focused on Sticks, zipped-in and mute.

"A death camp." Almost no sound came from her lips. She turned back to Jacob, had an urge to gather him up in her arms and take him home and lay him out peacefully, gently on the fresh sheets and pillow case on her bed. That was ridiculous, he would die. She turned her back to him, pins stuck in her back with guilt and ache. "Father." She palpitated with hope.

"Time's up," she heard reverberating from these subdued alcoves. "I'm sorry, you'll have to leave now. He has to rest." Jane's eyes filled-in with the blue-green of the attendants' hospital clothes, and she moved away like a banal ocean wave, unseen, useless, unrecorded, in disbelief.

One night a maid who had survived the Germans and who lived with us, came running in to the house yelling 'Mr. Grasgrun's been shot!' The partisans, peasants who organized themselves in the neighboring mountains and who generally blamed the Jews for their own plight and for bringing the war and hard times to Poland, carried him off and shot him in the Jewish cemetery in Nowy Targ, which had already been desecrated. More of these attacks started to happen to the few Jews that managed to return from Hitler's camps. We were finally given by the local police revolvers which we left loaded on the table during the night.

A few days later three boys and one girl were shot to death during the day on the road to the Czech border by men in a rented car. The bodies were brought to town by the police who told us to bury our own dead. We carried them over the river on the edge of Nowy Targ to our former cemetery, where Mr. Grasgrun was murdered, and we buried them there among the broken and overturned headstones that marked once the graves of our ancestors.

Soon after, we packed up our few belongings and left Nowy Targ for Krakow, where there was a proportionately larger Jewish population that had survived. And so we left for the last time, having survived the Nazi horrors and then having come back to our so-called country and home, and instead of finding our friends and fellow townspeople, we found murderers.

It was clear by then to Amy that she would continue during each break to read further. The moral pang of intruding had eased, her comfort present in the routine page marker she left each night — the printed hospital menu that was distributed to each room. Each evening when she came on duty she inquired about Jacob's condition. It had only been six days, but she knew it was too long to feel comfortable about his recovery. She knew more than she cared to admit to herself, and subconsciously, her nightly reading seances were sort of a race against a turn for the worse. Could she finish what he'd written not before he returned to his room, but before there'd be no returning. This was a thought, and in her silence death was a feeling, a nervous stomach, a threatening cloud, not a word or phrase. Privately, she had suppressed her guilt by acknowledging that her clandestine intrusions each night into the private affairs of a patient was a way of assuring this man, Jacob, a reader; his words would matter, at least to her. The diary became a communion. And from some inexplicable superstition she held herself from jumping ahead. There was more lurking in her engagement. She knew it. Her grandfather was unable....he too was a victim. The feeling was a larger one, imprecise as back pain.

Reading was an activity that she loved but after her marriage and all there was to do with Kevin — emotionally making room — there simply wasn't enough time. She tried to give Kevin the feeling of living with a mother, without denying the truth that she wasn't pretending to be his real one. She, at first, had felt it better that the child call her Amy, but soon after, maybe two months or so, he fell into the more comforting habit of making her "Mom." Reading now consisted of those skinny, adolescent volumes from the school library, *The Glass Catcher* by Matt Christopher, *I am the Cheese* by Robert Cormier, etc. The serious works of fiction that had excited her during her late adolescence in *Gymnasium* and then later while at university — especially in that survey courseon European Studies — demanded too much as a young "mother" and professional, and so reading time deteriorated in a way that disappointed her. Now she didn't read much of anything, with the exception of *Selections from Readers Digest*, which kept coming to the house by mistake. The subscription had been a gift from her in-laws not long after Kevin and his father had come into her life. "While he's napping you can relax with this," her mother-in-law had written on the gift subscribers card. She had wanted to be either a specialist in ethno-psychology or a speech therapist and had "almost finished" a degree with a double major: BIO/PSYCH. But with the crunch of wildly high tuition costs, guilt feelings in taking money from her grandmother, who had just a small retirement pension from the City of Frankfurt and a tiny allowance, 200 DM a month, from the State Commission on War Indemnities who had only awarded *Opa* a meager 10% disability allowance, claiming that the 18-centimeter round blood clot extracted from the right-forward section of his head had not necessarily been a direct result of the wound he'd received as a foot soldier in Russia. That and a disillusionment with the abstract prerequisites at university, was ample reasoning for her to decide to drop out. She would have been the first in her family to have attained a university degree. The options afterwards fluttered down to nurse, professional bilingual secretary, or guidance counselor, all required diploma programs and training which she could have gotten going part-time at a community college for a fifth of the price. She had picked nurse. And now the damn *Readers Digest* just kept coming; she had never renewed it and had no idea why it kept coming. At first she threw them out but now she found it just easier to read. She had the little ubiquitous mags stacked up neatly in her hallway, two back issues used to prop up the weak leg of the tv stand. She had pulled out the 25-cent coupons and kept them in a drawer in her kitchen. Stuff she never bought: Shake and Bake, Bounce fabric softener, Flintstones Multiple Vitamins, Captain Crunch cereal.... Other than those monthly installments, whose first-person accounts she started to become addicted to, there was the morning paper, which landed on her stoop at half past six, folded in thirds and held together with a thin elastic band. And then there was the occasional best-selling paperback, Jacqueline Suzanne novels and others like *The Thornbirds* and that whole wave of attorney novels, which she could tear through in a week and a half by reading over a yogurt at lunch and just before bed with her long, washed hair coiled into a white terry cloth towel. It wasn't so much literature that interested her but the characters that lived within it, and the things that happened in the world to them, and how they found their ways out of quagmires, or didn't. She loved queststories, preferred long, slow films the kind that played in only one or two d'art et d'essai movie houses in Houston where baggies of Trailblazer granola were sold in the lobby, and aside from the six or seven albums of Dizzy Gillespie, whom she loved not only for the genius of his music, but his resemblance to *Opa* and Yasser Arafat, whose charm touched her, she owned a small cassette collection of highly-soulful, international folk and popular singers like Angelo Branduardi, Julien Clerc, Milton Nacimento, Caetano Veloso, Cesaria Evora, and her fantasy boyfriend, an original new singer called Prince.

The handwriting was difficult at times, especially in the subdued light of Jacob's empty hospital room. Amy was tempted at one moment to take it home overnight, but decided without hesitation that that would be wrong. Instead, she returned to it each evening like a gentleman she knew she should stop seeing, but couldn't find a way or a concrete enough reason to say no. She pictured Jacob's face. A perfect stranger, yet there was an echo that wouldn't fade. The sound of a vacant building, the ache of memory never acknowledged. She didn't know, but it pulled lightly on her and she followed. Maybe she just sided with people who faced hardship head-on and despite weakness and vulnerability beat it. The same was true with animals; she loved them all, but defended mostly the voiceless ones, the pill bugs and centipedes and beetles and slugs and dragonflies, and the unclaimed ones at the animal shelters, the ones who were old and injured, had sicknesses or were losing their hair. A palsied parrot from Gabon that was kept in a dirty cage at her laundromat. These were her closest friends. The fact that her husband had gone into the processed-meat business depressed her. She had no reproach for vultures ripping apart the dead little bodies of lemmings, or eating horses that had died of old age, but processed-meat went too far. She had wanted to have a second child, her first, and adopt a third, any kind, race, nationality, or age; he or she didn't have to be a newborn like the ones most young couples seemed to want, and she would have tried despite her husband's protestations had the marriage lasted. No, a five-year-old or ten-year-old of any race or background would have been just fine, even desirable. She'd have taken in all the abandoned kittens and puppies listed in the lost and found column of the *Weekly Houston Gleaner,* the ratty give-away filled with supermarket cut-outs and used car ads that got left in stacks at every public place, if she hadn't already been evicted from two apartments for keeping domestic pets. She even lost an apartment once before she was married for lodging a myna bird in her kitchen alcove. Another time she refused a little turtle offered as a gift because keeping it in a dish seemed too cruel to her and she couldn't bear to have it die like Victor, the lizard.

And so we left for the last time, having survived the Nazi horrors and then having come back to our so-called country and home, and instead of finding our friends and fellow townspeople, we found murderers.

She reread the last line. Her grandfather, she knew, was incapable of such things. He was incapable of stepping on a caterpillar, of mistreating a car part. *We found murderers.*

11

Benjamin would be leaving in the morning for Houston. In his dorm room, as he sorted his laundry — a sock or two always clung to a sheet or towel — he heard Jacob's story-telling voice. Jacob's stories and songs and passed-on anecdotes and jokes, filtered and altered through time and personality and now translation. Growing up Benjamin didn't ever feel like an immigrant or the son of a foreigner, only American, but with something else, an option, tinted sun-roof or auto-reserve tape deck. And Jacob was thrilled that his stories interested his grandson; he certainly didn't expect it. It was just so, a blessing. Benjamin was a "vonderful boy." That's how Jacob described his grandson as he made a toast into the band mike at Benjamin's Bar Mitzvah, spilling medium-range, French white wine and not noticing it as he spoke, and his voice echoed around the friend-and-family-filled rented hall. A fancy function in a place that bordered between class and kitsch and was reserved mostly for nouveau riche Italian engagement parties and Sicilian weddings, Waspish graduations and Sweet-Sixteens, and white-collar company-motivation seminars. And there, standing on marble at the pinnacle of twelve decked-out tables with expensive center pieces and a three-tiered cake decked with porcelain bar mitzvah *chachkies* made in Hong Kong, stood Jacob in his best suit, well-shaved and scented with Old Spice, the tattoo having faded permanently. Harriet had been at the first table to his right, and Dzidzia with her husband and friends, mostly Jewish, in a white sequined dress and a tinted-blonde, Barbie-like hairdo that was the latest at the local beauty parlors, an aquamarine dangling around her neck, watched her father glowingly: JacobSimon, after two lifetimes of work, savoring the moment, a glass of French wine gripped in his hand as if it were the torch of the Statue of Liberty, in front of a microphone that amplified his accented voice, toasting his grandson upon becoming a man in the eyes of Jewish law in the United States of America. And God moved up a notch. To stand there free to spill wine was a gift greater than heaven. And so he was careful not to spoil or burden the boy's young, fresh mind with torturous war stories or murderous tales. A boy should think of his school, his friends, his parents, girls. Warstories weren't for children. They weren't stories at all. They weren't heroic or brave or even adventurous. Huckleberry Finn was better for that and even Jacob had read excerpts in the Newark Public Library when he was battling to build his English. He had never been on a raft. To talk about pre-war Poland pleased him because it told him that his life hadn't just started at the age of 43 on the dock at 34th Street on the West Side of New York, that he too had been a boy with a mother and father and good things to eat and healthy biological impulses. Poland before 1939 remained unscathed, if not glorified, in Jacob's recollections. September 1 was the dividing line, and every year on that date actually September 6 when the Germans took Krakow even while mixing paint or cutting keys or sitting on the toilet with *The Jewish News*, Jacob felt a little wave of dizziness ripple though him, a tiny murmur in his spleen, and he ate with less appetite.

Although he didn't deny life or facts that fell after that date, these he felt would spoil a healthy imagination. The only spoiling Jacob would entertain translated into expensive crab fingers at the Jumbo House in Greenwich Village with precocious Benjamin — age seven — sitting on a booster chair and cracking the shells, spoiled with exposure. Benjamin was a good boy, healthy and free, hair well-parted, a little gold-plated watch strapped to his wrist. Born in a special country to healthy, prosperous parents in an age of peace. "Why stain all this fresh possibility with the horrors of the past?" That was Jacob's conviction, and this was how Benjamin understood the beneficence of his grandfather. But the past was a part of the unknown and the unknown was within the realm of what a healthy curiosity tried to imagine and needed to know. Plus, the past could not be hoarded; it belonged to Benjamin too. It was his own history, his own story. And any child with an active mind not only wanted to know but required to know what preceded the Marine Falcon's arrival in New York on March 27, 1947. With Jacob in the hospital, seriously ill, Benjamin began to feel the fear of not having asked enough. He remembered the little stories that Jacob shared about his boyhood in the Tatras, the colorful townsfolk, mountain men, merchants, gypsies. Jacob would have to go down to the river on Fridays before sundown and cut the thick toenails of his superstitious grandfather Solomon, and then wrap the clippings in brown paper, and burn them to keep away bad omens called "canaries." Benjamin had encouraged Jacob to tell him the rest, but now it seemed like he hadn't insisted enough. He knew about the diary and hoped that the buffer of writing would allow Jacob to open up. Benjamin was eager to read those hand-written pages. The diary was Jacob Simon's entrance into the risk of letting feelings join facts. And now like an electroencephalograph connected to a dead brain, the line would go flat and straight as a western interstate.

Amy turned the page and found that he had remembered something and circled back.

When I came back from Russia in 1941 I did a risky thing. I buried in my parents cellar all of our family valuables — jewelry, gold coins, and a few thousand American dollars. While being in concentration camp in Plaszow one of my friends, related slightly to us through my wife's family, decided to run away from the group while marching to work through town with a wheelbarrow, not unlike the way those two guys stole the canoe. Before he escaped I decided to give him the plan to the cellar with a description of where the treasure was hidden. I asked him to make sure my baby daughter got the benefit of this small fortune. I found out later that he was caught and taken to Nowy Targ by the Gestapo, who forced him to dig it out, took everything, and then shot my friend. When I got back to Nowy Targ after the war, I didn't even look.

She sighed. Her back ached. That was enough for tonight. A bone cracked in her neck. She needed to make an appointment with the chiropractor, the same one who did work for the Houston Rockets.

Benjamin recalled Jacob saying something about the sketch of the cellar. He fantasized about that treasure, but Jacob would have nothing to do with any ideas of looking for it. He remained firm on this. "It no longer exists," he would insist. "The Germans got it. It's over with." There were moments when Benjamin, in a day dream, would be on his knees on the earthen cellar floor, scratching away the pounded smooth dirt with a hand rake. This was pure Butch Cassidy, and conquest rode on his baited breath. "It's there and it's ours." This was a way for Benjamin to still join the Resistance, to not give in. He wanted to be sure that he would have never walked to his grave like the others. "I will resurrect our memory," he proclaimed; "my mother will have her mother's brooch to wear plainly on her chest. She will walk down one day any Main, Center, Spring, or Elm, Jefferson, Washington, or Lincoln Street, Avenue, or Drive in the land with our memory gloriously present in the heirloom I'll bring back," he said one night to a mirror, stoned in his dorm room at college. Lord Byron's portrait sat flatly on a fat paperback next to the peanut butter and hash pipe. This was a liberal arts college where Jews had only attended regularly since the fifties.

Amy had been kind of surprised by the tone of disinterest in Jacob's voice on the page. But she didn't know why. Maybe the disappointment of being removed from these symbolic attachments to the other world was so deep that its power dissolved for good. Like electricity rushing into a ground wire. Even the authenticity of disappointment had been flattened. Survival flatness, the act of being unobtrusive as a plank in the floor, emotionally buoyant as a dead carp. Camouflaged as a rock fish. But she couldn't have known that at the fore of Jacob's thought was the protection of Benjamin. He didn't want the boy to risk a hangnail on that crazy, meaningless treasure, a stash that probably was no longer there and was only a demon from hell anyway. "Forget it. Forget it," he'd say with both temerity and playfulness, his lower lip going baggy on the second syllable of the verb "forget," his lower, grainy teeth testifying in the background. "If you want money, I'll give it to you." And he'd take out his squashed, brown-leather billfold and take out a fifty. There wasn't anything ostentatious about it; Ulysees S. Grant's head laying out on the ping-pong table just showed that he meant it. And in the gesture Benjamin understood his grandfather's wishes. "Become a doctor. Discover a cure for cancer. Or anything you want. Find a wife and be happy. Buy a house, a big one, solid and made of stone if possible. With two garages and a finished basement. Anything but digging in the tainted earth. Let it be." Jacob refused flatly to recreate a map of the old family dirt floor cellar, where potatoes and onions and apples and wine had been kept in the cool and dark foundation beneath the house on the *rynek*, like the cellar beneath Amy's grandparents' house in Frankfurt where *Oma* and her children hid during the air raids. There'd be no map. That was that.

Maybe Jacob had even confused the details himself of the Gestapo recovery of the treasure the way novelists blended reality and invention into one improved definitive substance. This theory would cement a convenient resolve to the mystery, one that he could live with which he could convincingly dissuade Benjamin's imagination. With no treasure in the ground there'd be no need for a map. The stolen treasure could just be mingled conveniently into all the other, worse, atrocities that the Germans were to be blamed for. Much easier to create one large guilt that could be negotiated, suppressed, forgotten in a lump. Or maybe Jacob, haunted by the fear of Benjamin, his only true continuity in life, venturing back into danger over a few thousand disintegrating American silver certificates and some trinkets of sentimentality, lost track of the real facts and order of events himself. The truth was no longer knowable or particularly desirable. But life needed meaning and at the age of retirement with the burden of free time on his callused hands, keeping a diary met these needs. Oscar was surely dead, and the whereabouts of his daughter Lala, thirty years later, were totally unknown. Australia, it was suspected. Dead perhaps. So the whole matter never got much further; it slid unresolved into that large, amorphous drawer of brittle memory superimposed on history, filtered through screens that both clarified and obscured and then superimposed the results on the daguerreotype imagination of a now American boy once removed.

Poland itself was removed. The idea of Poland had remained lodged in Benjamin's scratched-up print of a black and white film, a cold and dark non-place with no coordinated time and space. Had Gdansk not made it into the news so often for its shipyard strikes, and then *Solidarnosc*, and finally Walesa's popular ascent to the presidency, with the substantial help from the Pope from Wadowice, Amalja's village, Poland would have remained for him wholly in the shadow of a terrible ruin. A scar. An Old World place of black veils, dark clouds, gray ash buildings of heavy lichen-covered stone and cinder streets, inhabited by slow, limping people who unhooked wooden legs from worn stumps, and lived on hard rye bread and nubby vegetables, beets and turnips, that grew sluggishly in the cold, tired earth. A place with no way in and no way out, other than for the odd boat and screeching train car that carried sad looking people in tattered clothes and patched and mended suitcases and worn out shoes. Permanently November. To Benjamin, secure in his dorm room in New England, far from eastern Europe by a tiny generation of years — nine to be precise — Poland was not a homeland; it was the dull gray curtain, not even an iron one, that hung lifelessly over an empty stage of a theater in which no one would play again. A ship that could not call at any port. Silent, still, and frozen to that day in mid1947 when Jacob and his daughter broke for good from the land that had housed the lineage for 800 years! Now there was no coat of arms, no lingering cousins. To a first generation American Jew it offered no identity. Like a trick candle on a birthday cake, it flickered back. It was everything America wasn't, not even Polish like the way America was American or England was English. Even Jane after only two years or so

133

couldn't think of herself as anything other than — remarkable as it was — American. Certainly not Polish, although she was. Like the newcalf-length dress they had bought for her in Bamberger's downtown, she slipped into her new life. It fit. And felt good, like wearing a custom-made costume. It was simple in the fifties; learn its language and believe in the freedom of making money from your own energy, and America was yours for the asking. She stepped into that little dressing room, pulled the curtain, and walked out Jane Simon, Queen of her Senior Prom. And no one knew the difference, and Jane was afforded the luxury of oblivion.

As Benjamin prepared an overnight bag for the flight to Houston, Taj Mahal's voice proved the Doppler effect from a passing Datsun. Focused on Jacob, preparing himself for the pain he heard in the gravel of his mother's voice on the phone, he drifted into Jacob's now-defunct hardware store in Newark, the place that had for 25 good years replaced his homeland, had become his country: 18th Avenue Hardware, God's second chance. "Didn't that store ever remind him, haunt him even, of the first store, the family store, where generations of Simons would have kept selling tons of cement into the future had it not been for Hitler? Weren't there moments, strange deep moments perhaps while pumping a gallon of turpentine or filling an order, that he slipped and just forgot — just for an instant — which store he was in?" On Thursdays his wife would man the cash register, and when there was a moment of slack in the flow of customers she'd check the week's books, verify the inventory and prepare the bank deposits. It was Amalja that had had the head for business, the Simons were eternal hardware men, their minds riveted to the merchandise — once, at a Yankee Stadium night game with young Benjamin and his Dad, Jacob, in the wild roar of the crowd, completely missed Mickey Mantle's longest home run in his career because he was busy counting the bulbs in the brilliant panels of floodlights that beamed blindingly over the outfield. And Jane didn't get either the business or merchandise training; she was shielded from both stores, it was for boys, plus she was too little, and subsequently never learned how to change a trap under a sink or calculate the profits after deducting the cost of the goods and subtracting the overhead. She'd ultimately go to college and study Sociology and Government — American Government. She'd join a Jewish Sorority and wear lipstick and nylons. And listen to the motherly warnings of Harriet to please her father. Behind it all was "please father" and avoid the guilt of "hurting father." And thus there was none of that awkward and combative spell of adolescent rebellion that all young people needed to hurdle before settling competently into the healthy zone of adulthood. For Jane, the deprivation of childhood compromised the normal rage of adolescence, and by extension, catapulted her into adulthood and motherhood with dark and distant holes in her inner emotional galaxy. Now there was Harriet, eager yet blind to the shadows behind both Jacob's and Jane's eyes. Wasn't there at least one Thursday when he thought of Amalja as he watched Harriet with a sharpened pencil perched in her hair bun, a work-apron tied around her waist? There was a certain symmetry to the two wives. With Amalja, it was an arranged marriage; her family had paired her up with the red-headed Jacob Simon of Nowy Targ, and with Harriet, it was a matter of being at the right place at the right time, an entrance visa of sorts to legitimize their stay in the United States. Love and free choice were secondary in a world where the ability to continue "being" was already an achievement. Perhaps there was never any confusion. He knew what he had to do and he did it, like a bird carrying twigs to a nest. Even if it meant weakening his own health. Maybe that was the key to survival. A dead cat lay decaying in the empty lot under an Acme shopping cart that had been stripped of its wheels by kids making a go-cart.

Benjamin tightened the cap on his toothpaste and deodorant stick, scented with lime, and shoved the items to the bottom of his Adidas bag. He didn't have one of those leather toiletry kits like most of the other guys on the hall. In another generation this kind of school would be second nature to the Simon line, but for the time being, preppy toiletry kits and ivy-covered buildings were still dearly picturesque. It was clear that there'd be no hardware store in Benjamin's life, there'd be no savings of dimes in a converted coffee can to buy winter coats or textbooks. There'd be no trade for Benjamin to enter as an apprentice. His hands would never chaff and crack from the combination of cold weather and hard work. At eighteen years old he worried about the motivations of Othello, the blood-consciousness of D.H. Lawrence, and the use of interior space in the canvases of Vermeer. There was no Polish or Yiddish in his head, just the subjunctive tense in Spanish, which perpetually confused him. The hardware store he knew only as a place of play as a child, and now on the eve of this unique visit to Houston, a city he only knew for the Astrodome and the baseball cards he had collected, he recalled hammering aluminum roofing nails into the wooden floor and the powdery film they left on his hands after he'd run his fingers through the sharp keg.

Benjamin folded his bath towel, a Holiday Inn white and green one that he'd lifted once, and then unfolded it, remembering that hotels supplied towels and soap. He was going to the Hilton. His mind was still revisiting Jacob's old store and he sort of enjoyed going back there now, Proust-like, and seeing all the things he'd played with but hadn't thought of in ages. The silver and gold filings that he'd dusted off the key-making machine and saved in a Chase & Sandborn coffee can. The different sized Camp paper bags he'd fill with nails andbolts, stacked and tied in bundles behind the counter, and were excellent for making puppets because the bottoms of the bags would move along the folds and seem like nodding heads. And the way he'd weigh out those nails on the balance scale, trying to get it right to the last nail, while the customer waited. Jacob always tossed in another small fistful within the customer's eye-shot, which Benjamin didn't understand at the time, but later came to see as a key to success in America. Service. Jacob greeted his customers by their name, offered home delivery on even orders under ten dollars, (before Jacob got the '53 Chevy wagon, forest-green with a strip of laminated wood for trim, he delivered by Schwinn, a grown man on an 18-inch frame with a wicker basket and pedal brakes.) He threw-in always a few extra something and handed-out to the kids of Mr. Kubitsky or Mrs. Kowalchick sticks of Wrigley's Spearmint, which he bought in bulk at the Acme and stacked neatly by the drawer of the old NCR. And the people would make their child say "thank you," nudge them with a nagging, drawn-out whisper, "What do you say?" And Benjamin would have to say "you're welcome" and then the customer and Jacob could both smile proudly and feel good about the world and its manners. Jacob was a good neighborhood merchant, and people came back and the business prospered. There were no vacations at all the first eight years and the store stayed open from eight till eight, six days a week, with the motto steciled in glossy exterior trim on the heavy swinging metal sign above the door that advertised Cook & Dunn Paints: "Service is Our Business." What did that guy, Mr. Antonelli, the one who would return unused nails, ever know or care about Jacob's past? Or Nick, the grocer? Or Bart, the overweight and suicidal soda jerk who ran the luncheonette next door and resembled Khrushchev? These people, the citizens of Newark who spent the war years in Newark, what did they know about what Jacob had come through before being able to deliver gallons of exterior semi-gloss by bicycle? And Jacob would only smile, inquire about their mothers or children and car problems and thank them for their business.

Re-visiting the scene ten years later, Benjamin pictured the Everready Battery dispenser, which was shaped like the roller coaster at Olympic Park, itself later condemned and turned into scrap-iron and sold to the country of Bangladesh. He heard the clunky 1.5 Volt D-size silver-papered batteries scuttling down the gravity feed. He filled the plastic-rimmed tracks and then one by one removed the bottom battery causing the whole line to start rolling. And there was the tub of sponges, real sponges, course and each differing in size and shape, varying prices printed on in black magic marker. And the pegboard near the front covered with Master locks, whose combinations, written in pen on tiny paper tags tied to the barrels, Benjamin tried a hundred times each.

"What should I take?" He gloated over his stack of required reading. They all wouldn't fit. For a second he complained out loud; there was an "unreal" amount of work, a ton of reading, and two ten-page papers, the philosophy one a "bitch." He loaded a few key volumes into the pouch inside his bag, and removed the pack of ribbed Trojans that were still there from that weekend at Norton. "Won't need these in Houston."

Then, heading down with the same slight trepidation the steep wooden steps to the cellar, he switched on the light on the dirty wall to the right — past the thin plywood door that 18th Avenue Hardware shared with Bart's Luncheonette. Jacob had to punch open that door once when Bart held himself hostage on his toilet seat in the luncheonette bathroom with a barber's razor raised to his throat, and a second time when he was on a soda fountain stool with his belt around his neck reaching for the blades of the overhead fan. The wood on the steps creaked. And into the tunnels and tunnels of stacked merchandise and spider webs with rat traps set in the corners and planks of lumber to walk on and straddle where puddles of rain water and ground water had seeped in. And the scary boiler room behind the back of the stairs and up front near the street with its row of jagged blue-black shark teeth forming the flame. The cold, dusty coal heap with its metal chute poking up into a grate that opened up onto the sidewalk above on delivery days. At the base of the wooden stairs were two alcohol-smelling metal drums, one with turpentine and the other with the less refined, cheaper sub-terps. Cold metal pumps jutted from each and rows of dusty brown gallon jugs and white metal caps which held the prices marked with thick grease pencils that could only be sharpened by pulling a string that wound around the thick, waxy lead, cluttered the dank floor space below. Jacob would always poke the snout of a jug up to his nose before he'd fill it with one of the two solvents, cautious of chemical fires. Once Benjamin cranked the pump before readying a jug, and the sub-terps splattered onto the drum top and jumped up into his eyes. He thought he'd certainly go blind, but Jacob wiped away the spirits which always felt weirdly dry on the skin and nothing happened to Benjamin's sight. The ceilings were low like in bunkers and Jacob, no taller than six gross of Lestoil stacked in cartons four high and six deep, often bumped his head on the steel and wormwood beams, forcing him to wear wide band-aids on his exposed scalp. It was better than war.

Upstairs there was a paint-mixing dispenser that spit colors from a little nozzle. And a funny machine that locked the paint cans in and shook them frantically in a blur.

Benjamin flipped on the switch and jumped back. The whole floor vibrated and cans or boxes sometimes shifted and fellfrom shelves. Then Jacob opened the can that had been shaken, and checked the new hue for the customer. Sometimes they'd have to add a tad more black or white to meet the customer's liking. The customer was always king.

With every gallon of Cook & Dunn he always gave a paint stick for mixing, and with big orders a nice wooden yard stick that had the address and phone number of the store stamped in red on the back, along with "Painting's fun with Cook & Dunn".

Benjamin smiled to himself, saw his lips rise up in his college mirror, tucked a few more school books into the outside pocket of the Adidas bag. He had to read Hannah Arendt's *Eichmann* but decided it was a bad idea to take to Houston. He replaced it with Conrad.

Jacob had glued onto the corner rounding the counter by the cash register a wad of rubber padding so Benjamin wouldn't take his eye out. It was Harriet's phrase.

There was a small back room too, which he reentered now for the first time in over ten years. The store had been sold and the merchandise liquidated ten cents to the dollar. What had become of the space? In the late Sixties there were the race riots and then the great exodus out of Newark by the whites and better-off immigrants who tried to hoist themselves out and into the better towns in and around the hills of Essex County. Jacob and Harriet finally left too, opting for a more comfortable garden apartment on the way to Morristown, where George Washington had once slept. Benjamin sat at his desk, his bag ready in the armchair, and played with the on/off button of his tensor lamp. There were lots of wooden crates that held galvanized pipe and loose plumbing fittings. He used to sit back there among all that threaded metal, screwing the male parts into the female ones, jamming together iodized elbows and straight

pieces, building contorted structures that Jacob would ultimately have to dismantle and sort.

Out the back door empty paint and merchandise cartons were tossed rudely into the alley, where they collected
throughout the day. At night, just after closing, or when
Harriet was watching the store, Jacob would have to break
them down, collapse them and tie them up flat near the
dented trash cans for the garbage men, invariably Italians,
to tote away. There was a big black cat with yellow eyes
that lurked around back there and always looked dangerous. There were no cats in the Simon heritage and Benjamin
never learned to like or understand the one out back. Rap-
ping on the water pipes that ran between the store and the
apartment upstairs was their signal, there crude but eco-
nomical telegraph system. When Harriet rapped twice from
downstairs it meant that Jacob should stick his head out the
kitchen window. Harriet would hurry out into the alley beneath the window by the garbage cans and crushed boxes
to tell him that a salesman ormerchandise rep was there to
see him, or to check the price of a caulking gun or the five
gallon can of ceramic tile cement, or to tell Jacob that a
delivery had arrived, forty cartons of assorted hardware
from Stanley Tools in Irvington. And Jacob would hurry
down, his hot lunch half eaten or still warming in the oven.
And sometimes the salesman would leave a key chain or
penlight with the company logo on it as a little gift which
Jacob would save for Benjamin. Four raps on the pipes
meant there was a call to be made, since the phone upstairs
only got incoming calls and the only way to call out was to
use dimes in the pay phone at the back of the store, behind
the counter. Jacob would take Mercury dimes out of the
register to call out.

Between the counter and the back room — Benjamin
was now over twenty years old and a split major — opposite the pay phone, there was a dark and cramped corner

141

that had a sink with only a cold water faucet. There the water was always freezing, even in the dead of summer, and hard and metallic-tasting, calcium deposits caked around the base of hardware. There was a dirt-stained bar of ivory soap that Jacob used each day to remove the grime and grease from his hands before coming upstairs, which dried with dirt stains every evening, a roll of course paper towels that smelled when it was wet, and a red metal drinking tumbler.

Up front there was a panel of kitchen clocks whose hands Benjamin arranged and disarranged. And the stacks of graded sandpaper, discs for the electric floor sander that Jacob rented out by the half-day. And the rotatillers and the rows of wooden and steel grass rakes and garden tools and rough straw brooms and wedgie mops that were displayed on the sidewalk on 18th Avenue to show that the store was open for business as usual. And the folding lawn chairs so popular at the time with the stringy plastic weave that held the stuff together. And the manual lawnmowers and green garden hoses, coiled and tied with hemp. And sprinklers and grass seed spreaders and 25 pound sacks of lime. At closing Benjamin and Jacob pulled the stuff inside the store, cluttering the two aisles, then checked the lights, and locked the door, the big Yale bolt up top and the ordinary round one below. Two turns to the left and yank. No alarm; no security. Just an honest lock for form and dignity. No need to tempt the Devil.

The bells of the early 19th century steeple clock on top of the chapel that towered peacefully over campus clanged six times. The recollected images receded and Benjamin let them retreat on their own, forcing nothing. It was six already. He grabbed his meal card from his dresser top and trotted down in tennis sneakers to the dining commons to choose between chicken tetrazini and veal cordon bleu.

12

Harriet was taking her nightly bath, resting her tired legs in the hot water — she could stand it very hot. It was as if temperature didn't reach her or if she was composed of some other substance created by Dupont. Withered skin circling her thighs quivered in the filled tub on the nineteenth floor of the Hilton. She was frightened. She had married late in life, well after she'd become resigned to the idea of finishing out life as an "old petunia." Oh, there had been a few men, local Jewish boys, that she'd seen once in a while, but nothing much had come of it. The Tischman fella had proposed sorta, but kinda didn't follow through. Then there was the accident on Route 23 just above the Raritan exit, the Studebaker that had jumped the median. That had changed things for a long while. And Harriet had become resigned to taking care of her arthritic mother and her baby brother after her father died. When papa "left us" it was like her whole image of men evaporated. And no male in Harriet's life would ever seem right or good enough or available — like papa — to marry. Theycouldn't come up to "here" (and Harriet would emphasize the word and hold her right hand up to her left shoulder) next to him.

She would be talking about character, not size. In a drawer cluttered with black and white photographs with bent, scalloped edges, Benjamin had once spotted her, strutting in polished riding boots, flanged pants, a bandanna, and a silk shirt, lips painted red, eyes pitched downward between the cracks, and a filterless Old Gold perched between fingers, strutting from somewhere, going somewhere, moving down the wooden boardwalk at Atlantic City. There, only in that one photograph, taken by G— only knew, Harriet was her own person, smoke in her lungs, muscles aching in a satisfying way from the staccato of the horse's canter. Elsewhere in that drawer Benjamin kept a pair of silver and mother-of-pearl cufflinks; they had been Harriet's father's. And he, curiously enough, to Harriet's great pride, was called Benjamin too. There wasn't a single French-cuffed shirt in Howard Perley's Men's Shop in Benjamin's suburb, where all the kids got their man-tailors, banlons, and Nehru jackets, but he liked keeping them in his drawer nonetheless.

Harriet was a curious creature, surprisingly bold and adventurous in some ways — she'd once crossed the country alone by car and then a second time on horseback in the 1920s — and yet repressively cowardice and nervous in others. She'd never made the break from a shift car to an automatic, threw out milk products if they'd been left out for more than an hour, never argued with an authority figure. Change frightened her. She'd not change her brand of coffee even when it had ceased to please her. Nor would she leave her Thursday hairdresser although dissatisfied with his results for fifteen years! "Maybe he had had a bad day?" she'd pontificate each time beneath the sticky hair spray.

Marrying Jacob in June of 1947 and adopting young Jane was a rare stroke of luck. Brilliant luck. Instantly, amidst the lonely years preceding menopause, she became a wife and mother, equipped with an already installed sense of purpose and a challenging set of goals. A new lease. She'd adopted a man with child and they became hers without the investment of the early years. The time she'd written-off now rejoined her, and the traditional cycle of love, marriage, family, grandchildren, retirement, the cycle she'd first sought and then had abandoned as lost — "not in this life" — she suddenly stumbled back onto and picked up in the middle.

Who needed whom more — Jacob or Harriet — was a senseless question. An uneven draw, a moot point. Jacob and Jane had landed in the Port of New York in March of 1947, St. Patrick's Day to be exact. Imagine arriving in America on St. Patrick's Day, in New York where the customs and immigrations inspectors and the Port Authority cops were called Mack and Timmy. And the streets were confetti-strewn and unusual doses of thecolor green were everywhere. Just two more Poles with a tired-looking suitcase and worn clothes, that would soon be dumped neatly into the Good Will box in the Acme parking lot. Those tattered and bulky European objects just wouldn't make the grade in this modern country of new and improved styles, louder colors, and quicker drying fabrics. In Jacob's passport an alien looking, messy stamp in blue-black ink read *"Visa residencia para Venezuela."* What could Venezuela have meant to a Polish concentration camp survivor? A way out. In New York, they were "in transit," granted the famous sixty days to continue on. Others went to Cuba or Brazil. Many docked in Montreal. Thousands migrated the other way: Australia. Or any place else. Durban, Johannesburg, Stockholm, Mexico City, Shanghai, Tel Aviv, Montevideo.

Paris after the war was a live swarm of displaced souls. The ninth *arrondissement* hummed with eastern accents. The back streets jutting east from the Gare de St. Lazare, where the trains from Alsace, Germany, Hungary, Poland screeched in, teamed with chaos and excitement. On the rue Richer there was a huge second floor cafeteria run by a Jewish entrepreneur from Warsaw where Poles ate hot plates of *purée de pommes de terre* and *saucisses cacher* for one franc. And there they could talk and spread rumors and tell about schemes they had for landing visas. Or for making money quickly. Or of lawyers they knew or cousins they had who had friends or brother-in-laws who knew of ways to book passage to the United States. *Toujours* the United States. Many stayed put, found menial jobs in Paris's *quartiers populaires* washing dishes, mopping the *couloirs* of dingy hotels with *serpierres* and *eau de javel*, helping out in stores, eventually starting their own. Jacob had paid a hundred-dollar *pot de vin* to get the resident visas for Venezuela. He didn't flinch seeing those last few bills, the ones that represented the last bits of wealth from a life of work go into the vest pocket of a crooked *huissier*, who kept repeating, *"Quelle chance vous avez, monsieur, quelle chance." "Oui, monsieur,"* Jacob replied knowingly. Language was mobility and mobility was survival, and thus vocabulary grew quickly. Jacob handled himself in German, Russian, Czech, Serbo-Croat, and superficial French. There was no pain nor indignation now. No selling of soul; he was far beyond that. He handed over the American dollars and the crushed blue-black passports. In twenty four hours they were back in the secure inside pocket of his overcoat with the blotch of ink that let them board the Marine Falcon in Le Havre, and bounce down that ramp less than two weeks later in the United States of America.

His brother Hank — he had wasted no time becoming Hank from Henryk — and his American wife Lily were waiting on the 34th Street pier on St. Patrick's Day when the Salvation Army-sponsored vessel steered its nose into that wide New York City boat slip. The boat had made the crossing in eleven days — one day for each of Dzi's years — and then spent the last night trolling slowly off the coast between Nantucket (the most un-Jewish spot in America) and Long Island so as to arrive during Immigration working hours (even on St. Paddy's Day), as the captain had been instructed via radio. These were special missions, bringing war-shocked eastern Europeans into the United States. No one was exactly enchanted with the cargo, and had the Marine Falcon not belonged to the US Navy and the passage not been part of a paid Salvation Army humanitarian effort to assist immigrants displaced by the ravages of war, perhaps it too might have been refused entrance into the Port of New York and then wandered around at high seas like barges of urban refuse searching for a place to dump its tonnage. Harriet, then, for example, would not have been taking that scorching bath on the nineteenth floor of the Houston Hilton. And other things.

Hank and Lily were there waving handkerchiefs. They had their story too. There were no shortage of stories in those days, and only the truly brutal or miraculous impressed anyone. The rest were too banal. Hank had been a student preparing to be a textiles engineer in Milan when his Polish passport expired in 1939. After the September 1 invasion, the Polish consulate refused to renew passports to Jews, so Hank found himself sequestered in Italy, unable to return home. Each day, the world was growing darker and more dangerous. Fascism in Italy was in full swing. There was a rapidly shrinking list of places in the world still accessible and offering relative safety. One was the free-city of Shanghai. There was a boat leaving from Trieste and Hank joined it. And from Shanghai, he managed to get himself on a freighter to Manila, knowing that The Philippines were under American control. But, there, he very nearly shook hands with death; the island fell under a Japanese siege and Hank found himself under the cruel regime of a Japanese concentration camp, where he remained for three years. Released in a general amnesty at the end of the war, he sneaked onto an American battleship heading for California. New York was riveted to his desire; he had a cousin in New York. The ship docked in San Diego, and with his invalid Polish passport, he was confined to ship. Pleading successfully for the right to one phone call, he risked it on the closest Polish consulate in the US, at the time located in Chicago. Luckily, he got a sympathetic consul on the line and the response, "Send me the passport and I'll see what I can do." He dropped the tattered blue document with the coat of arms of a government no longer in power into the US mail and returned to his stuffy cabin on the ship to wait. In a week, the passport came back — renewed. With legal title he was granted a five day shore leave. There wasn't a second of hesitation. He made a cardboard sign marked NEW YORK and leaving on Christmas morning hitchhiked across the United States, making it to the mouth of the Lincoln Tunnel by noon on New Year's Day. It was 1946. With his last bit of cash he bought himself a professional shave and an Arrow dress shirt and the very next day walked into his cousin's law office in Brooklyn as if he had an appointment to sign an important contract. He was like that. Almost immediately, he took notice of the young legal secretary, Lily, sitting at a desk with a stack of documents to file. Now she stood next to the always-dapper Hank shaking white handkerchiefs as the tired Marine Falcon glided into the dirty, tire-padded slip. It had been Hank who had wired money to Jacob in Paris via American Express — as always, on the rue Scribe near the Opera — and Jacob paid a hefty premium to get his and his daughter's name on the ship roster, with the invaluable help and generosity of Sala Barusz, a captain of Polish origin at the *Armée de Salut*, whose family had been in France already for some time. The Marine Falcon threw its lines ashore and some forty minutes later, Jacob Simon and his daughter, Dzidzia, Gustawa, formerly Krystyna, came walking down the gangway to the pathetic-sweet brass and percussion sounds of the Salvation Army Band. Below, in the murky New York water, less than two miles from the Statue of Liberty, gray carp-like garbage fish poked their wide, wormy mouths at the floating objects on the surface. Jane noticed the unruly overcrowded mob of fish, as they competed for the bits of dirty stuff.

"Final destination, Venezuela, huh?" the immigration inspector confirmed.

"Yes, sir," Jacob lied with honor, admiring a uniform for the first time since his father's departure for Albania in 1914, and the authority of the polished brass buttons.

"And her?" He pointed to the pig-tailed Gustawa.

"Yessir," she mimicked on her own. He smiled.

"Okay, sixty days transit. No work."

By the end of that year Jacob and Jane were in threat of deportation. Venezuela had never been a serious consideration. Its virtue was purely the fact that it wasn't Europe. And the marriage, in no uncertain terms, was an arrangement, although Benjamin grew up wholly unaware that such things could happen. Wally and Beaver's parents seemed to love each other. So did Ricky and Lucy Ricardo. Even Ralph and Alice Cramden and Norton and Trixie. His parents had clearly chosen each other, despite the bickering. He had seen endless times the 8mm home movie of the wedding in Harriet's mother's house, the cake being stuffed into happy mouths. And the pool-side pictures of the honeymoon in Miami. (They had made the three-day journey by train; Jacob forbade their taking the six-hour trip on the Pan-American propeller plane. There'd be no risks.) Harrietand Jacob would kiss when they greeted each other at the end of the day or before going to bed. Love, had figured in later, kind of grew into place. First, it was aquestion of getting everyone's needs filled. Tenderness and affection were bonuses, offshoots of the primary components of the arrangement. Benjamin had never asked about the honeymoon. Did arranged marriages have them? He had heard about Jacob's honeymoon in Dantzig and Copenhagen with Dzidzia's mother, and that was an arranged marriage. It was Copenhagen, in a guest house not far from Tivoli, in fact where Jane's first cells began to divide. But with Harriet perhaps they just said let's just begin by making house. And so Jacob and Dzidzia became legal aliens and the buck stopped there — in North Jersey, where Benjamin would be born only nine years later on a Sunday morning after a night game in which the Brooklyn Dodgers clobbered the St. Louis Browns in Ebbetts Field, later to become a welfare complex and a dangerous parking lot.

As Harriet swung the stainless steel piece to the right and the bath water began to rush out beneath her, cruising down the plastic PVC pipes through the modern hotel's guts and finally nine minutes later into the Houston sewerage system, and Benjamin finished packing for the morning flight, Amy read about those early days.

Through my cousin Anna, I met my future wife, Harriet Neiman from Carteret. We were married on June 5th 1947 in her mother's house, the day after Dzi's birthday and we lived for a while with my sister-in-law in Rahway, and then with Harriet's mother.

How gracefully he turned strangers into "sister-in-laws." Nowhere did he mention how he felt or what he thought about the idea. Each new turn of events now was a matter of carrying-on like being transferred from one camp to another, or building a second house after the first had burned down. There wasn't love, but there was hope and the luxury of being un-pursued. It was a natural process, normal to keep going, to do what was necessary. There was nothing in his spirit that fought the drive to continue.

Jacob enrolled his daughter in the local public school, and not a week later she became Jane. The guidance counsellor, a spinster who had an associate's degree from Stevens College, and who had found "Gustawa" a bit too "foreign," strongly encouraged a new name. "It is in the child's best interest," she argued looking over the pink ridge of her inch-thick glasses, a woman who'd later die of undetected breast cancer. "The teachers all agree and so does our principal, Miss Oxner." Jane would soon hear the jokes about Miss Oxner's blue hair and scaly skin. She had little objection to becomingJane, and took on the new one-syllable with the same ease she'd changed names from Dzidzia and Gustawa to Krystyna and then from Krystyna back to Gustawa and Dzidzia again. Watching her long braids of blondish-brown hair become detached from her head, however, was a bit more complicated — although she said it didn't bother her. All those long strands fell limply to the ground in a pile around a mahogany kitchen chair and were gathered up in a day-old copy of *The Newark Evening News,* Eisenhower's face bearded with a blondish grin, and tossed out in an Acme shopping bag under the sink with the skins and tops of peeled carrots and the empty tins of Libby's French cut beans and Delmonte canned orange juice. So Jane became American with a pair of scissors and the advice of a primary school educator. And the frayed but handsome sheepskin coat — of quality unknown to the American lower middle class to which they now belonged — which she'd lugged around and hid her face in since the end of the war, was carried off and placed in one of those uninviting bins in a shopping center parking lot. In the wavy mirror in the apartment above the store, she contemplated her new look. She was like one of the girls in the monthly magazines now. And when she didn't talk, just stood there in short hair and modern synthetic fibers, long Bermuda shorts in the summer, all the differences were invisible. This excited her; for once she'd be like the rest. Miraculously, even her accent faded like the way the old uncoated Polaroid images did when left in the sun.

Her friends talked to her about clothes, boys, ice skating at Weequewaic Park or Saturday afternoon at the movie house on Clinton Avenue. "Do you want popcorn?" "Sure," she answered, never having had it before. "With butter and salt?" "Of course." By the time she reached the middle of the deep paper cup, it was like she'd been eating popcorn all her life. What fun! And her friends never thought to ask her about her other life. They weren't just being polite or discreet; they didn't think of it. What other life could they have asked about? Nor about the two weeks on the Marine Falcon. All those misplaced eastern Europeans and the smells of the kitchen and the scary night air on the deck escaped — or retreated — from her thoughts as if she had spent everyday of her young life in and around Newark, New Jersey. And Jacob was pleased with this. Just let her be happy. Just forget. It's better. Just forget. And he used quarts of hand-packed ice cream to help everything be smooth. If he had been running for office, Howard Johnson would have been Jacob's presidential choice. One night a week after they all had bathed and were warmly fitted into their nightclothes and slippers, the three of them would sit in the living room, Jacob with his naugahyde-covered feet perched on his hay-filled hassock, and eat scoops of Howard Johnson's hand-packed ice cream on top of Harriet's home-made apple sauce. She used lots of cinnamon and cut tiny squares of orange rind into the pot. It had been her mother's recipe.

In 1949, Jacob wrote with a penmanship that moved across open space like the swift movements of a trapeze artist, swirled and looped above and below the line in its American vernacular. Small but typical faults in grammar and spelling, and an underlying style of European training characterized the page. The way characters were first formed by the hand of a child was the way they most often remained. His capital Ss and Es and small gs, ys, and js could only have been made by a hand that had first learned to write in eastern Europe.

In 1949, we bought a run-down hardware store on 18th Avenue in Newark, with an apartment above the shop. In the beginning the business was quite hard, mostly because I was handicapped by my limited English. Of course, my dear Harriet was at my side constantly trying to learn hardware nomenclature and helping me out in understanding the customers. We, or actually Harriet, scraped up all the money she could to be able to buy enough merchandise to accommodate our customers. We were open from 8 a.m. to 8 p.m., seven days a week, anxious and willing to make a go of it, acquiring the motto 'Service is our Business'.

I forgot to tell about my first job as a salesman in the sporting goods department at Macy's, I had been hired because of my European accent which was considered chic at the time in that skiing especially was still a very European sport. On my first day, I experienced my first lesson in the American retail business. Two men picked up an 18-foot canoe in front of me and I watched them walk out of the store. I couldn't imagine stealing a canoe just like that. I came to understand quickly that the key to America was to think big.

Harriet rose from both the bath and the fog of nostalgia, still fearing vaguely that the happy cycle that she'd given up on and then was graced by once again, would be removed, swept away like it had never happened. She wasn't aware of the source of this fear, only of the deep discomfort and sense of vulnerability that rode through her weak veins. She was very far away from knowing what in fact generated her nervousness and thought only of Jacob and his health. Down the opened drain the soft water kept turning and pulling clockwise into the hole, like twisters, which weren't uncommon in Texas. She stepped squarely into the middle of the embossed **H** on the bath mat, and rubbed her sagging body vigorously from habit. Nothing felt very vigorous at the moment. The mirror was still steamed up and she couldn't see her own image in it. She hadno need to see anything. Her hairpins were by the sink where she had left them. When the last of the water had been sucked down the bottom of the tub clockwise and had given off a loud *slurp* like the noise children once made with paper straws when they'd reached the bottom of their goblets of chocolate milk, Harriet rinsed away the film of dead skin and silver hairs and dried out the peach-tone sides of the acrylic tub. She left no sign of her having been there. There'd be nothing for the maid to do. Without looking, she held three bobby pins between her creased lips and one by one sunk them into her gathered hair, firming up the thick bun that sat at the top of her head, finally appearing like a good imitation of an Albrecht Dürer portrait.

Jane sat quietly at the desk in the room, biting her fingernails and spitting the ragged pieces into the Hilton ashtray. Then, oddly, she withdrew a sheet of the thin, white, rag-bond hotel stationery from the drawer — beneath the black vinyl covered Holy Bible — and started to write out with a miniature golf pencil that she'd found in the gray-lint at the bottom of her handbag, what she figured roughly must have been a poem. She'd never written a poem before, but now, suddenly, intuitively, she found herself driven to find words and pieces of sentences that carried her emotional overload. She tried to write down what she felt, but her grammar crumbled and what was left were words, sorted or strewn with their own logic, like how shards of glass ended up when a glass hit the floor. Her poem was strange. And not very good as a poem. Three and a half blocks away at the Creative Writing Center at the University of Houston, graduate students would have cut it to shreds in one of their poetry workshops, calling it all the things they'd learned to spot and banish in a close read — sentimental, clichéd, obscure and inaccessible, too private, too abstract in its use of images and language, ridden almost exclusively with catch words like 'dark' and 'night' and 'love' and 'true' and 'Hell' and 'evil' and 'why' — words that she thought had belonged in poetry — and words that were the product of hundreds of unrealized details from the past and present, from Poland and Houston, hybrids that were formed by experience and now mercilessly concentrated themselves beyond individual recognition (peace, love, truth, death), massive, monolithic extrusions that stood now and here for all of human condition and yet showed nothing of it. "Show, don't tell," an instructor left on the board all semester. They would have been right about these things, but she wasn't trying to write well. Her father was dying eight-tenths of a mile away in a big and prestigious hospital while she sat powerless and lost on the nineteenth floor of an expensive hotel, moronically tapping her ring finger on the Room Service menu. She could have actually had a dozen oysters staring in front of herwithin ten minutes! Or a piece of Viennese *torte* with bitter chocolate shavings and a swirl of *chantilly* cream topped with a coffee bean! Or french fries or veal marsalla or a banana split!

The bathroom door clicked open and Harriet stepped into the cold, air-conditioned room, and Jane's first instinct was to dash the paper into her handbag, crumpling it out of sight as if she'd been thirteen and had snuck a cigarette or had been admiring the little mounds of flesh that were growing around the pink circles on her chest.

"What should we do now?" Jane popped forth illogically, smoothing over her nervous reaction with false spontaneity. In the moment that the question was up for grabs she realigned her equilibrium and settled the adrenaline surge. She'd not look at the poem again for months but would always be sharply aware of it like many things she and others kept in drawers and wallets. She'd know that it lay there in her handbag, creased and taking on smudges beside a hair brush and a make-up kit, a pack of green Chicklets, outdated receipts from Bloomingdale's and Alexander's (the huge one in the Paramus Mall with the world's largest mosaic), and a dispenser of artificial sweetener. She wanted to cry like a child but couldn't do so with Harriet. Somehow, after all these years like stone she knew there wasn't enough intimacy.

Harriet didn't sense anything different. Faithful to the logic of conversational dialog, she answered, "We could watch a few minutes of the television, Merv Griffin or one of those fellas. Then, I'd like to go to sleep. I'm absolutely exhausted."

"Okay, mother," Jane replied, as relieved as a concert musician who has just played the final note of a symphony and now momentarily waited for the end of the finishing rest an instant before the rush of applause. And Jane pulled the silver-plastic knob of the Quasar, the set still bolted firmly and inauspiciously to the furniture, sending a crackle of electricity into the components within the simulated wood-grained box, and a pre-recorded voice from somewhere behind the snowy, zagging pattern, as the image gathered its druthers, caressed them. "Johnnie's guests tonight are..."

13

Benjamin watched Houston appear out of nowhere and thought it odd to see the city sprouting from the vast spanse of burnt dusty earth, irrigated with laces of interstate and sporadic mall complexes. As the jet banked to the left, south of the city, he caught a view of the Astrodome, round and small like an Oriental tea cup. Just then a deep male voice, mid-fiftyish, seeped out and pervaded the cabin from somewhere above the overhead storeage compartments, which were limited to 40 pounds. "Folks, this is Captain Becker, we've starting our final approach and should be on the ground in about sixteen, seventeen minutes. For those of you lucky enough to be seated on the left side of the aircraft if you take a peak out the window you'll see that you have a prime view of the LBJ Space Center just off the left wing. Challenger 2 can be spotted if you look carefully to the right of that octagonal dome." About half of the passengers craned their necks towards the doubled plastic port hole windows. One young woman ina Denver Broncos sweatshirt even snapped a picture from 12,000 feet with her new Kodak Disc camera. "Other news, the tower is reporting 89° fahenheit with a humidity count of 73%. For those of you continuing on with us to Tucson and San Diego, we'll be on the ground in Houston for just around 40 minutes and we ask you to remain aboard the aircraft. For those of you whose final destination is Houston, Texas, on behalf of Delta Air Lines and its crew I'd like to thank you for having chosen Delta today and we sincerely hope that you do decide to fly again with us in the very near future."

Benjamin then felt the landing gears untucking and first thought of the way a duck crashes onto the surface of a lakeand then of those sixteen tires bearing themselves from pod-like bays like grinning bombs. "Crew, prepare for cross-check." The wide-body Delta righted itself and Benjamin caught a glimpse of the Space Center. Houston had always been "Mission Control." The rockets themselves would blast off from northern Florida but the guys who threw the switches were always in Texas. And those early morning lift-offs would undoubtedly pre-empt the morning programs, usually re-runs designated by a capital R at the end of the description in the TV section of the Sunday paper. The thought fixed in. "We were one of those families that didn't get the *TV Guide*. It was only twenty-five cents on the line at the Shop-Rite but still we considered it a waste of money and a symbol of Waspy bad taste. The same stuff was free in the local paper for crissakes." In the middle of "Our Gang" or "I love Lucy" or "Gumby" the picture switched to the launch site at Cape Canaveral and a dramatic voice would say in a loud whisper, like the sportscasters who narrated the tense, 16-foot putts for the birdies on the greens of the 18th — the kind that separated the men from the boys, certainly sinkable, but not all the time — "T minus seven minutes and counting," and the digital time would flash on the screen. And then everything would go fuzzy and snowy for a bit as Dad would switch on his Norelco with apologies to knock-off the night's worth of stubble. Then the big mechanical arm would back away from the sleek, white and silver rocket body on which big American flags were printed. At T-minus ten seconds the engines would begin firing, and flames and smoke would erupt at the base, melting the platform. The voice would gain intensity, and the craft with three guys scrunched up in their Pop-Tart compartment would ease up and off its pad as if animated, and as the sleek but still sluggish-looking vessel cleared the top of the launching gauge and roared forcefully into the air, slightly arcing over the Atlantic — a minute later breaking in two with the boosters having done their job and then falling into the sea, killing a few fish probably — all those serious guys in black-frame glasses and white short sleeve-shirts and thin dark ties at control panels at "Central" in Houston would start walloping and cheering and chugging unidentified substances like spiked Dr. Pepper from opaque plastic mugs as did football fans after hometeam touchdowns, not scientists. And the camera would follow the spaceship into the blue sky, which was gray on a black and white set, with the voice of Gus Grissom, who'd be killed in a cockpit fire on the ground two years later, patching in and out, with his words being typed in white on the screen so we could decipher the message, saying that everything was "going beautiful," until the capsule separated from the hulk of the second chamber and the dot on the tv screen became lost in the grain of the tube. Andthe announcer would return us back to our regularly scheduled program, already in-progress, promising to keep us posted. Lucy's face would jump back on; Lucy'd be wailing; and the canned laughter'd be wallowing; and no one'd know why. Or worse, it'd already be "My Little Margie" and we'd never know for another three years when the re-run ran again what had happened to Lucy's problem and if Rickie Ricardo ever found out or what.

Seven days later the same thing would happen so we could witness the splash down and be proud of our country and admire the brave, anonymous frog men who fished around in the cold Atlantic near the SS Nimetz and hooked the capsule to a tow line that dangled from a United States Air Force helicopter that whirled overhead which would then swing the bobbing top out of the sea and onto the deck of one of the two aircraft carriers on hand. And the astronauts could then pop out to the Marine Band's rendition of the "Star Spangled Banner" and show off their bearded faces and make funny speeches and the president could thank them publicly by a telephone hook-up that everyone could hear, and we'd know then that we were the strongest, the best, and the smartest country around. Often in the afternoon in those pre-cocaine days, Gene Rayburn's powdered-for-the-camera face would jump on with a smirk as he read a little card from packet number 4 on the Match Game answer board. Johnny Olsen, who'd later go on to bigger and hipper things, would cut in to tell us about *New and Improved Family Size Salvo* "for those especially tough stains" — blueberries and Georgia red mud — and it would all unfold just like that, as if nothing had ever happened. And those guys had circled the earth and had successfully made reentry without burning up. Our plate of Oreo cookies, each black disc twisted apart and scrapped free of white icing, gone, blackness still around orthodontured-to-be teeth. Or handfuls of dried Cocoa Krispies or Lucky Charms. The stewardess put Benjamin's tray in its original upright position as required by federal aviation regulations with a canned smile.

The movie screen illuminated and suddenly Benjamin was watching the thick white line of the runway approach and the backs of the pilots' capped heads and their hands touching levers. It was a film with no reflection, no editing, no maker. Out the window to his right was the now quick moving sight of oil storage tanks and ranch houses and school buses, cars (flatbeds of Hondas), electric lines, Nuclear Power Stations stalled in litigation, Wendy's. The profile of who they were, what it was, that plane landing just then, while on the screen, together, was the front view, startlingly direct like if each passenger was gripping the throttle. Now airlines would bring you more than just the latest films, good meals, and beverages, reading materials, *People Magazine* and *Redbook*,piped-in radio programs, playing cards, stewardesses with tinted hair who'd fetch your every request, they'd give you the vicarious, existential sensation of landing your own wild bird. This was how the technology would continue to serve the democracy, equal access to information.

The jet tilted downwards with the graceful illusion of having all the room in the world. That there was a Western Airlines flight from Salt Lake City breathing a thousand yards off its tail didn't spoil the effect. Out here, Benjamin thought, cities were spaced out like stars. There was Houston, unable to be confused with any other city, the way cities ran into each other back east, exfoliating into each other's domain. There, below, was Hobby Airport, alone, with plenty of space beyond the end of the runways, which were made of dark black macadam, smooth and straight and relatively unscarred, unlike the gray, worn and repaired surfaces of Newark, La Guardia, Logan, Bradley Field, Philadelphia, National, tired, salt-stained and cluttered. And there was Houston proper, the city sitting out past the right wing, an outcrop of contemporary building materials, aluminum, brown glass, oxidized steel, reflecting like an oasis pool, relieving the monotony of the surrounding desert sprawl. An immense movie lot, piggie-backed to a Star Wars-sized U-Haul trailer, an elephantine tennis ball protecting the massive hook-up joint, when not in tow. The Astrodome had grown now suddenly from tea cup to crater. Soon it would be stadium. Round and colorful, empty except for the crew doing infield repair and the spreadsheets doubling over onto themselves on the Wang in the front office upstairs. Benjamin peered down onto the crater roof. He thought of how the artificial grass now grew rampant forever in complexes from Louisiana to the Jersey Meadows. Scores of new injuries, new treatments, new artificial knee parts and internships to learn how to install them, sprouting healthily into being. That would be a good paper, he thought. "Marx, Astroturf and Visions of Decadence." The whole astro *schtick* may become a significant pivotal point in understanding the origins of artificiality of experience in contemporary American life. "Poor Walt Whitman and his leaves of now-fake grass."

The country was really immense, he felt it for first time. All this out here was his country too and he was privately claiming it. The sixteen, eight-ply steel-enforced radial jet tires, made by a subsidiary of Goodyear, or was it Goodrich, the one with the blimp, or without it, rolled down the smooth tar and creosote surface, routinely as cold Diet Coke, the original, rolled down dry throats in those parts. The air outside the hatch window rolled and buckled transparently from both the heat rising off the black and the rich mixture of jet fuel fumes. That critical point ofre-entry, when the vibrating fusilage seemed to cease taking on greater velocity and the brakes and flaps pulled hard on the mass to corale it to a stop, had passed. It was a short taxi to the gate, not like one of those hour safaris that often followed the arrival of, for instance, an Indonesian 747 or a commuter plane from Bar Harbor at JFK.

The hatch opened and the Texas air galloped in, moistening the crisp pressurized stuff they give you during the flight. Benjamin tasted the fine dust on his lips as he bounced down the carpeted tunnel ramp. For a brief instant between the airliner and the terminal he felt enclosed by the density of heat and thought he could imagine what it was like to be trapped in a fire. A hot chemical fire where the plastic in the ceiling panels and the lino on the floors melted and bubbled on you. "I shouldn't have worn my vest. That was stupid." Tears of sweat tickled his sides as they gained momentum between his armpits and his kidneys. They seemed to disappear, though, dry up, form icicles, the moment he reached the moving ramp inside the terminal. Whoosh, it was freezing, air conditioners doing their stuff, whirling away in total anonymity. "Glad I took my vest." "Couldn't live down here without air conditioning," some guy remarked as they pushed into a shuttle bus headed for Terminal A.

The name of the hospital was printed in yellow electronic letters on the forehead of the super modern urban vehicle. They were no longer called buses. The new cities got new vehicles, the others just kept repairing the smelly and smokey buses. Taxi cab drivers approached Benjamin with calculated nonchalance, offering rides to the medical center; they knew instantly where he was heading, as if it had been Mecca or Orlando, like the way Jews knew each other in a glance. Jews had some secret brotherhood-bonding device like secret-society handshakes that didn't require contact, and membership was a thing that came factory-installed. He thought of that trip to Rome with his parents when he was eleven. On the steps of that dark basilica behind St. Peter's Cathedral in the Vatican, the one that housed Michaelangelo's Moses in Chains, he remembered his father and a postcard hawker eying each other, smirking and sending knowing glances, then smiling with inexplicable warmth, then risking being misunderstood with some words. The password: *Red Yiddish? Shalom*, the souvenir salesman answered with a shrug like to say "Was there ever a doubt?" How did he know, Dad? How did you know? "We just know. The nose knows. What can I tell

163

you?" The cabbies knew by the overnight bag, the skin color, the look of clear purpose, that it was a medical trip. Half their business was transporting heart patients and their friends and families and staff members, employees, and visitors to the Texas Medical Center. The taxi industry was an auxilliary of the medical profession. Thedrivers even knew about the by-passes and valve jobs and could talk about them the way they exchanged info on traffic conditions and detours. They even knew the surgeons and could talk about them like they could about the Astro pitching battery or Oiler Quarterbacks.

"Methodist or Southern?"

"Methodist Hospital, please." Benjamin fumbled for the paper on which he'd jotted the information.

"That's good for you."

"Why do you say that?" Benjamin replied in mild defense.

"Southern's on a losing streak. Had two ladies this morning that weren't talking too much. Overdressed and mostly in black too. Cooley, I think. Probably wasn't fully rested."

Benjamin replied, "Uh huh," not disinterested, just speechless. And the driver flipped on his radar detector as he veered onto the South Loop and then took the Gulf Freeway ramp a bit too fast, squashing Benjamin into the corner, his face flattening against a gummed window sticker that read FOR NON-SMOKERS. "Sorry about that." And he gunned it towards the city center, overtaking in a matter of seconds a loud and sagging Pontiac stuffed with black people. A twisted coat hanger acted as radio antenna and a Pink Panther doll hung over the back ledge.

"You seem to know a lot about the hospitals here."

"Cabbies even keep stats like batting averages and yards per carry on the heavy hitting docs, ya know."

Cavenaugh was an ace reliefer; Debakey was unstoppable in the early innings, Cooley had the most touchdowns per season. But also the most interceptions. What that meant in medical terms, Benjamin didn't ask. He turned north on County 288 (or Almeda as the locals called it) and Benjamin looked out over some fields. The corners of the parking lot for a Century 21 ranch-style office were rounded with coarse sand. Anyone who had taken a semester of Intro. Geology could tell you that the topsoil was thin as unleavened bread in these parts. And the water table was low. There was a big billboard for the Church of Tomorrow, Sunday Brunch Service on Channel 56. There had been a marquee once outside the reconstructionist Temple Beth El in affluent Short Hills that read "Spend the High Holy Days With Us, We're Air Conditioned." The driver crossed over Old Spanish Trail and the Brays Bayou, which led out eventually to the Ship Channel and the San Jacinto Monument and the Battleship Texas. "I'd take you out to see those places for only fifty bucks but I bet you just want to get to Methodist."

Almost out of nowhere the city was upon them and the taxi cut through the Texas Medical Center's Ben Taub Parking Garage complex and then swung around the Baylor College of Medicine and Rice University campus. In the distance Benjamin saw the imposing sign for the Texas Heart Institute-St. Luke's Episcopal-Texas Children's Hospital and he thought of theinternational celebrities, men who had made their names by changing prestigeous vital organs. "That over there is Shriners' Hospital for Crippled Children. A lot of them in town now."

"And that, which is that?"

"That, over there, is Dunn Interfaith. That comes later."

"A hospital?"

"No that's a chapel. I've already had to drive big flower arrangements over there. It's funny when you got a fare and no one to talk to, just some flowers sticking out of your trunk. Tip's already included."

Benjamin swam through the few feet of heavy air and stepped through the parting electric doors of Methodist Hospital. There were a few plaques by the entrance, thanking the hospitals' founders, etc. The instant coolness made his perspiration tingle and freeze for the second time. He moved through the corridors as if he knew where he was going. He never liked asking for directions; he didn't need them. Being lost was a state of mind. If you didn't feel lost, you weren't. He rode the central elevators feeling that he had rights, slightly mocking his own seriousness with the thought of the television sitcom spy Maxwell Smart, and almost in the same second chose to repress that bit of irreverence.

He stepped out and followed the signs to the ICU Waiting Room, which was the opposite direction to the Sidney Kaplan Rehab. Center. "How do I know Sidney Kaplan?" Benjamin thought. "Wasn't he the guy that took your money for getting you extra points on the SATs and GREs? Right. I wonder if it's the same dude. Naw," he then remembered, "that's Stanley." He readjusted his shoulder bag and walked on past the nurses' desk.

Just ahead, he spotted his mother and grandmother, sitting there on the plastic chairs near the back of the insulated room, far away from the day outside. He slid into their view and they jumped up to greet him, relieved to see his face, relieved to diffuse their attention. They felt rescued. In the Bible Benjamin was the youngest and favorite son of Jacob. It was no accident. In Hebrew, "son of the right hand." Jane just liked it. And now she felt such a need to hug him. Her embrace slightly exceeded normal affection, draining all its neediness into the boy, and Benjamin, who had just three weeks earlier started to "see" an art history major named Gail from the neighboring women's college, and thus had female anatomy freshly engraved in his psyche, perceived against his thighs, knees, and ribcage a trifle too much of his mother's body. Harriet then kissed him so hard on the cheek, far from the mouth, that it hurt the bone, almost at the ear, because she was petrified of giving him her cold or hepatitis or something else that she didn't herself have, but figured she might and thus didn't want to take any risks. Hebacked away to give his eyes a chance to gain a wider scope. Then he focused back on his mother. Her make-up wasn't hiding a thing. He saw the tired lines under her chin, the spidery creases running like tiny spokes from the corner of each eye, delicate arteries running away from the Arc of Triumph in Paris. He remembered Avenue Foch.

"This is Fanny," Harriet established, pulling at Benjamin's hand, pride abounding. Smiles flashed back and forth like the reflection in two compact mirrors. There were others in the room Benjamin was introduced to and whose names he had instantly forgot to remember. He heard about the wonderful Italian lady and how she danced and laughed and rose the spirits of the other families. Jane now had her hand in Benjamin's, squeezing it sporadically, showing her love, testing its quality of being alive, clutching it as if she were two and it were a transitional object. Benjamin didn't say much; they'd tell him about Jacob in the minutes to follow. They'd ask about his flight but he'd not want to say how it was exciting flying off to somewhere new, alone, which he'd only done once before, a ten day cultural exchange in high school to Paris, where he lost his virginity, not to a sassy cancan dancer at the Lido but to a senior on the trip who lived in his same town and carried her own contraceptives. He was embarrassed thinking of himself. Fanny offered gum and he accepted. Trident, the gum recommended by two out of three oral hygienists in Orange County.

At two o'clock he had the numbered ticket in his hand like a customer in a bakery and waited nervously, both hot and chilled, by the entrance to the dim ward. The others all agreed that it should be Benjamin that should go in this time.

Jacob was bearly recognizeable although the nurses and doctors that passed-by didn't seem to notice this point. They'd grown accustomed to the sight. Dying bodies were like leaves on trees that had started red, yellow, green, outstretched and full and then turned slowly brown and gray, shrivelled then, bent and hung on, weathering the change, waiting ultimately to fall. The sight of Jacob was like having a limb pushed down his throat, like having to eat a third of Bosch's "A Garden of Earthly Delights." In a second, all the strength and composure that he had thought that he had had — others thought of him as emotional cement, even-keeled and steady — would crack like a clay façade hit from below. He'd never witnessed the decay of a loved one. The inner picture that he had of Jacob from the last time he had seen him jolly and in bedroom slippers, his teeth already out and soaking in a glass of water by the bathroom sink, and now the mass that lay prone in the whitish sheets, one against the other, jolted him. He bit his lip voluntarily, trying to keep his facial muscles from cracking. It was important to pretend now, hethought. Words were needed. With words he could make contact and help Jacob come through this wicked labrynth. He'd pull through. He'd pull him through. Benjmain had grown up in the halo of the Hollywood movie and the pulse of the American Dream in the mind of the Self-Made Man, and at college had begun to learn to identify it, dissect it, and deflate its hot air. But still, until you do some real living the myth continues to stand up on its own, propped up like the angle hung on the backs of travel alarm clocks. Just getting a deep paper cut or cracking your knee against your desk hurt like hell. Next to having your chest sawed open, though, what were they? Now at the bedside of the underdog, he suspended his scientific veil and hoped and tried to believe even in the pleasant positivism of lies.

"What have they done to you?" Benjamin actually mouthed the words, trying to both choke and scream, to vent the outrage. This wasn't the same man. On the jetty once in a place called Safety Harbor, near Tampa, he had tried to remove the two fine filets from a freshly caught, sleek, red snapper that had minutes earlier been cutting through the clear bay water in the refracted late afternoon light. The knife wasn't sharp enough, the pale flesh ripped instead of being sliced off the bone in clean whole flanks. He had taken perfection and ruined it. A perfect life lay in his hands defiled, useless, and he felt sickened at his debauchery. Embarrassed for the human race. No one understood. Someone suggested that they go out to Arthur Treather's Fish and Chips. "Bread it and freeze it," a cousin in the insurance business chipped in, with a wife named Tilly.

"Gramps," he then cried out, "it's me, Benjy. You can hear me, right?" He touched Jacob's right hand and squeezed it, having the perverse insight that there was nothing to stop him from squeezing too hard, beyond reason, hurting the hand, breaking the bones that hung in his, and thus he knew instantly the utter vulnerability of Jacob's life, of his life, of all life. In the movies, a touch of the hand, a slap in the face, a pail of water, a loud voice, was all it took to revive someone, even if it was only long enough to hear the words or say the words "I love you" or — "I'm innocent" or "I'm sorry" or "Get me a priest." Or else a peak under the eyelids, a quick check of the pulse, an ear to the chest, was all it took to pronounce death. Now, the only way to discern if life was in fact still present was the activity of the lit panels and the banal hums on the gaggetry, the spastic line on the oscillator.

"Gramps!?" But it was neither a question nor an exclamation. He paused. "I don't know if you can hear me but I'll just keep talking. Okay? Okay!" He could have asked a thousand times. His voice proceeded as his eyes drank up with the healthiness of curiosity the details, horrible and all —the ghastly incision of Jacob's collapsed chest, stapled together roughly back and forth like the large teeth of a zipper on a baby's homemade snow suit — the waxy yellowish skin like the peel of bruised mangos — a tube taped into his nostril and the mouthpiece of the respirator that pulled on the corners of his mouth — the blue-black holes of the intravenous running into the thick vein above his left thumb, through which medication and clear liquid nourishment dripped. The left arm was tied down to the bedrail with a hank of guaze so that the tubes wouldn't pull out when his body rumbled from the pain of each cough. He coughed, and it was like a subway rushing under him. The earth trembled. Benjamin's eyes watched as if confronted directly with poverty or torture. And he realized that if he could stand there and watch and learn to feel nothing at all, to be untouched, he could condition himself to tolerate anything, no matter how terrible or wrong. And the more he wanted to be part of Jacob's pain the more the mechanism in his brain blocked him from feeling a thing. The more removed he became, detached, and alone.

"Let's get out of here," he whispered to his grandfather, wanting to gather up the bones in the sheet and sneak out into the sunlight near a lake. He heard his own voice soak into the hidden, echoless world around him, be blocked by the ugly portable curtains that created privacy at tense moments in hospitals. His voice couldn't reach further than the thick plastic barrier. And the motionlessness of everything, his voice included, began to take hold. He felt his morale drain away like the juice in a car battery, the motor off and the high beams glowing. It was like walking away from a lost battle in which you yourself didn't die and yet your side technically won, you were the good guys, the Allied Forces. But still you were stuck behind enemy lines. Where was there to go? It was foreign surviving like this. This was the backroom of a malignant regime. Where wonders were celebrated and atrocities were quietly noted. Cavenaugh's not Mengele's. He looked at Jacob's shiney, artificial face and heard its accent. It was like talking to a Barbie doll all over again or GI Joe, and now as an adult being forced to believe that the flesh-toned plastic really appreciated the tiny polka-dotted outfit or battle fatigues you hung on it. Benjamin ripped away from the morose circuit of similes that rushed for the front door of his thoughts but skinned its ankle on the broken screen door.

"Gramps, do you want to hear about College?" He didn't wait for a reply, fearing the silence that hid like a kidnapper between his phrases. "The fall semester is already in full swing. I have mid-terms coming up when I get back." His words were pathetic, empty letters standing without a spine, characters without a role. Any sensitive human who had overheard him at that moment would have had to cry or gag."I'm taking Intro to Philosophy, and..." He was just filling the void. He knew it. There was no place on the Graduate Record Examinations where this kind of knowledge could be recorded. He waited and then started again, noticing just how little difference it made. "My room is pretty nice. You'd like it. I share it with a kid from Pennsylvania. He's not Jewish, but he did write a paper this term on the Dybbuk and he likes bagels. Yes, of course, everyone in America is circumsized! In any case, you'll be back in action by Parents Weekend and you'll meet him.

171

I've already reserved rooms at the Inn in town. We have a soccer game against Bowdoin next Friday." Jacob had played soccer as a boy. Left Wing. He was fast, despite his asthma, although it was hard imagining Jacob, who was heavy in the upper thighs and had large bones, gliding down the field, calling for the ball, charging for the net, red hair blazing first. He was the secretary of his Jewish sports club, the *Hagibors*, the Strongmen, and arranged matches with other teams, often in Losencz, which was on the Czech side of the border. Just the sports club certificate, no passport, was needed to cross between the two countries. Very easy, and everyone followed the standings of the teams, even the border police. "I wish you could come see me play."

He paused. It was getting hard to carry on. How long could he maintain the illusion of a second party. It was easier talking into his cloned Walkman, making a tape to a friend. His voice faded in volume and spirit and everything seemed comatose. Suddenly, he wished that the room would fill up with molten lava like at Pompeii and everything and everyone would be preserved instantly, at once, in rock. He moved his jaw. Stillness like deafness, like the calm in the eye of a tornado. Benjamin was afraid. Maturity fell away, it was always a stancheon, the scaffolding that painters stood on as they worked on the building. Beyond and beneath, he was afraid like a child.

"Can you hear me, Gramps?" His voice was thin, and his power of concentration was strained.

Jacob's hand moved. With an orthonographer's attention to detail, Benjamin observed the small movements, back and forth, with the thumb and pointer and middle fingers slightly pulling to form the suggestion of a bunch. The arm, too, shifted, as if motioning with the utmost discretion for a waiter to bring the check, a gesture that was never elegant, even when it was minimal and discreet.

"What is it? What?" Benjamin was talking to the hand. And then he understood; Jacob wanted to write. "You want a pen. You want to tell me something. "Wait!" In a rush Benjamin scoured the area for a writing instrument, in a frenzy far more frenetic than the rush that overtook people when they searched their domestic landscape for a pen with a longdistance caller dangling on the other end. Anything, often settling for a connect the dot colored pencil, a dull Crayola, an eyebrow pencil, a safety pin that would scratch the number onto cardboard...a blade of grass. Benjamin didn't want to leave Jacob's side even for an instant. The impulse would be lost. But there was nothing to write with so he placed his own forefinger between the thick pads of soft flesh but nothing happened.

"I'll bring you a pen, I promise, I'll bring you a pen, tonight." Then with a spasm, Benjamin squeezed his own flesh into Jacob's hand like drawing ink into the barrel of a fountain pen. "*I'll* be your pen. *I'm* your pen."

But Jacob's hand did not respond. And Benjamin slowly withdrew, stunned by the implications.

14

Amy knew that things were very bad. A week in ICU was already too much. Recovery from open heart surgery had to be swift and dramatic or it wasn't to be at all. She accessed the computer patient file and read the symbols. She was computer literate; she'd taken a night course in medical information systems at a technical community college. The hospital paid half her tuition. The symbols were clear. Now at work, she scanned Jacob Simon's life according to Methodist Hospital. Dialysis had begun that evening. The kidneys weren't yet functional, output insufficiency. Thirty seven units of O-positive blood he'd already taken. It was all there, in lines and columns running down the greenish, high resolution screen in yellow and blue. With more units on call. Into his second week, already. She knew, then; there'd be no miracles. But you had to play it till the last out. Medical ethics.

On her break at eleven she slipped into Jacob's empty room, his slippers still lined-up under the empty bed, and returned to the marble-covered diary, leaning against the windowpane so the artificial lights from the night combined with the beam from the round-white moon would illuminate the page. Reading now took on another dimension, a pathetic voice bubbling up off the page from ten floors below, narrating its own written testimony, the voice of a man no longer with us, breathing at the insistence of parts built in factories all over the country, and her country, and working as programmed.

Jacob had tried to follow the chronology of his life, however, the events, subjected to the adjustments of human recollection and the phenomenon of selective memory, had jig-sawed in spasms in his mind — pre-war to post-war, Polandto America, historical facts to moral evaluation, witnessed events to hearsay information, items long inscribed in memory to items revisited for the first time, geographic facts to the ingredients for *matza brai*. The text went back now to the early months at the camp in Plaszow, the period after he had last seen his wife. Something had driven him back. He had filled-in the plot line all the way to America, to the beginnings of Benjamin, a first generation American, perhaps the symbolic end of his story, and then back-pedaled, not out of any style or notion of narrative art, but rather like a watchman doing his rounds; when he got to the end he started all over again. Without thinking, he treated the more complex writing problems — person, voice, point of view, treatment of time, narrative structure — by remaining immune to them. He just recorded or deposited thoughts as they arrived, a safe-deposit box of sorts. He figured he'd go back, with Benjamin's collegiate help, and make everything sound good, put it all in good English. For the time being, it was just like taking inventory; you don't worry about your window display while you're un-stacking cartons. Amy sensed the end. She approached the pages of the marbled diary that were empty, white, and smooth, the unfinished symphony, and then backed up into the veiny pages of writing, textured with ink and the pressure of a hand and arm still strong, at the end of a brain. The pages were thinning to a close, and she felt a hollowness and urgency that scared her. The void of it being all over...

One day shortly before liberation we were awakened by sirens announcing an air attack. We were told to run outside. The whole sky was covered with Allied Bombers, possibly American, and bombs were falling and exploding from all sides.

They opened all the gates and we were told to run anywhere we wanted to go. We were a mixture of all nationalities — French, Italian, Russian, Jews, etc. A lot of people, before running outside, went to the stockrooms, smashed the padlocks, and grabbed anything they could carry with them and then ran.

The first impulse was to flee but after the air attack was over and the planes disappeared, and since we didn't know which direction to choose to reach the Allied Lines, most of us returned to the barracks. Since most of the factory and sleeping quarters were burned down and destroyed our living conditions changed considerably. There was a shortage of everything. If you had a piece of bread hidden under your pillow it was a miracle to find it there in the morning. We lived like rats.

We were often told to send thanks for our conditions toour American friends.

Amy's inner picture turned to her grandmother's bombed house, the gaping hole in the garden, the caved-in roof, resurrected into an image by stories of *Oma* and the children huddling in the *Keller* with the planes hurling overhead, wondering if they'd die. Her mother had told her that dying didn't scare her. It was okay if everyone was together. There was so much she hadn't yet asked.

Harriet and Jane had agreed that Benjamin should be the one to go in again to see Jacob, although it was he who had gone in at two and up until then neither Jane nor Harriet had made two consecutive visits. Plus, it was Benjamin that had surfaced with the news of Jacob's attempt to write a message. If anyone, it would be Benjamin who'd be able to reach him, they fantasized with conviction. Had either Jane or Harriet insisted on going in twice the same day, there would have surely been a tiff. "You're being unfair, Dzi!" "But, Mother!" With Benjamin, there was no resistance. As predictable as quick-drying mortar, he hurried into that No Man's Land with a big white pad and a blue felt-tipped pen. The ink would slide more freely with felt and the chance of a communicated message might be heightened. It was pure religion.

Harriet and Jane sat anxiously in the waiting room in a stable of tense new faces. Privately, neither wanted really to go into that gray, dead place where time took on new dimensions. And reminders of the deepest human fear hovered. Twenty minutes meant nothing, the time to eat lunch, to regain the urge and readiness between orgasms, to drive an automobile at 50 mph from Chatham Center to Newark Airport.... They let Benjamin go in there, knowing righteously that it was, might be, better for Jacob. They would wait out there with the others. Jane looked around; the new faces increased her nervousness. She searched for those she knew. There had been comfort in their familiarity, the tiny Italian-American woman, Fanny, the man in the Thom McCanns, for as long as they were all there together it meant that there wasn't something special going wrong in the gray zone beyond the swinging doors. Waiting and worrying was standard procedure. Everyone had to wait. Now with the fresh looks and immature expressions of concern, the little comfort that she had found there in that plastic world was ripped out from under her like a conspiracy in a dream.

Who were these people? Abandoned again. Alone, only with Harriet, who searched her pocketbook for a tissue, refusing to use the silk handkerchiefs Jane had bought her one vacation in Italy. "They're too good. I'll never use them. They're too lovely," she'd insist. The long week that they had spent in that world of visiting hours, cafeterias, shuttle buses, tasteless dinners, local television news, seemed like a major part of their lives, twelve years with the same damn company, twenty six years in the same split level in West Orange, six years of night school, four years in concentration camps, four years at the same liberal arts college in New England, six years of psychotherapy...

Fanny's knitting bag, marked "Big Shopper," saved Fanny's place next to the dense, sand-filled ashtray, as she too entered the morose zone, inexhaustibly, to see her Bobby.

Benjamin hurried in, handed-over the numbered ticket, and moved in a near-run like a greedy shopper hustling over for the ten-minute K-Mart special to the cove where Jacob remained. But upon resting eyes on the form in Jacob's bed, his excitement drained from him as if his own blood was leaving his body in a hurry, and death was taking him in the swift yet gradual way it claimed a kosher chicken. The dialysis machine had just been disconnected and Fraser, the renal specialist, and his young team, a gaggle of baggy-eyed med students, were finishing their work behind a screen. The specialist emerged and an intern wheeled the bulky apparatus away. Benjamin, feeling useless as a boy before a forest fire, watched them pack the thing up, un-gingerly, as if it were an industrial vacuum cleaner, Big Suck, as they called the terrible one stored in his dorm back at school, the one that could aspirate into its iron chest puddles of stale beer, ralfed grinders, half-dissolved Quaaludes, and ill-digested pepperoni and sausage pizza.

Moving closer to Jacob's side, he smelled a strange yet unfortunately human scent. Clinical smells were one thing, but this was something hauntingly human, that only those who had come close to evil and survived could identify in their memories. Benjamin wanted to avoid it, to block it out by closing down the censors that picked up and translated smell. Animals, even ferocious ones, knew in the presence of certain smells, to back away, to leave at once. It's all in the scent. The guilt of cowardice cornered him and he fought the sense to block out anything. "This man had come through, had survived, had...I can't stand a....Fuckin' wimp," he chided. Falling into a survival mode, fearing the weakness of his stomach, the terror of nausea, his mind ravaged its options and broke into the repetition of a learned mantra that a TM master had planted there a few summers earlier. The simple, two syllable Sanskrit word that he still wouldn't share with a soul flim-flammed back and forth like a shutter in his head, dissolving stress like an unwinding mainspring, absorbing it like an antacid. Jacob's skin radiated with a yellow, waxy tone. And then he saw the IV needle; now it had been planted securely into his stiff right hand. The hand that had motioned for a pen at two! Tied down to the bed rail with white gauze, unable to shift, unable to transmit a thought, the hand wassilenced with a shunt. A defeated prisoner, the hand bound and gagged in its own slums. There was no more resistance at all. "Mengele, the bastard." Rage, Benjamin felt.

He called out to his grandfather's consciousness. He tugged a little on the bound arm. He even peaked under a shut eye lid, splitting with embarrassment the frail lids of skin with his fingers, finding only a stained, limp pupil hanging in a veiny cream-colored white. What if one of the hospital crew had glanced in there and spotted him doing that to the patient? How grossly they would have misunderstood! And there would have been no way to explain.

His grandfather had gotten away. His spirit had started its journey, either ascending somewhere or going nowhere at all. At two, there had been the suggestion of the spirit communicating outwards through the body, of contact however small, of recovery however remote. Now, at eight, as new prime-time television shows were breaking into their pilot episodes, network executives settling-in with flutes of California's best champagne around large screens with a few close backers and hand-rolled Cuban cigars, hoping like the devil for a winner, Benjamin trembled at Jacob's side. How Jacob would not have wanted this. "Go play with your friends," he'd order with false authority.

"Gramps, gramps," he called out, keeping his voice down and hating the world for making him think that it was necessary to keep his voice down, wondering if this was a movie and detesting himself for watching himself instead of just being. The unit was empty. Emptiness bounded. Benjamin pleaded in a prayer that was as useless as asking God for a bicycle or to grant wealth or sunshine or anything else, a postage stamp or five minutes more on earth. "Don't die," he screamed in thought. Benjamin's eyes backed out of his head for an instant, made a mental k-turn, and saw the sight of a grandson at an old man's death bed. The voice of an art history professor amplified out over the scene as he watched himself as an oil painting on the auditorium screen and followed the tip of the black pointer as it scratched at the details of his shoulders, the bend in his neck, the subtle suggestion of a tattoo on the back of his left hand, the strange smile formed by the disposition of knobs on the respirator controls, and the self-documentary touch of the written name plate hung at the foot of the bed frame: Jacob Simon September 9, and then the year. Benjamin's eyes re-joined his life and he felt something he identified as shame, and cursed, "You can't play with a person's blood!"

A cough came up laced with pain and dark, serious phlegm. The *Urschleim*, the last, personal substance one emits, post language. Beyond words and sound, phlegm. The thin legs fluttered and the right shackled wrist tightened the knot. Whya knot? To keep him from ripping the intravenous needle out of his hand. Of course, it all made sense. And anger bubbled; it was like they had gotten him in the end, robbing him of dying finally like anybody else, with the dignity of just not being fucked-around with, taking his clothes, glasses, shoe polish kit, false teeth, suitcase, address book, address.... "No, stop;" this was death by natural cause. "Don't be ridiculous," he whined, and his brain defying reason mocked his life, and slogans from television fried him with popular audacity. This was Houston during a Republican Administration. We have rockets in the atmosphere and live tissue coming in from Muncie, Indiana landing on the roof. Cardio-vascular procedures costing megabucks; this is the best of the best. The sphere from Wheel of Fortune appeared spinning with Ronald Reagan's face centered in the middle, fascinated by the possibilities. And the insurance co. is footing the bill, all but maybe ten, eleven percent. Those animated All-State hands rocked in front of his eyes. Things were disconnecting. Defenses were reinforcing. Denial came crashing down the bob-sled track of his mind. This was just one routine, civil, gave-it-your-best-shot, death. Knut Rockne, Vince Lombardi, Lou Gehrig, Charlton Heston, and Pete Rose-in-uniform arrived at the conference as the century's leading philosophers. So, just grieve like a normal human being, and get out your best suit and show respect. He was a good man. Dustin Hoffman would be casted to play Jacob. And video rights would be sold off to the new Polish market for an undisclosed amount.

In the waiting room Benjamin did not show his disappointment nor his horror, guilt, nor anything. He was as steady as Mahatma Ghandi in those final seconds in 1948 when he knew his end had come, an extremist's bullets lodged there peacefully in his flesh. *"Mey Rama,"* he whispered, thirty years earlier to the day. The white writing pad and blue felt-tip pen were under his arm, unused. "Jacob was resting," that was all, "tired after the dialysis session." What more was there to say? Why horrify the others? Why heighten their vulnerability? "Plus, what do I really know?" he thought.

"They changed his IV and so Gramps couldn't hold a pen.... I can try tomorrow." Hope waited at the end of reason. Were there any known societies where the concept of "tomorrow" or "future" didn't exist, where hope was incomprehensible because there was no idea for anything beyond now? He knew of a few languages that didn't conjugate verbs. He looked down as he spoke to his mother and Harriet, holding back the mercury, doing the very thing with his feelings that Jacob did in his diary and Jane continued doing from Krystyna Antoszkiewicz onward.

"What had he wanted to write, damn it?" Benjamindemanded, haunted privately by this lost chance. "What was the last thing I'd want to say if I knew it would be the last?" Benjamin wondered, Brando at the end of *Apocalypse Now*, followed by Orson Wells as Cane, fluttering up from the visual archives, he, like every subject in his culture, carried around permanently-installed, hoping that that in fact hadn't been Jacob's last attempt at being human. "Goodbye? Water? Did he want to ask something? A last request before the volley of bullets?" Benjamin thought of that powerful story by Borges in which a man on the firing line lives out the rest of his life and dies between the order to shoot and the arrival of fatal bullets. "A proclamation? A guarded secret? He would have left us with a word; instead he left us with the image of a word un-revealed." The last time Benjamin had seen his grandfather alive and well had been several nights before Jacob's flight down to Houston for the exploratory catheterization. It had been time to leave, everyone had said good-bye and was out on the sidewalk heading for the car. Jacob stayed back in his garden apartment drinking a glass of ice water from the refrigerator. Benjamin had gone back to get his sweater. There was Jacob standing beautifully in his slippers, clean undershirt on under his robe. Benjamin grabbed his sweater and turned for the door, stopped, and for some awkward reason gave his grandfather — of all the weirdest gestures in the world — the Black Power raised fist, and chanted from he'll never-in-his-breathing-days know where, with white fist clenched in the air, "Keep the Faith." What faith had he meant? How could he have been so trivial at that poignant moment? The last good-bye and he wasted it with that empty bit of passé, mock-power, jargon? It didn't even belong to their cause. Now, it haunted him. Maybe that was what it meant to be human, to be vastly inappropriate, to be inexplicably off-the-wall?" He tortured his spirit now at 8:25 PM in Houston. "I saw Dr. Fraser, the renal specialist, but he didn't have anything new to say, other than the dialysis is still necessary until the kidneys start functioning on their own."

Fanny returned this time as bright as a helium balloon. Filled with encouragement. The bleeding had stopped. For the first time in two weeks things had stopped getting worse. Benjamin wanted to be pleased and it bothered him that his own ego was so pitifully fixed in orbit to his own concerns that he could not truthfully participate in her joy. He was glad, sure, but he didn't really share her joy. He was only caring about Jacob and himself and he was ashamed that that was the plain truth, ashamed of himself and ashamed for the species.

Harriet's face lit up as Fanny announced that Bobby's cheeks were red with life and that she'd brushed his Bobby-brown hair and made a neat part and doused him withlime-scented Vitalis. Benjamin watched the soft wrinkled skin on Harriet's cheekbone rise with elation and he couldn't help but wonder if that was rooted to her desire to believe that her Jacob, too, would show new signs of life.

Amy, was reading all about the judgment of the International Claims Settlement Act of 1949, which had jurisdiction over claims of nationals of the United States included within the terms of the Polish Claims Agreement of 1960, ten floors above.

"Claimant, Jacob Simon, submitted a letter dated June 15, 1948, issued by the Pocztowa Kasa Oszcwednosci, *reflecting that "Vita-Kotwica" lost their rights to continue home and life insurance activities; and that Jacob Simon's claim had been registered with the* Pocztowa Kasa Oszczednosci *as liquidator. No other evidence with respect to this item of the claim has been submitted. The Commission finds that claimant has not met the burden of proof with respect to item (C) of the claim, in that he has failed to establish ownership rights of property and interests in subject life and property insurance policy. Accordingly, this item of the claim must be and hereby is denied. A photocopy of what purports to be a "note" for $784 signed by a Rajski Mieczslaw" was submitted in support of item (D) of the claim of Jacob Simon. It appears from the record that this represents the balance due claimant from the sale of some books. No other evidence with respect to this item of the claim was submitted. This item of the claim is hereby denied."*

'Some books' they say! After we left, Rajski got the entire house and all the land, made a deal at just the right time, with the Polish State, which expropriated everything

left and right. Jaskierski, of course, had already made away with all the contents.

Amy paused. The moon would be nearly full and the crime rate everywhere would be upward and mobile. Amy'd see a hit muskrat by the side of the road on her way home, which someone would stop for, take home, and cook, while the next day's sun would be creeping up behind Sacre Coeur in Paris and street repair was commencing in the *rynek* in Nowy Targ.

15

In the air conditioned Arby's that had been slapped together in a week a year earlier halfway between the hospital and the Hilton, Benjamin sat coldly, mechanically, morosely, tearing off bites of a nitrate-preserved, pressed roast beef sandwich. The world had come a long way. The sesame roll was fresh from another part of the country. The little slice of pickle that had sat first for a month in a warehouse in Harrison, New Jersey, was in fact quite tasty. The lithographs on the walls could be found in a thousand similar structures from Florida to Guam. As his jaw ground-down the food into a useless gray substance he heard elsewhere in his head his father and mother yelling at each other, bickering over a poorly washed head of lettuce and the subsequent exchange of increasingly caustic allegations and counter-allegations. To shock them, Benjamin would have eaten the dirty lettuce; (it wasn't really dirty). Sometimes, as a child he had wished he had broken an arm or leg as a means of making them stop. In the context of something else, something more grave, everything could be seen as trivial and stupid. "Let's stop this; look what it's doing to us. C'mon, okay? Okay?" " You're right, I guess. But...it was you who started...." A tape played in his head. He sat there distantly in that public place like the schizophrenics that frequented the all-night coffee-n-donut shops, walking to the beat of a different drummer. He withdrew the cruelly-unused, felt-tipped pen and started filling-up furiously the back side of the paper place mats that were used to line the ugly plastic trays.

"I was born 1066 Sundays ago — a Taurian day of rest inmid-Spring. I am told it was a brilliant yellow morning and that I arrived with my hands laced behind my melon-shaped head. As my weak, red ankles were pinched overhead, my fresh, clammy infant lungs were initiated with the smog-filtered air of the already crowded Northeast. The busy doctor struck me with crisp smacks, which was customary if not necessary, and I began.

Unclothed and unnamed, I made noise. My eyes were christened and I was carted off to a white room, where the other babies that had recently hatched from their mothers' cul-de-sacs were being charged up for the trip home. I gleamed through the print-smudged glass into the foggy visages of goo-goo-eyed fathers. I didn't wonder which was mine. I lay in that white, synthetic universe, innocent and hungry, not yet knowing that already, for sometime, I had been a beacon of meaning.

I was a first child. I was on schedule. I was a boy. I was a ready-made King. Pre-natally-indulged at first, the treatment continued. I was nurtured, bathed, nursed, rocked...

Upon my arrival, my mother became a mother — no longer an abandoned child herself. My father, respectively, became a father — no longer an ignored son. My mother could now become the mother she missed and my father could replace the father he secretly hated. I filled the void of my mother's destroyed siblings and of my father's estranged ones. Instantly, I was a way for my parents to leave the past and to surge ahead into the excitement of their own independence. My start was also their start. I was what they had done without any interference from undesirable consequence."

He stretched the muscles in his right hand, took a bite, and continued.

"Not long after, they took me to a place called home. It smelled from fresh paint, but I didn't know that. Then we moved from the city to the suburbs. Our apartment became a house and my crib evolved into a complete room. We got a white station wagon for our drive-way and I had a special seat in the front with a horn.

The cut of our dinner meat also improved. The garments in the closet were replenished. The old family piano was refinished. Our income swelled, then doubled. I stood, then walked, and then talked. It was a big deal. Then I rode with training wheels. Later, I rode without them. Then my parents made another me — a she. Then came school...and bag lunches, new math, baseball card trading. I was in the class play and was given the part of General Wolf on the Plains of Abraham, singing 'God Save the King.'

My father was in the early innings of a career in the New York financial district as I came into being. And, as my little life began to crescendo my father's career began to mature, prosper, and make impressive gains. A proud, informal man of considerable wit and invention, he had given up (and not without regret) an offer to pitch for the Newark Bears. It was a question of practicality, he always told me. He had played it safe, rounded the bag, and held-up at third. There was his young family in the stands to remember. So, he sat all day at a desk in a cubicle, surrounded by the roar of business. He hung onto the old cherished lingo and the strategy, although the ballpark had changed. He found that the rules of smart baseball jibed well with winning all over, and he stayed in the field until the Wall Street world made it too difficult to win and remain honest.

His telephones, five in all, rang and flashed. They looked silly when they dangled and were left off the hook. One or two were always lodged between my father's ear and chronic collarbone. He was on the mound always, throwing strikes, keeping the ball low. The phones rattled in their seats. More orders. He told his clients what he had known in the dugout — go to bat thinking you'll get a hit, wait for your pitch, play for the easy run, protect the plate... The day-old box scores were buried under his voluminous paperwork, and a bit-into corned beef sandwich (extra lean, but never lean enough) waited on the corner of his desk.

My mother stayed home and sorted the colors from the whites. She sprinkled water from a coke bottle onto the crinkled collars of Arrow dress shirts; manufacturers' seconds, purchased on the lower East Side. The ironing board with the scorched, gray-metallic pad, squeaked open each afternoon in front of the 19-inch Zenith. 'As the World Turns' crept along in installments.

She walked the baby in a plaid stroller; she redeemed her ticket at the cleaners and picked up her order at the butcher's. He often placed a slice of that mauve, Kosher bologna in baby's pudgy fist. The butcher's boy had his leg in a brace; he was born the year before me, three months before the vaccine was ready.

Back at home the baby napped beneath a formation of plastic birds. I peeked in to watch the little bundle drool. My mother rested on the bed with a fat novel, usually one of Michener's.

At five o'clock she put the dinner up and I had my piano lesson. The exhaust fan above the stove sucked out some of the onion smell. She wrote a check for the piano teacher and left it on the stand in the hallway. My Seth Thomas metronome counted time with beats while in my head I distinctly heard the silent pauses between the beats. But I didn't tell my teacher. He was there for the check and yawned a lot.

My mother stepped out to snip some lilacs from our bush. Crab apples made the ground bumpy on the side of the house. It hurt stepping on a crab apple with bare feet. Weeds were always crawling back in between the flagstones of the front walk. I had to cover the sandbox at night so cats couldn't shit in there, and then we'd get sick. Sometimes I pulled the tops off the dandelions instead of getting them by the root so that they wouldn't grow back.

The timer gonged. The meat was done. Or the chicken. The thermometer held steady at 300 degrees. I set the table while my mother messed with the baby. She reminded me which fork Daddy didn't like or was it the spoon? And washed the lettuce. There was a six-pack of Tab at the base of the broom closet. One calorie a bottle and no deposit, no return. My mother returned and fed the baby. Then she brushed out her tinted hair in the upstairs mirror and slid with her foot the fuzzy slippers under the dust ruffle on her side of the bed.

A car turned in the driveway. It was my father; I knew the sound of gravel his car made as it turned in. 'I'm home,' he yelled. I carried his briefcase to its spot. Then, my parents kissed lightly on the lips."

Another bite. Benjamin looked up, and grabbed another place mat from a nearby table.

"My mother had been dragged through a motherless childhood. She had been passed around secretly under a false identity like a forbidden book. It had been a tyrannical and savagely insane epoch in Eastern Europe. But that was all over now. She had a diploma, a four-bedroom split level, several subscriptions to women's magazines, and above all, children. Her tiny accent hid in only a handful of awkward syllables.

My father had been the brunt end of reproach. As an unwanted sixth child, he arrived with hunger and curiosity like everyone else, however, there wasn't much waiting for him. The good times were finished; the family business had collapsed in the Crash. There was no time for his questions. His siblings moved away. There was the war, then, that terrorized the tenuous life of the little girl he'd later marry. His father chided his young courage and punished him unconsciously for the failures of the nation. My father learned to ignore the lovelessness of his father and banked on his interest in striking out batters and hitting the white, seamed ball over the right field fence for approval and acceptance.

My father feared the severity and missed the love of his unreasonable father, while my mother feared the truth and missed the honest nurturing of her sacrificial mother.

So...I was a new start, freshness, independence, and an original lease on life for both my mother and my father. I was the future (and my future was already at the time of my birth being invested wisely). I was health and safety. I wasprogress. I was the hope of tomorrow and the joy of today. I was memory-less. I was to have it better than they did. I was to have every chance. I was what being American was all about.

I was sent to a good college...in the daytime. I had spending money. I had a car and no insurance bill. I studied the things I wanted to. I experimented with women and drugs. I wrote poetry. I missed the draft."

He stopped, and then decided to play out the scenario beyond the present, just for the hell of it.

"After four lovely years had passed I graduated on a sunny day. My proud mother and father were there. It wasn't an unusual story.

Instead of accepting one of the high paying jobs I was offered in the advertising industry, I traveled, wandered, I wondered. And somehow I realized that I was filled with resentment. Anger buzzed inside me like trapped bees. It was the plan that bugged me; no one had asked me about it. It was done to me. I was symbolic. My parents had depended on me to complete themselves. I had a controversy with my birth; my life was started for reasons other than me. I wanted to have had control of that decision. I had been robbed of that struggle. I didn't know what was really mine, what was my doing, what was and wasn't me. I was overly connected to the hopes and histories of my creators...and I thought I would always be. This was my great denial. I quickly identified with the purposelessness of high art.

Art seemed like the only realm in which the past and the future could be leveled. I journeyed around the world, worked at little jobs along the way. I felt as if I were an artist, an artist that hadn't yet made any art. And I imagined my art as being the re-creation of myself. If my mind was really fertile, I thought, I could experience and render a Renaissance of self. Art was the urge to be my own maker!
I set out."

He looked up. An hour had passed and three menubacks were filled with blue ink. The hot apple pie had a warning on its holster: CAUTION THE FILLING MAY BE DANGEROUSLY HOT, a provision that'd be useful when the lawsuits hit. The apples on the colored packaging

193

looked good, red and shiny, but the apples inside the sealed pouch of pastry were soggy and lifeless, cellularly decomposed by microwave and asphyxiated in a starchy and gelatinous fluid. Benjamin left the specimen steaming on his paper-lined tray, folded his confession into the back pocket of his Levis, and walked back to the hotel to join his mother and Harriet, who had taken the shuttle bus and were numbly watching Dick Cavett in their room when he arrived.

Jay-walking carelessly against the blinking orange command, Benjamin watched the massive mauve clouds that were gilded with the final rays of sun. In California there still were bodies on the beaches. Soon there'd be margaritas pouring from blenders into salt-lipped glasses and sushi pieces sculpted on microwave-safe platters, and then after-dinner snifters of Sambuca, tanned, fit bodies would be bumping on waterbeds and futons. Horns were honking at Benjamin who stood frozen in the middle of John Fitzgerald Kennedy Boulevard. There were people in those cars speeding home or speeding back out. Going places, there were lines on the pavement, broken ones and solid ones and double ones in yellow and arrows. Who was running the world anyway? The question sifted through him, while sets of cars stopped and then gunned away as lights flashed colors and the backs of cars lit up red and then went off. And someone gave him the finger. And someone else was getting head in the back of a rust-bucket Bellevere to the voice of a Jim Morrison clone.

"Gramps, watch-out, you're going to get hit!"

"It doesn't matter; I have insurance." It was the voice from six-months back that just at that second made sense. He understood the joke, the disregard. The policy, it was true, was paid up to date as always, carefully filed with photocopies of all the correspondence, properly dated and placed in chronological order in the deep bottom drawer of his desk that held file folders that slid on ball bearings. It was the insurance that mattered to him, the form of doing things right. His life was something to joke about.

Jacob had died so many times in his mind, had said good-bye to his own life so often, had prepared his body for the journey to oblivion so regularly — only to be touched by chance (or something else) and not die — that death no longer brought on uncontrollable shivers or miserable wailing or loosening of bowels. Death to him was what it meant to a convicted killer who'd been marooned on Death Row for half his life. Death was a joker, a court jester, the sage of nothingness. It had lost its seriousness in a card game with the Devil. And Jacob had shared his life with him, had been sodomized by him, had tasted him. Jacob had shoveled corpses with the tedium with which day workers shoveled ditches. He had hid among them, cold, stinking, infested, dismembered corpses, until he'd lost his certainty if he wasn't one of them and death had become less fantastic than bread.

Daily, hourly, he'd been forced unhaltingly to digest the knowledge that his wife, his partner in life, the woman who'd taken his name, who'd opened her legs at will for him at night, who'd given him a daughter (and thus a lineage), had died, was dead, wholly, certainly, and eternally, and had died a terrible death, and that the daughter, the last bit of meaning, an innocent, defenseless child of seven, was perhapsdead too. What was worse than this knowledge was that he was simultaneously condemned to live-on helplessly day after day, repeating the horrific truth of this knowledge, being constantly reminded of it, until it became by the cruel obligation of sadistic repetition, unremarkable, trivial, commonplace. And even worse, he was forced to live on until the idea was so normal that he simply forgot to think of it. And then to have to live on further with the shame and self-hate of that!

Benjamin kicked a dented Colt 45 can across the Hilton parking lot — angry and defiant now. "If I had a child I'd want everything to be just perfect; one bad experience, one irrational fear caused by a stupid accident would spoil everything. Four years — out of my sight, with no news — I'd machine-gun the planet!" Beneath the energy that surged in his imagination lay a liquid mass of acid. The guilt of not knowing death first hand, of fearing it terribly, of not being immune to it, of being the soft and padded aftermath of someone else's annihilated hell. A shadow. "I'd like to live till one second before the end of eternity and then experience death," his girlfriend of three weeks had written with a fountain pen on the inside cover of his Vintage edition of Joyce's *Ulysses*. His life was just the ephemeral jelly that lolled about in privilege, the disgusting stuff that encased gefilte fish pieces in glass jars. He didn't know anything or feel anything bone-deep. He didn't have to go to Vietnam. He was an American in middle America, where the good times rolled, where chicken came in buckets, and entire years were played out in imitation of Coke commercials, and no two consecutive days had been experienced without the comforting visual caress of the bube-tube. When Jacob ate a chicken he cracked the bones in his teeth. He sucked out the marrow and chewed up the gristle and cartilage. He usurped all the energy from the small animal's life. There was no waste, he was what a Sioux was to a buffalo. Everything was transferred, and trash was really trash. "Eat the bones and throw away the meat," he'd tease, and Benjamin would laugh. It was one of those lines that just struck kids as funny. Its repetition predictably brought smiles every time. It carried the irony of this second life. The truth of everything turned on end. He knew something.

Benjamin spun through the revolving door and reeled through the lobby. He rode the silent elevator while watching the light jump from number to number above the thick doors. He knocked at the room and found his mother in her bathrobe already. She was a full-grown woman. He'd never known her as that abandoned child from Europe. Soon her periods would stop, he thought, and he'd be the only remainder of this story of generations, the only one who'd be able to make it go on. Hehugged her and smelled the apricot cream she had rubbed into her face and neck to prevent her skin from drying out. There were wrinkles already on the side of her jaw and her skin was soft but no longer taut. "Someday I'll make you a grandmother," he voiced internally with a sort of dread of fear, embarrassment even, lurking beneath in his subconscious, suspecting absolutely nothing on just how soon that occasion would be. He didn't want to make his mother old. She had been a young mother and he wanted to keep her that way. His real grandmother, he remembered, was dead already as a woman younger than Jane now, the woman in the doorway. She'd met death by gas, by breathing in the air that her body demanded. Gas, pollution, chemicals. "The Jews know already about the fantasy of nuclear Armageddon. All your life, you live trying not to get hurt. You walk in the right places; you eat good things. You cover up in the winter air. You take precautions. You follow doctor's order, get plenty of rest and drink lots of fluids, have your teeth checked regularly. For what? To be destroyed on purpose." His thought went wild as his body hung against the body of its mother. Whatever the age, the cause and effect would remain the same; he had come from her.

"I love you," she whispered at him and he remembered oddly her breath when she was 26, fresh with instant coffee and a powdered creamer. Cremora, a Carnation product, a non-dairy creamer, the company boasted. The country had gone nuts, letting concerns who wanted to make more money twist its people's needs into warped directions, a non-dairy creamer! She'd sit at the breakfast table in floppy slippers and a bathrobe and dunk slices of industrial raisin bread in her mug of freeze-dried decaffeinated coffee before embarking on the tasks of morning housework. All the cleaning supplies were stacked haphazardly beneath the kitchen sink. Brillo, Cascade, Spic-n-Span, Lestoil, Lemon Pledge... They were all there, the battery, cluttered around a sack of potatoes that grew roots out through the red mesh rope.

"I love you too."

Truman Capote lisped, slouched in a studio chair across from Dick, his legs crossed at the thighs and his socks sagging a bit. His thighs were probably very white and freckly, Benjamin thought as his eyes drifted onto the screen. Cavett asked a dated but predictably popular question about *In Cold Blood*, Capote, unknowingly close to his own end, shut his pink eyelids, gathered his words like they were wild flowers growing in a field, and responded in a slow, queer and ironic way, almost black in its humor, certainly off-color, toyingly ambiguous with lovely overshadows of sado-machochism, and the studio audience laughed, following the electronically flashed cue, and Harriet rose to change the channel without asking.

"Vile," she said with a grimace. "How can people likethat?" She had missed the irony and responded directly to the horror of the generation-old, Kansan crime that had shocked the American imagination before weird and rampant and irrational killings had become as everyday as cancer or fax machines or missing-kid cases printed on milk cartons, while flipping past a police story, Marcus Welby, M.D., a classic re-run on a new re-run network, and the Astros-Padres night game. "Oh, certainly not one of those violent football games," Harriet muttered as she crunched the tuner. The color was off and the nicely swept infield as it jumped past was indigo-cranberry.

Benjamin plopped himself down into the brown nougahyde chair, crushing his story, and air hissed out under his weight, making a compromising noise like the one made by the whoopee cushion advertised in the back of *Mad Magazine* in the sixties.

"Who passed air?"

"No one, it was the chair, Granny."

"Oh, mother!"

"It can happen to anyone, dear."

He took his philosophy text from his overnight bag and opened it to his assignment. He read a few lines from that William James essay, "Does Consciousness Exist?" and then snapped shut the expensive softcover, unable to concentrate.

"Dung...." And then, as an afterthought, asked, "Where's Gramps' diary?" inquisitively, without accusation. He knew Jacob had been writing in it over the past months, although he had not read much more than the few passages that he convinced Jacob to read over the phone.

"Mother?" Jane redirected the question to Harriet. In a sudden fluster, Harriet searched around the room with her eyes, her chest rose with panic and then quickly settled in an exhale.

"Why it's in Dad's room in the hospital." She breathed deeply. "Why did you scare me like that? I thought I lost if for a moment. Do you want me to have a heart attack?" She knew as she spoke that her words had been poorly chosen.

"You left it there?" Jane asked with slight and unjustified annoyance. Then, realizing that she had needlessly upset her stepmother, she quickly changed her tone. "I'm sure it's fine."

Benjamin hurried to her side, out of kindness, and reassured her, careful not to crush her chronically aching feet, which she had buried under the fire-resistant bedspread.

She could be so easily unnerved. She was as brittle as the cold taffy she'd bought regularly on the boardwalk each summer at Bradley Beach. Taffy was just a taste from the past now that her mouth was filled with costly dental work. Her fillings were all gold; it was sort of an unreasonablesuperstition. She, at least, would be buried someday peacefully with the gold still in her mouth. No one would be tugging out the fillings for the *Führer* with extraction pliers and rendering the gold back into nuggets or coins. Why gold and not the more common silver/alloy mixture? She couldn't say, but just wouldn't scrimp on her teeth. Gold would never rot; worms didn't stand a chance. It all came back to that, immortality.

Benjamin's embrace was blissful to her for the first two seconds. Then, she herself soured that good feeling with her own perverse thought-process. "I'm exploiting Benjamin's kind will. How villainous of me!" He had tried to shelter her from feeling guilt, which she shouldn't have felt in the first place, and as a result, she ended up bringing upon herself a deeper sense of guilt for having Benjamin shelter her, which secretly now she blamed on Dzi. Softly, he backed away, sort of repulsed slightly by the ease in which seemingly normal human communication could be short-circuited. There was no simple extradition either from the smallest misunderstanding. Additional comment made the thing bigger, longer, wordier. A flaw almost always led to some larger and unmanageable neurosis or worse, which lay dormant but volatile in the psyche. Try to mend the flaw and the whole personality split wide open. Do that and be prepared for a long and treacherous therapeutic haul. Life was like sailing between icebergs.

"I'm going out for a little walk, okay? I can't stay in here. I need to walk around."

"Where, darling?"

"Don't know. Out. To breathe."

Benjamin couldn't read or talk or watch television or sleep. He had nervous energy pent-up inside him which needed burning off. A treadmill would have been fine. The Hilton Roman Club sauna just didn't cut it, stretched out there in big towels with dripping Shriners and artificially-sweetened Piña Coladas. "Outside, I need out." Colorado, Jack Kerouac out. He resisted the confines of the room, of his life, of history that condemned him to a time and place. He eased out the door. There seemed like nothing to do in the world that made a difference. He couldn't imagine suddenly how people had fun or convinced themselves that they were having fun. A door on the long corridor half way to the elevator opened and a woman dressed like Cleopatra, but with Nike running shoes and one of those black and white cotton scarves that tacitly showed solidarity with the Palestinian cause, stepped out. A look of surprise spread over her face, and a smirk saying 'I don't always dress like this; you can tell it's for a masquerade ball, can't you, schmuck?' The schmuck part Benjamin's inner-dialog made-up. She was probably from Little Rock where very few schmucks were seen in public. As she bentdown to fix her shoe, her shoulder strap toppled and Benjamin couldn't help see the northern rim of her right nipple, actuallyher left. "A nice one with a wide, rouge corona and a frisky apron of bumps." What was there to do? Deny? These things happened. In the elevator not a word was exchanged. And yet in the Anglo-Saxon world such insignificance could seed destruction. Both retreated to the safety of commonly acknowledged superficial behavior reserved for adults. Each watched the numbers light up. Benjamin checked to see when the elevator was last inspected and made sure the certificate was signed.

As his shoes rubbed against the carpeting, gathering static electricity which would spark against the elevator button panel, the previous and pervading mood grew back:

there was no way to have fun now in the world. He wanted to laugh, but feared that he could only produce the sound of laughter. He craved a real laugh and was sure that had he laughed spontaneously at the human awkwardness of the encounter, the woman too would have had to laugh as well. The doors opened on six but no one was waiting. He smelled the ice machine that hummed in an alcove at the end of the floor, a red electric sign required by ordinance and a requisite for Mutual of Omaha marked the Emergency Exit. Somehow in case of fire these things always seemed to be locked or blocked or missing.

At least outside in the warm, restless, darkened end of day it would be easier to believe that there were real, important things to do. He turned left out of the elevator on Lobby; Cleopatra jogged right, turned her head back, and Benjamin, like a macho asshole winked at the Egyptian queen from Arkansas. She smiled out of pure civil protocol and her metal earrings jingled while her well-protected feet were silent.

On the pavement out past the runners of green indoor-outdoor carpet, and a flock of Budget and Avis four-door sedans and some handicapped parking, there were lights that drew eyes to them and didn't stop. Cars were going fast. Music was over-spilling from extractable car radios with auto-reverse and Dolby B, and the around-the-corner bars were coming to life. Beer was flowing from taps, although the heads were still a bit too foamy. It was early. The night, as they say, was young.

Benjamin hurried across the parking lot, powered by an idea. He rushed back past the pre-fab Arby's, his uneaten apple pie now cold in a hefty black garbage bag, sitting limply out back beneath the air conditioning unit and kitchen exhaust fan. Grease dripped like honey from the grill. He didn't care, found it almost beautiful, even. He added the folded pages from his back pocket to the pile.

"They were cathartic but dumb. Fuck that," and hurried back towards Methodist, as Cleopatra was tightening her straps in themirror in a padded little powder room marked 'Dames'.

16

He took a short cut and passed through an alley that ran the length of both Methodist Hospital and the Texas Medical Center Parking Facility No. 2. There was a back door to the hospital — not for visitors — and Benjamin made a quick appraisal and then entered. "The backs of hospitals should be avoided," he mouthed out loud to himself, "as should the backs of restaurants, hotels, mobile home complexes, theme parks, and other tales of ordinary," he chuckled and acknowledged the irreverent Buk before correcting himself, "...establishments that served the public." Here, behind the scenes, in the back of the "house," the public image of the place had no façade. The model without her make-up. The amoral guts of a user-friendly machine. "Hitler was obsessed with the *Tanzania* of Eva Braun's anatomy," he added in absurd self-amusement, genuinely interested in that mini-second in the naked ass of the German woman who had actually grasped the *Führer's* erections with her sphincter.

Benjamin entered this inverted zone of expectations and was greeted by a clutter of medical garbage. Anything ugly on the public floors simply got covered over with sheets or tied securely in opaque plastic and wheeled away. Here they arrived: amputated limbs; lanced, bulbous cysts; removed and useless organs; the sack of aspirated pregnancies..."The poor Pope." The lighting was dim and there was evidence of heavysmoking. Workers who lugged ruined kidneys, pouches of gall stones, sacks of afterbirths, weren't going to be told not to smoke their Lucky Strikes. The unions wouldn't have it, plus this wasn't California.

Benjamin heard the presence of hospital employees but he didn't see them, like mice in the walls. He moved along the gray, ill-lit hall, eyeing the signs for the boiler room and electrical power facilities. His mind went zany as he pictured the circuitry of wires and pipes and tubes and cables, intestines that snaked through the structure, feeding and sustaining the functions of the complex, like a large body. If he polluted a line or ruptured a hose, or blocked an artery, or wrenched open a value, would they be able to locate and repair the ailment before lives were mysteriously lost or the building was condemned? Would Mutual of Omaha cry foul play?

He reached a pair of scratched up elevator doors. Someone had engraved with the precision of a gas cap key, a warped heart, the name Maria, the head of a generously-hung circumcised penis and a phone number coming out of the hole. A cave painting; it would mean something someday, to some academic, as would the Miller Lite can, the Bic Fine Point, and the floppy disk. He jabbed the plastic Up button. It arrived. The penis slid into the wall, and Benjamin stepped into the long and narrow echo-filled chamber, the sort that you were suppose to exit on the far end, the floor worn thin and smooth in most spots like Buffalo nickels, and the walls scuffed with the abrasions of the corners of carts that wheeled. The letters on the black checker-sized buttons, he couldn't decipher. Where was H2 or CAP? The doors opened again at ER and Benjamin bailed out. He hurried down the corridor as if on call, a young intern who hadn't had time to submerge into the arms of his white coat. There was massive hemorrhaging to halt. This wasn't the heart clinic where recuperating ladies and gents wore their own terry cloth — sometimes monogrammed — bathrobes and leather slippers in the hallways, asking if the mail had come yet. Where Interflora delivery men with flowers and wrapped packages with half-pint cards looked around impatiently for room numbers, double-parked outside. Here, the aisles were lined with chrome and rubber buggies filled with mostly off-white and black bodies clothed in ripped-away street clothes and bleached-out hospital issue. Emergencies, they called these. He'd emerged unknowingly at the back of the Emergency Ward. Loaded stretchers he wove among with eyes as wide as a young rural male's in a big city sex shop. It took very strange things to cull-out the last untouched zones of innocence. Someone wailed, moaned, and hugged his knees. Another sat with eyes rolled towards the ceiling, waiting, blocking out, dreaming. It was the beginning of the night and the rough edges of the city were sharpening their blades. A lanky, black man withwild hair, no front teeth, and a tattoo of a cobra on his Adam's Apple, lay on a stretcher bleeding from the mouth with his wrists cuffed to the aluminum bars of the bed. "He raped an eighty-year old woman and then ate glass," a younger man with a rag wrapped around his hand blurted out. "I captured him," the man added, as if there was a bounty. When the rapist swallowed, the bump slid along the insides of the digesting snake. Benjamin hurried through a series of doors, fire doors, and then another and plowed up a stairwell, spooking himself with his own echo.

He sprinted up the cinder-lipped stairs without pausing between floors and tried the door on the sixth where he thought he might find Jacob's floor, or at least a corridor that led him around the same level to a recognizable part of the hospital. It was locked, so he galloped up to the seventh. He pushed. The cylinder hadn't settled into the lock; it opened. He went through and turned right. The corridor was dim. He didn't recognize a thing. It was like being in a different city, a different life, perhaps a different century. The smell was wrong. It was like being lost on the upper floors of a downtown hotel in a city that salesmen no longer called on. Where the whores were cheap and honest. He was nervous. He longed for the street, for the parking lot, for the sight of Arby's. There was a plaque on a door. He read it. Psychiatric Wing — Authorized Personnel Only. This was worse than ER, the invisibility and the silence of illness. The smells weren't clinical, they were of soiled clothes, of packs of cinnamon chewing gum that had been run through the wash. There were eyes suddenly pouring down on him and that thing that made both Polansky and Stephen King hits in the world fear-market worked on his nerves like Draino in a clogged sink. Wild men, he pictured, with messed up hair banging into the padded walls, and women with knotted hair twisting up their faces, scratching, screaming with no sound coming out. And the smell of the fire-proof carpeting and sweat-matted lambskin-lined house shoes harassed his already overcharged senses. Way out, how to get out of here? He barreled back down the same stairs, hair-raised, taking three steps at a time, banged out the first unlocked door he tried and exhaled with relief upon seeing a human being, a guy with a cart-full of cleaning supplies and a scar on his chin, the shape of Florida. He'd gone through a glass door as a kid in Santo Domingo.

With directions in an English that was missing all its Rs and most of its Ss, Benjamin hurried around two corners, took a left, skipped up a ramp — equipped with banisters for the handicapped — linking two buildings, and came to a better-looking bank of elevators, which he happily halted at. When, the doors opened he stepped out onto a plush residential ward more reminiscent of a Ramada Inn than a hospital. It wasalong here that he'd find Jacob's room. And the grief of the unpleasant labyrinth he'd just negotiated faded. "God, it's so damn easy to get into this place after visiting hours. What security!" he thought. Some afternoon soap opera serial was pressing on his brain. It was only in those that hitmen and jealous lovers were sent in to finish off poorly executed first attempts and terminal patients who might reveal the dreaded truth, the bribe, the motive, the night of incest, and the heir to the will.

The nurse's station at the corner of two arteries wasn't manned. He bolted across the hall, found the right number above the veneered-oak door and tried the handle. It gave. He pushed it wide open, stepped in, and the door settled shut behind him. He turned.

"Whoa!" Gasp and a ruffle.

Startled.

Movement in the brush.

Shoot.

Hold on!

"Hey!"

"Shhhhhh....I...."

"What the..."

Benjamin's skin went taut and another sound came from his throat. A figure in the dark. He went weightless. "Gramps!" his first thought, impossible.

No. Who? Wait.

Amy slapped together the two halves of the marble-covered diary and set it down quickly on the night stand, obscuring her act as if it wasn't true, but knowing that she'd been seen, caught in the act. Who was this? Nothing was clear yet. How would this unravel? Only the sealed beams of vehicles and the neon over-spill and weak phosphores-

209

cence of billboard lights and street lamps down below illuminated the otherwise dark room. The two pairs of retinas adjusted. Two dark masses faced each other. Almost in unison they realized that they had no idea who the other was. Benjamin wasn't the shift supervisor. Nurse Stadler wasn't Jacob, clearly. A thief?

"What are you doing here?"

Instinctually, her defense took to the offense. "Shhhh. What are *you* doing here? *I* work here. Visiting hours are over. How'd you get in?" she delivered in a forceful whisper.

They both spoke like they had rights. But neither voice held any real command. They were bantering in patterned responses.

"This is *my* grandfather's room; but what are *you* doing?"

"Nothing." Looking for a better word she repeated, "Nothing, why?"

He reached to his right and felt with his fingers the slight rippled texture of the plastified wallpaper. Where's the light switch? He'd see who this was. She perceived the shadow of his arm reaching. "Wait, I'm a nurse, I'll explain." So this was the grandson from college, Benjamin. She knew him as she collected her words. He'll understand. She preferred the subdued light.

Why was she in the dark and trying to whisper if she worked here?

He stopped. There was silence except for their breathing. His eyes were adjusting and the contour of her figure gained definition. Her hair was tied back and the mass where the bunch was tied looked like a nest in silhouette. The rest of her was appearing like an under-exposed photograph agitated in a darkroom tray of chemicals. She wasn't old, but not young either, and her hair was dark and there was a lot of it. She hemmed. He waited.

"I met your grandfather before," it sounded so queer in words. She hardly knew the man at all, only what he'd written. "...before his surgery, and..." Benjamin held himself from interrupting, "and, well, I've been reading his diary. Kinda secretly." She felt better having said it straight out, and now waited for whatever response she deserved. "I also know that it's dedicated to you. You are Benjamin, right?"

"That book is personal you know. Did he tell you that you could browse through it like that? Do you think you have the right to go through somebody's private affairs? Just because he's not here?" It was Benjamin speaking, but if he didn't know himself he'd never have guessed it.

"No no no, wait." She was shaking her head and the shadow of the nest diffused light on the wall. You really don't understand. Listen."

He heard then her pale accent.

"Well?"

"Well," and she began again in a cadence of calm that she felt she'd now earned, "you see, your grandfather told me about his diary and it, well, I'm interested in it...." Benjamin watched her talk, sound coming from an undefined source, still not knowing why the lights had to stay off. "I'm not from here, originally." Nothing yet had begun to make sense. "*My* grandfather, well, he was in the war too." She swallowed. "So you see what I mean? You're a Jew, right?" Her tone wasn't unkind but only a Gentile and a European would say "a Jew." The woman continued before Benjamin could formulate a reply. "Stop telling me all this," he was thinking. "The diary, I find it touching." There was silence. "I'm sorry." She was. This was awkward.

They reached emotional ground level. His impulse to battle receded as if the batteries were drained. There was no reason to argue. The planet was too noisy already.

"No, I was wrong. It's not my property. I was justinterested. And he seemed like such a sweet man." She thought of her *Opa* and *Oma* and what she grew up hearing, the way tears welled-up in her grandmother's eyes when the subject of the war surfaced at the dinner table. The way he'd been broken. Things never got returned to normal. The letter from the other woman in Berlin, near the front.

The past tense unnerved Benjamin as he couldn't think of his grandfather as a thing of the past, but it occurred to him that it was hers that she was thinking of. What had come of him? What did he do? Where had he been? What accent do you have? He wanted to know all this, ready to blame him or forgive him. He said nothing, looked down at the marbled notebook and then back at the woman.

"Well, how much did you read?"

"Nearly all of it," she replied with some embarrassed delight, then tried to retract any hint of enthusiasm thinking that the omission enlarged the guilt.

"You've read more than I have, you know." His eyes saw her better now. His aggression was nearly all gone, like the dissipated rage of a caged animal. Resignation.

"I've been reading in segments.... Mr. Simon is one of my patients." This she thought softened the blow. "I'm sorry if you're angry." And with that she felt she'd cleared herself. She was a member of the hospital staff on duty and he was the emotionally strung-out grandson of a patient, who had violated hospital regulations by sneaking into the building after hours. She could call Security. Her word would hold up. The boy was just upset and oversensitive. That was her official line if she had to have one.

"It's okay." Now, he felt she owed him something. "Can I ask you something?" And he approached the window maneuvering himself into better light in which she had read. He slid past the empty bed and leaned against the window. He could see her face and thought of that French Canadian actress in *Kamuraska*, Genevieve Bujold. The hair was tied back and held in an enameled hair clip. A bird of sorts. It had belonged to her *Oma* in Frankfurt. And on her finger of her left hand was a white metal ring which *Opa* welded for his wife while a prisoner-of-war. A belated wedding band banged out of a fired-down cafeteria spoon. To Amy it was a touchstone, a token of love. She pictured her grandmother sitting in front of the television with the sound turned way up in the house she had spent her entire childhood, in that carved up neighborhood in north Frankfurt, originally part of that progressive Social Housing Program that Hitler created. Solid, respectable stone houses with steeple roofs and yards for flowers and gardens with healthy rows of potato and tomato plants, climbing green beans and heads of lettuce and cabbage. And fruit trees. It was a sane vision and it won support. *Brotund Arbeit!* Amy had heard the words come from her grandmother, tears welling up around her eyes. They had been so hungry. And he promised food and he gave them their house. That's all. Benjamin ran his fingers along the smooth, cool pane. A faint breeze drifted up through the filters of the air conditioning unit which at night was on the fan cycle and was powered by large rotary units deep in the hull of the complex, near where he had entered. The pale haze of bluish-neon colored like television-studio make-up the side of Benjamin's face, and Amy observed the scarceness of the boy's facial hair. She placed a hand on his shoulder and squeezed a bit as to say, "C'mon, trust me, I'm an ally." She knew him. It was like a transfusion He smelled her soap and watched the soft cord of muscle

213

that joined so elegantly below the ear and the throat and then disappeared below her white collar and united with her chest. He looked away. She was older than him. The HILTON sign was flashing and he thought of his mother in one of those windows, behind a thick pane of glass that did not open. He felt guilty for being there in Jacob's room with this nurse. Amy tried to follow his line of sight, but caught a glimpse of the Interstate and followed it east to where the large road sign read in nitro/radium letters that headlights picked out at night: Beaumont Eastbound lanes. Kevin was already asleep, his own dreams circulating freely. She looked at her watch. A bit past ten thirty.

"Listen, I'm off in about a half an hour. I have to do medication before I go, but why don't you meet me for a coffee? There's a diner about two blocks from here that I go by on my way home. It's called The Hen House." She smiled, thinking how these American places were so funny. The place was shaped like a hen house and painted red and white, and you could get scrambled eggs and hash at 3 AM. Perfect for a late night.

"I'll find it." He headed her off as she tried to give him directions. And his concentration momentarily went out of focus. Would he even remember the name of the place. The name of a bird. The wires were all crossing in his head and confusion followed. The impulses were over-loading the circuits and dashed away like a mad, surrealist painter or performance artist. "What if we're living in the world of the two small words that you can still type on an electric typewriter after the power has been shut down?" he asked without sound, weirdly to himself. Mentally, he shot Hitler in the head with a retarded *Ouzi*, licked madly that soft muscle below the nurse's ear, headed-in the win-ning goal of the Europe Cup for the Barça Club, thereby spiritually liberating Catalunia. Swords of a recurrent dream skewered him through the back and chest but didn't kill him and didn't hurt, somewhere in between current day Iran and El Cid's Castilla. And he saw theparamecium-like squiggle that reappeared between his field of vision and his iris on bright, sunny days at Beach Haven, with his eyes closed, a dead cell floating in its own reality. He hurried out and down the hall, hearing the words Hen House. And then regaining focus, the diary, he remembered. "Shit." And impulsively decided. " I'll leave it in its place." Amy moved to the doorway and watched him approach the elevator. "Funny boy." And the door settled closed. Then, pleased by the naughtiness, she returned to the marbled book before slipping it back into the night table drawer, knowing that it might be her last chance.

The living and working conditions in the cable factory were not too bad at first. I worked on a stream-controlled press machine manufacturing all kinds of bakelite items like radio shells, shoe paste boxes, and electric wall plates.

It happened a few times that one of the inmates forgot to take out from the press the ready item and the press jammed up and would not open. This happened to two inmates during the day shift and both were taken outside by the Gestapo and shot for sabotage. It happened once to me too but during the night shift at about four in the morning. Fortunately, I had a foreman who was very nice to me, and he started to work on the problem immediately, taking the whole press apart. And we finished it before 8 AM. when all the big shots came in, and my life was saved. The Chief Engineer, a Volksdeutscher, who was very strict, never found out and that's why I am still alive.

Also while at the Kablewerks, one day after we came back from work, two Werkschutz came to pick twenty of us inmates to unload several carloads of saw dust, which was used in the pressing system for manufacturing the bakelite.

I tried to save my father-in-law's brother, Gustav, who was old and not well, from being picked, but one of the Jewish Capo noticed what I was trying to do and, as punishment, I was picked instead. This work was terrible. filling sacks with sawdust, our eyes and mouths and throats filled with dust and we coughed and choked up blood. But, unfortunately, we had to take it and make the best of it and be happy every day that soon it would be over.

It was the Day of Atonement, Yom Kippur, and among us were two rabbis who refused to eat anything, trying to fast. One of the Werkschutze, a Ukrainian and a mean anti-Semite, brought us a twenty-quart pot of hot soup and forced us, the rabbis included, to eat it without spoons with our bare hands, hitting us as we ate the scalding soup with our fingers.

Amy, not religious at all, baptized of course like allChristian babies, a Catholic from a Protestant country, crossed herself for the first time in years and closed the diary. "That's enough." And prayed for *Opa*, whose asthma was worsening. He had once told her that he desired to be buried in his overalls in a pasture where goats grazed and fruit trees were free to bend with the heaviness of ripe fruit, and it was the most poetic thing she had ever heard. Although she knew that one day the family would send him down in the one suit he hated, arranged in a polished casket that clashed with the aesthetics of his soul, and decorated with bouquets of cut flowers that would have made him sneeze. She felt love for him, as she heard him wheezing thousands of miles away at the plastic tablecloth slurping *Oma's Knoblauch* soup. "The poor rabbis, the hairless face of Benjamin. *Lieber Gott*. I better go." There was medication to parcel out into tiny Dixie cups that patients needed.

17

Benjamin followed the movement of her white hospital shoes along the concrete path as if the shoes were detached from the body. He simply followed the feet into the cluster of early postwar garden apartments. Past the Super's place, Christmas lights, un-lit of course, still rimmed the gutter and front window. Red-brick facing, concrete, slightly ornamental wrought iron on the balconies that were large enough for a lawn chair and a modest hibachi or miniature Weber grill. Here was one of the many neighborhoods that didn't figure into the pictures in the brochure packet that the Houston Chamber of Commerce sent out to interested parties for a dollar, attracting new businesses and professionals. A toppled tricycle, obviously forgotten or abandoned that day by a kid, was stuck in the middle of the lawn of coarse Southern grass, wide-bladed and painful on bare feet. With its front wheel up in the air and the handlebar butting into the ground, red plastic lanyard strips hanging limply from the plastic grips, the tricycle had an oddly sculptural look about it as if dropped by a sculptor from a helicopter to define the space.

The evening was warm but Benjamin felt chilled and felt the need to steady himself to prevent shivering. In a burst, he might easily have cracked into an uncontrollable chatter. He breathed deeply and perceived the sweet waft of marijuana fumes seeping from the direction of the Marvin Gaye tune. He resisted the chill by concentrating on the shoes, a mantra of sorts, forbidding his eyes from wandering higher than the lower calves.

Amy was older than him. Although not more than six or seven years, in terms of life experience if she was closer in age to Jane. She had been married, had reared a child, had learned a profession, had uprooted herself from her country and language, and lived alone in a large American city. Benjamin sweated while he shivered, and worried about his perspiration. This was the kind he thought that dogs detected, sweat from fear, not heat. The coffee at the Red Hen hadn't calmed him. They had slid into a cracked red-leather booth, him on one side, her on the other. She looked straight at him; he looked back periodically but couldn't maintain more than a few seconds of insistent contact. The light was too bright and the width of the table slightly too narrow for Benjamin to feel at ease, to wield the questions. He leaned deep into the corner and fiddled with the salt shaker, dumping some grains on the simulated-teak Formica and then stopping, realizing how young he was being. Before anything else, a napkin and a spoon was plopped down in front of them. Mugs of coffee, "regular" which meant a shot of Half-n-Half and two sugars each, came dangling on the bent trigger finger of the waitress, a veritable expert at video games and a novice at airbrush painting of vans. A moonstone and a puzzle ring crowded her middle finger.

Benjamin stopped her with, "Black for me, please."

Amy accepted hers like usual.

"So, where are you staying?"

"Hilton." He pointed out the window in the general direction. The hotel was actually the other way, but it didn't matter.

"And..."

"With my mother and grandmother."

"Dzidzia?"

This was weird, hearing a stranger pronouncing his mother's childhood Polish nickname. Only her parents called her Dzidzia. It brought him back to the thought of Jacob, but he hadn't yet the courage to ask, or more like he wasn't ready for the reply. He sipped from the massive mug. The coffee was pretty terrible.

"So when did you come to this country?" he asked after nodding yes to her question. She told him and then a little about life as an NCO's wife, about the boredom, and about Kevin. "You know the thrill of shopping in the PX wears off very fast." But he wanted to veer deeper into Germany, pre-marriage, her interest in Jacob's diary, and Jacob. What was her grandfather's story? "At least you have a grandmother!" he thought but refrained from screaming at her. It wasn't her fault. "You can call me Amy, you know." She smiled gently. He smiled back and considered French toast, then cole slaw, before settling for nothing.

"Tell me, Amy..." They both smiled, and the coffee didn't seem so bitter; "was your father in the war?" She knew what he was heading for, that perversely yet understandable magneticurge to assign guilt. She was used to the guilt-by-association attack and shared at moments some of that collective feeling. It hadn't been easy sitting in the tv room with her husband and his family at Thanksgiving watching those war films with the exclusively German bad guys. The simplification of guilt annoyed her.

"No, he is a painter. He went to Paris to study at the *Beaux Arts*. He was 17 and stayed. That's where he trapped my mother." Benjamin thought it a weird choice of verbs, but he didn't say anything; this wasn't his concern.

"She's French, then?"

"No, she's German too, but she left Frankfurt as a young girl just after the war and went to Paris as an *au père*. I think she found it hard staying at home after my grandfather returned from the war and the Americans took over."

He could have argued over her use of "took over" but it was the part about the grandfather that now got him interested. "Tell me about how he didn't know what was going on and all that," he thought toyingly. He asked, and she told him the story about his being a drafted soldier injured in Russia, about how he had been knocked off the *Strassenbahn* time after time in the thirties because he was suspected of being a Jew, — a detail she was proud of — he being of a darker complexion and so very un-Aryan. Before the war, both he and her grandmother had worked for a prominent Jewish family, the Kohns, as driver and seamstress. But in 1935, they lost their jobs when the family, they were told would be emigrating to America, and they never believed it, although the Kohns didn't get futher than the *Hauptbahnhof! Oma* spoke affectionately of that house and the lovely embroidered linen! Benjamin listened. And sipped the coffee. And little by little his anger resided like a tide going out.

"How about a beer instead of this coffee?" Amy suggested, eager to get out of her white ripple-soled shoes. "I'm parked just outside."

"Love it." Benjamin grabbed the sloppy bill and paid at the register and they walked out into the muggy air on even ground. He still wanted to ask her.

Amy unbolted the door and slid back the rod of the police lock with the ease of habit. "You need one of these around here. I learned the hard way. Twice. They didn't get much." She flipped on a table lamp and quickly collected a few glasses, an aluminum tin of Lean Cuisine, and an ashtray from the glass coffee table, and spun into the tight kitchen to free her hands. Benjamin thought for a second, hesitating, not knowing where to sit? He picked the couch, thinking that if he'd picked one of the two battered Victorian chairs (that she'd picked up at an auction for fifty dollars a piece) it would have looked as if he'd been afraid to pick the couch. Which was true. The soft cushions failed to absorb all his tension, despite their plushness. He sunk, like a rock in the sea, right to the springs. The cushions were the sort that robbed men of their pocket change. Benjamin wondered how many coins were down there in the dusty crease. His eyes scanned the walls, picking out the repetition of a child's face in the snapshots. The child she'd mentioned in the diner, he assumed. There were many photos of the boy, always in color, printed on that permanently unsmudged mat texture. Some also captured a man, the father, Benjamin guessed, but only where the central image was the cute, dirty-blond, creamy-skinned kid. Always in a football jersey or a college sweat shirt.

The paint at the top of the walls near the ceiling was peeling. This was the South, where the humidity did its number even on the good places. There was air conditioning everywhere in the South where strong breezes up from the river didn't rush across open porches — Americans were always overcooling or overheating, temperature-controlling to the point where their natural range of resistance diminished to a thread — but Amy only had a cheap window fan in the bedroom that blew back the plain cotton curtains that she'd hand-sewn, and displaced the junk mail she'd left on her desk top. One envelop had her name printed in red along with the news that she was going to Hawaii for two!

She returned to the living room and dropped a cold green Heineken bottle down in front of Benjamin on her way to the bedroom.

"Be right back."

In a very short amount of time she stepped back into the living room, metamorphosed into a girl. She had shed her nurse things and now wore pants and a thin Indian cotton shirt. Her hair was down, and she had brushed it out. The white shoes were gone and a pair of backless sandals had replaced them, the cheap kind from India with the leather strips between the toes. She'd been so swift that Benjamin's mind excited as it pictured the clothes rolling off her like a snake shedding its skin. His eyes then took another tour, finding it hard to stay where they had wanted to. There was a sprout jar on her window sill and an unruly spider plant or Wandering Jew suspended from a wall bracket. There were some books on two small shelves, although some of the volumes were really photo albums and nursing manuals, the textbook from her computer course, and a sleeve of air mail letters, *flugpost* printed in deep blue. And a book on how to fix your VW, although she now drove a maroon Cutlass with rust spots and an under-inflated spare tire and a loud muffler. Her husband had taken the Rabbit. "I'd never fight over a car. I'll take the Olds, you take the VW," she'd told him.

There was something about her furnishings that announced uprootedness, the thinness of permanence. They hadn't been bought for that apartment; they'd been lugged from other cities in rented U-Hauls from a single family house, a basement storage bin back East, Newport News, Virginia, a container that had slowly made the journey via military shippers in Bremenhaven. Now, in Houston one had to wait longer than a menstrual cycle to rent a U-Haul; there were just too many folks trying to move away. With the radical fluctuations in the price of oil people came and fled in spurts. The by-passes, though, continued selling out weeks in advance. There was a mix of things from both her girlhood days and her married life, and now other things too that she had never had before, like the sprouts and the bong that Benjamin spotted behind the end table. She was deciding all over how to live alone, and now her place showed inadvertently the chronological and psychic delineation of her life with the latest stage only a few stops from what seniors did to dorm rooms at private colleges. A thin, printed cotton spread loosely covered the couch.

The Heineken felt good, real good, going down, but the cold, beaded bottle sent a flurry to Benjamin's brain. A hundred little spots on the top left side of his scalp pricked up like stiff points of water on a wind blown inlet. He was attracted to the nurse. She took a beer too and sat in a bean bag chair opposite him. "She's pretty cool," he thought again, eyeing the red enamel on her toenails.

"So," she pronounced in a great exhale, the first real breath she'd taken all day, treading through the stillness with ease. So, this was the grandson of the voice in the diary. Her body was tired but it felt good not having to go to sleep just yet.

"I'd like to," Benjamin false-started. "My grandfather..."

"Don't think right now about," she wanted to say "him" but heard it first in her mind and thought it sounded kind of callous, "your grandfather. You're so tense. You'll see him tomorrow. There's nothing you can do. I'm telling you."

Benjamin, for the first split second felt defensive, felt hurt, felt as if she'd been out of place to say what she'd said. "Who's she to..." But before that response could fix into place other possibilities presented themselves. Was she being therapeutic? Or seductive? Motherly? Social workish? Who was she anyway? German. "Why did I follow her here? I'm not one of those who'd refuse to buy a Mercedes or Braun coffee maker. Or set a foot on that country's soil." We can forgive but we'll never forget, they used to say at confirmation class at temple. "What do I have to say to her that doesn't have to do with my grandfather?" But when words finally came out they weren't any of those.

"So, how long have you lived here?"

Since my divorce. Almost four years," she answered and then looked surprised. Had it really been four years already? And she wondered herself why she hadn't even thought of going back to Frankfurt. Kevin, for one, but something else too. "I couldn't live there." But she missed her *Oma* terribly and cried with sentimental tears when the heavy brick of a package arrived each December with *Oma's Stollen,* a dense fruitcake loaded with candied cherries, rum-drowned raisins, condensed milk and a pound of margarine. And the metal chest of *Lebkuchen,* a pretty assortment of spiced Christmas cookies prepared specially by the Schmidt & Sons Company of Nuremberg since 1859. They never missed even one year. When Nuremberg was overflowing with the inspired masses converging on the rally grounds to hail Hitler, impressing deeply Lena Reifenstall, Mr. Schmidt and his bakers were preparing for the Christmas season of 1940. Now his wares, packed and buffered so well they'd endure Armageddon, came to Texas every year, unscathed. *Oma's* swollen knees as she hobbled with the heavy package to the *Bundespost* office between the Bonames S-bahn station, Angelo's Pizza and the Drake Edwards Kaserne, United States Army and once temporary home for at least 450 Hispanic Americans, 290 NCOs with illiterate Asian wives most of whom worked part-time bagging groceries at the AAFES Commissary or the Mini-Mart, where even Halloween pumpkins and Jiffy Pop were airlifted regularly from food warehouses in Norfolk, Virginia, fluttered through Amy's thought. That was another world. She pictured Frau Schultz in the Dog House, a sausage shack in the commissary parking lot.

Suddenly, Benjamin felt himself wanting to leave. "This is wrong. I'm socializing." The contrast of juices that were running through him confused him and created discomfort. He was just a boy trying to be big. His emotional state was overloading and he didn't know what he felt or wanted. He was afraid. Afraid that he was feeling or would start feeling or wanted to start feeling like a male instead of a grandson, the family of the patient. "I came here to find out more about Gramps' condition with this woman who had secretly read his diary. Guilt struck. His mother, Jane, and grandmother were back at the hotel, in ragged pieces, like Jane's cuticles, unable to sleep, consumed by the sour taste of nervous stomachs, and now to complicate matters, uneasy too that Benjamin was out alone in a strange and big city. Jane's ulcer, in its infancy, would grow and worsen and for years she'd not be able to drink any alcoholic beverages, coffee, or tea or eat spicy foods, without consequences. Her weight wouldincrease and she'd use sugar substitutes in Morning Thunder or decaffeinated instant. Benjamin knew he wanted to kiss her, knew especially that he had the urge to try. To holdonto someone, something, warm and living. His saliva thickened and he thinned it with a sparkling swallow of Dutch beer. But his grandfather, Jacob, was alone and dangling, and there was some moral barrier there despite the humanness of the urge. Benjamin thought of the tricycle he'd seen outside — in New York it'd be gone in the morning — lifted and sold for parts — and then hated his mind for being so loosely constructed, flimsy, able and willing to dart like a bee from thought-bud to thought-bud, taking a little from each stamen yet faithful to none, for having not only the capacity for but being bound by necessity to wander without discipline from to from to from to from back to to and then off to from, thought, distraction, distraction, digression, and so on. He couldn't hone the activity of thinking to singularity, the way he had learned a mid-19th century American novel worked. One plot, one voice, one real reason for being. And then without thinking he closed his serious, brown eyes and readied his lips for hers. As much as he loved Jacob and was frightened by the thought of losing him, his mind moved on, responded to the stimuli around him and within him. He drank from the green bottle and tongued the rounded curved lip, amazed what a machine could do.

"Why'd you tell me about your grandfather before?"

"I don't know. Probably because I'd read personal things about yours and I thought it was fair that you should know something about me. To balance things off, I guess." Her shoulders rose and her upper lip tightened, gestures that corresponded with her earnestness. It was a good answer in any case, although she wasn't sure if it was the whole truth. "I guess I've been thinking about him since I started reading the, um," she didn't know what to call it.

"But you didn't have to," Benjamin replied, and just then noticed deeply just how young she wasn't; she could be one of several ages. It was like the eyes and mouth came from the early Sixties while the chin, cheeks, and nose hailed from the fifties. And the hands and toes from the reflected foreground of Velazquez's Maids of Honor (1656).

Amy wasn't used to talking about her past. She didn't relish finding words for feelings. Just let them live their own life down deep there inside her head. She hated talking too quickly, over-articulating after a movie. Or over-dissecting a book. It wasn't that she had no ideas; she just preferred thinking them than diluting or spoiling them with language. It was a mechanism for avoiding too, she knew herself at times but wasn't ready to dismantle.

"Did his sickness have to do with the war?" Benjamin asked, feeling safer now that the conversation took a sharp corner. He felt less scared, less feeble, more in control. He was getting more information, building his understanding. Now it was she that had to risk, to talk.

"Uh," she began to make a phrase with a sound while theimage of Jacob eating boiling soup with his hands splashed by. "Uh, I'd have to say yes," she said and then unfolded her legs and rose from her lower back without the use of her hands. Benjamin thought of a praying mantis. They were a protected species. There was a five dollar fine for capturing or killing one in New Jersey. She'd taken a yoga class once at the *Volkshochschule* in Frankfurt. That's where she learned to stand like that, breathe deep into the muscle. "I guess so, but he never talked about it. He'd just gestured with his hands as to say 'what's the point. Forget it. Maybe he was ashamed. Maybe it was too traumatic. He'd been hit in the head with shrapnel. Maybe that caused the blood clot. It certainly provoked the epileptic attacks." There was a pause. "Would you like another beer?"

Benjamin checked the sweating green bottle.

"Sure, if you're having one."

She entered the tight kitchen. A knife sharpener was screwed to the side of a cabinet. It had been there when she arrived. There was one like that in Harriet and Jacob's kitchen and their knives showed deep signs of being drawn fiercely against the stone edges. Silence, except for the hum of the refrigerator, the handle of the round-shouldered Frigidaire clicking open, the crumb-lined rubber stripping sealing the door shut again, and then the motor kicking on, sucking out the hot air.

She came back and placed the fresh beer before Benjamin, and handed him the opener. She hadn't taken one for herself. It had been a while since she'd served anyone anything other than medication. She sat down next to him this time, Benjamin was intensely aware. "Did she know Jacob was going to die and felt sorry?" he wondered.

Benjamin felt the pressure to respond, although he wanted to run, to center the heat of his presence. He'd read into this. She'd just wanted to sit closer; she was a helping person and what she didn't do with words she usually did with her silent energy. Benjamin felt his heart pounding, hating the irony, blood jetting through unblocked arteries, valves clapping — he'd seen this once on a sonogram screen — and thought of the excited hands of gospel singers. "Am I really going to do this?" He forced his eyes to meet hers at close range. There were dark spots around her iris like in the eyes of Persian cats; and there was an instant chemical understanding. Age fell away like backdrops in a theater.

Suddenly, she was mostly yes. And the only thing left to do in the world was to kiss. Even her understanding of this lost its footing. But there was no larger question in her mind. Ethics had no place here. Their mouths opened quickly and their tongues slid against each other like playful seals. Benjamin's eyes shut. He fought to stay with the briskness asshe became enmeshed in the good feeling. The tongues circled and dove, playful like dolphins, pulling away and jumping out to sea. Stress dropped into the tops of Benjamin's thighs. He stretched and then there seemed to be no room left inside his clothes. It was good to kiss, but both he and she felt, or knew, the feeling of sadness in the full wetness of the kiss. Just the two mouths were kissing, the people were spectators. The mouths were organs, oysters making pearls. Benjamin was scared to stop or slow down or back away. In a different situation he'd pull sweetly away to see the moist face of the one he was loving; now, here, he didn't want to give his eyes a chance to undo the haze of what he and the nurse were doing. He kept close where life was out of focus. It was important to his ego that he kept up with her, a proficiency that accompanied her history. Years of marriage were different than the few weeks Benjamin had spent with a senior with a less-than-cooperative roommate. He neither wanted to lag behind nor appear as overly eager as he was. She would turn him into a little boy. He surged ahead, exciting her, surprising her and himself. In the same thought he joined 'what am I doing here?' and 'This is nice.' He ran his right hand quite naturally over her left breast, feeling the nipple veiled tightly on the other side of the thin cotton.

She let him roam as he liked, as she liked. He was gentle although he thought he was being bold. Her former husband had been bold, pushing her head down into the pillow with both hands, as if to submerge a volleyball under water. She braced her hand against Benjamin's back, a gesture which seemed more serious to him than the kiss. She was holding him like a grown man. More adult than the time the El Salvadoran live-in, seduced away from her husband and her two *niños*, by an agency in New York that placed "industrious women from Central America with a sense of full service and domestic excellence in your home," pulled herself down on his bed, a Joe Namath poster grinning overhead, and stuffed his Spanish homework, exercises in the difference between *ser* and *estar*, into her worn bra cup, coaxing him to fetch it. She was 25, he was 13 and it was his first live breast.

He let his hand roam in deliberately expanding circles, cautious but determined, until it broke its pattern and pushed gently into the warm V where her legs joined. More than passion, what drove him was his desire to fulfill what he thought was expected of him. It was harmless; and it felt good, so she eased her muscles and sat way back to help him. Benjamin opened his eyes slowly. He wanted now to see her, to evaluate the look on her face, without letting her detect that he was checking. He pushed all other thoughts to the corners of his thinking. He slowed-up, hesitated, made nervous by her willingness. "Reach for the elastic?" He had already pushedevents further than he thought they'd ever go. He was more than ready to stop, edge away, smile, and reach for his beer. But she gave him free run; it was harmless, it felt nice, and it was good for him. "He is so tense," she thought, seeing the tightness around his closed eyes. When he caught her eyes open he was freed. "Had they been open all along?" he wondered. She smiled and rubbed his back. He smiled back and forced himself to maintain eye contact. They hugged each other, caught between mother and son, man and woman, strangers yet intimate. It was weird, but nice. Very private. He'd never tell anybody. He'd not know what it meant.

Over her shoulder Benjamin spotted the boy in the photos, Kevin, stalled in happiness, the colors vibrant as in the new commercials for Fuji. He thought of the tricycle outside. Outside. Houston. He was in Houston. His mother. Jacob. "I gotta go," he thought in a panic. And the moment was over. He wanted to leave, to climb into his bed and rock himself to sleep. They disengaged. Benjamin sat back, reached for his beer it was still cool and took a long slug. His lips ached a bit.

"I should get going," he suggested.

She didn't try to dissuade him. She knew it was better. The taste of temptation had been nice though.

"I'll drive you back," she offered, straightening her shirt. He removed a strand of hair that hung in front of her eye. She squeezed his hand. It was gestures like that that mattered, that you remembered forty years later, with grandchildren of your own.

"I can walk," he replied ridiculously. It was a good four miles back to the hotel.

"Really, I don't mine. C'mon." A slight foreignness was still caked onto her articulation of colloquialisms.

"Well...."

She'd already grabbed her keys. She would have liked sex, but....

In the street by her complex the full trees hung low and were cloaked in shadow. She fixed her seat belt. They sped off and made a quick right. Amy knew the way blindfolded; she had made the trip at every time of day and night. She knew which lights to steal and which ones to honor, where the cops were and where to gun the accelerator. The Cutlass made noise. It hesitated. Knocked a bit from that lousy cut-rate gas. Benjamin sat passively, slightly changed, slightly bowled over by the world. He watched the lights go from red to green, green to yellow, and back to red as he had watched her white hospital shoes move along the pavement. He left back there the tricycle. Piles of Pearl beer cans were littering the highway at a stoplight where ugly little mounds of crushed butts had been dumped by irreverent motorists wholly ignorant of the great litter campaigns of former First Lady Lady Bird. Crazyhedonists were zooming by, hanging out of car windows, hollering, passing joints, blaring The Doobie Brothers. The American joyride after dark. Nine out of ten of these creatures would be given high school diplomas thinking, light was spelled lite.

The Hilton sign soon came into view. There was so much he hadn't asked, so much she would have liked to have known. They both heard the sounds of the gears shift automatically inside the engine, and saw the advance green arrow, the Winn-Dixie and the Spur Station.

"Tell me," he finally asked, as the car pulled into the circular drive of the hotel, "is he...," he hesitated, superstitious and afraid to finish the question. She shook her head minutely before Benjamin had a chance. He let himself out of the car by the revolving doors and the sad run of artificial grass. Inside his chest there was a lump as large as a softball. He shut the car door without slamming it, avoiding unknowingly that pet peeve of hers.

She drove off wondering if she'd see him again and returned the same way, instinctually avoiding the interstate, which to the east, of course, led to Beaumont. She couldn't deal with that thought just then.

The hotel lobby was brighter than Benjamin would have liked. The absence of human voices permitted the rigged-up sounds of electronic games and computer talk to spill out from a side arcade by the cocktail lounge, a dark place with leather bar stools, The Nautilus. Even the Hilton had capitulated and installed those horrid machines. They had to keep up with the demands of the times, private entertainment, HBO movies, an aging Ms. Pacman in the lounge, in-room mini-bars and shoe shine machines. Several Shriners with their drinks with swizzle sticks balanced on the top of Space Invaders, *oowed* and *ahhed* as bits of light, darting images of self, were eating and conquering and being eaten and conquered by more aggressive shards of composed light. The enemy, forever some generic sort of Russians, were thinly disguised and unnamed although still red and angular. And the winners reached the sequined, white honey with unnaturally full and suck-ready lips. To destroy or to possess, the late-century electronic American cream dream. Both consequences were reduced and spoon-fed to the helmsman with a buck to blow and an hour to kill. Antony and a paper maché model of the Sphinx passed by. A frozen daiquiri with a lime-green collapsible umbrella toothpick rode in the Sphinx's gloved hand. It was easier like this.

Benjamin boarded the elevator in a particularly cynical mood. The doors eased shut. He was alone this time. The last apparition had been a foreshadow. He stood face to face with another panel of buttons. Buttons everywhere. He closed hiseyes and pretended to be blind and jammed his finger into the panel hitting the one that meant his floor as if the history of the world depended on it, wondering how any human being could ever deal with the power of that decision. Like that, he wiped out Pittsburgh. Then Lvov. Osaka. Krakow. And finally Houston. Invisible to the consequences, loving your grandchildren but not seeing the enemy as having the right to them too.

"It's only an elevator," he muttered as his guts rose quickly up that shaft of vertical non-space. The smell of Amy fresh on his mind. Would he see her again? Up he went, his weight sucked out of his feet. Jacob's life ended then. A trillion heart beats and then the last one. A countable number in the end. And then anything that was, was no more. And they changed the sheets and tallied the final bill. And those that knew you began to adjust.

No argument.

18

The phone call came in the early morning. It had happened in the night.

Jane's face changed, went distorted, filled-up with pain, took on years. The words jolted her like what a surge of electricity did to loved ones at an execution. It was all in her cheeks and eyes.

Harriet's face crumbled. A building demolished yet caught in that one last second before the mass crashed to rubble, held there for an instant by nothing. She became an infant again, stuck for a long moment in a silent, breathless cry, suffocating, deprived of air and the ability to comprehend. Then her voice went squeaky and she began to whimper, miserably. The tank that contained belief for her burst, and her body and mind were drowning in one uncontrollable fact. She rubbed her face, scratching with the heavy gold links of her watchband the spotted-apricot skin of her cheek.

Benjamin watched his mother and grandmother make sounds in each others arms, and felt anger and sadness crest inside himself, yet tears hadn't yet come. Ninety thoughts stormed to the front of his thinking, canceling themselves from becoming valid speech by the overriding censor: the thought that it didn't matter. Nothing mattered. No thought was stronger than the fact. The present tense had no power in the past, and Jacob's life was already in the past. "Our tenses change and we lose our reflexive verbs; the first person, singular and plural, abandons our persona. I don't feel a thing; there was so much to feel," he babbled silently his defense.

And then he didn't want to but couldn't help it and he cried fiercely, without restraint and his face musclestightened and began to ache and the taste of his tear-water spread into his nose and everything was mixing up and...

Jane pulled Benjamin into the embrace. The three of them formed a huddle of tears in the carpeted space between the two Hilton beds. An anthropologist from another world would have found the scene strange and phenomenal. Perhaps there was a short article there, a cultural footnote on grief in the homo-sapien.

The way Jane held Benjamin awakened something in him. A shift was already happening; Jane could no longer look to her father for anything. She could no longer look back for support, look to his invincibility for her own survival. Although it had been thirty years since he'd stopped saving her, in her mind, he hadn't stopped. He was always there hiding her from the relapse of isolation. Now, he had finally died — not in Auschwitz or Plaszow or the *Kablewerks*, not in hiding in Sara Zollman's attic or in the broilers of Teresenstadt, not while fleeing from Niepolemice or while huddled in the urine-soaked boxcars in the winter of 1943 or from the maddening grief of living through the torture and demise of his wife and mother and father and brothers and cousins and best friends, not even from the Lugar bullet of an Ukrainian prison guard which had smashed his cheekbone and stayed there lodged in his head until 1947 when it was finally extracted in Elizabeth General Hospital, where his grandson would be born nine years later. It was a $27,000 heart operation and seventeen days in a Disney-like showcase of modern medicine that finally did the trick. The American Dream was complete with the right to an expensive death. In the grasp that Jane's hands had on Benjamin, the transference of emotional dependence from father to daughter, mother to son was already taking place. Benjamin felt the intensity of his own importance in the hold his mother had on him, relieved that at his age, such maternal presence couldn't make him gay. "You're all I got, it's up to you." What did she mean anyway? The heaviness of the responsibility began to bear down on him like his shoulders were squared off beneath a massive bale of hay meant for a pack animal. "I know, mom, I know."

There was a loud, but cautious rap at the door. And just then a loud, Black, and southern voice intruded.

"Maaaid." Benjamin had hung the plastic sign on the doorknob with the wrong side showing. Instead of PLEASE DO NOT DISTURB, the plastic card showed in both English and Spanish PLEASE MAKE-UP MY ROOM.

Benjamin's strange face at the door was enough to send the maid away. She kind of cowered away, the way a dog backs away from a corpse.

"Not now, thank you."

"No madda to me, chil'," she chuckled. "Deres a ho flawhea ta do." A chariot-full of sheets, towels, bars of herbal scented soap, toilet seat wrappers, Hilton matches, and plastic garbage bags housing the corporate logo waited like an indifferent goat by its round shepherdess. She was thinking already of lunch, pressed turkey slices, mashed potato buds, buttered corn, pre-sweetened Salada iced tea, and an Almond Joy from the machine in the employee lunch room.

The door shut.

Silence and whimpering. At what point could one begin to think of oneself again and the progression of the day, the next step forward, and without being clobbered with guilt. At what point did one have to break from the realm of suspension, of emotional rafting, and rejoin the previously-scheduled world already-in-progress? Let the maid make the beds, call the family with the news, put deodorant on. There were funeral plans to make. To be civilized meant burying your dead. Were there enough folding chairs in the hall closet?

"Why why why why whyyyyy whyyyyyyy WHY'D he have to die?" Harriet began to repeat, rocking slowly in her heavy shoes. "He was such a ..." Emotion choked off her words. Why? Benjamin watched, consumed by general lousiness and sadness and wishing that Harriet would grieve more privately. "Let her be," he scolded himself with interior talk. "Don't judge." But he judged.

Jane got the hotel operator, a male, by dialing 9, and placed a collect call to her husband. He was shocked, having refused to believe that the situation had really been so grave. Benjamin listened to his voice seeping out of the faded Southern Bell ear piece.

"Why couldn't it have been my father?" the voice said. It was a strange remark, that one. Benjamin couldn't imagine making it himself. He thought of the story he wrote in Arby's. He was sorry he threw it out. He wanted to re-read it.

Jane spoke in a matter-of-fact tone, compensating in excess for the inundation of terror and anger that gathered at the base of her throat and everywhere else in her body. Chemicals were acting chaotically, like a perturbed sea before a tidal wave. Messengers from the brain were running into each other. She held everything down with a tone that came across oddly flippant, an impervious defense mechanism whose sound, not words, communicated "I knew it all along. The world is unfair." If she had let her voice carry the full weight of her feeling, she would have broken into incommunicative pieces.

"Yeah, yeah," she added in monotone, "later when we know when we're coming. Call..." and she muttered the few names of those it was imperative to tell in the first round. And thus the circuit of action that followed death began. There was protocol and ritual to respect. The bank and the safe deposit box would be high on the list. That dark, humorous half-truth that his parents quipped as they left for the airport onvacations, "If we go down, clear out the safe deposit box first; you can cry later," echoed in Benjamin's head — "Jews were so practical about these things — " then thought of Harriet's cousin who had made off with a Shop-Rite bag of Uncle Leo's best silk ties and leather belts two hours after Leo'd been lowered into that fine New Jersey earth, cufflinks and tie tacks discretely loaded into his pockets, a box of shoes waiting at the door. Harriet would have to get directory assistance, (201) 555-1212, for the number of Menorah Chapels in Millburn, "One of the Largest Jewish Funeral Chapels", rudolph h. kindel, mgr., all small letters on his stationery head. That showed style. Rudolph himself would say over the phone, "Mrs. Simon, you know how we work; you don't have to worry about a thing. Now, I just need a few pieces of information from you and then you can leave everything to me." Three weeks later the bill would come: $695 for arrangement, supervision and conduct of funeral, Out-of-State professional services (Texas) an extra $545. Removal from Newark Airport $150, Hearse $210, Airline: Delta from Houston to Newark $399.21, Merchandise: Orthodox Pine Casket $205, CMAS Airtray $150, Newspaper notices, *Star-Ledger* and *News Tribune* and fifteen Death Certificates $176.70. Total $2530.91.

Jacob had left at the rear of his filing cabinet, a numbered list in a brown file folder marked and underlined, THINGS TO DO AFTER I'M GONE. Some twenty items he had listed, including point six, *"Cancel my subscription to the Jewish News,"* and point eleven: *"Send contribution to the Salvation Army Fund Drive."* Jacob gave annually since Lieutenant Barosz in Paris had assisted the passage on the Marine Falcon. Jacob hadn't forgotten. Point fifteen: *"Add date and then send attached letter to the West German Bezirksamt fuer Wiedergutmachung."* And the brief note simply referred to Jacob in the third person announcing his death. The 821DM monthly payment that the Bonn government issued against damages inflicted by the Third Reich, Jacob was entitled to receive until the end of his life. Twenty eight days after his death, Harriet sent Jacob's letter along with a brief note of her own addressed to the Deutsche Bundesbank in Frankfurt. "Gentlemen: I am returning the enclosed check for $443.12 which is made out to Jacob Simon. Mr. Simon died October 1 of this year. Very truly yours. Mrs. Harriet Simon. She'd even paid for registering the letter and requested a return receipt. In his file, Jacob had listed one after another each payment he had received. Over the years, he continued spelling December with a z. Point sixteen stated: *"Take car in to the Chevy Dealer in Madison for 20,000 mile servicing (or 30,000 if the case may be).* Point 22, and his final point, was: *"Give Benjamin my diary."*

"We have so much to do. What are we going to do?" Janesaid into the air. Harriet, although devastated with chagrin, knew what to do. She had buried her parents: Papa Benjamin Neiman in the Benjamin Neiman Plot, the family plot which had a potential of 21 grave sites in Mount Lebanon Cemetery, Box 135 Iselin, New Jersey, along with her mother Rebecca Neiman and her brothers Morris Neiman and Chas. Neiman and brother-in-law Leo

Steinberg. Now she knew where Jacob would soon lay and where she'd be taken one day too. This was comforting.

There was a very thick folder which she kept back home in Jacob's desk file, maybe a hundred pieces of correspondence from Mount Lebanon, a stack of Care Order forms, each marked in bold type at the bottom NO GRAVE CARE WILL BE GIVEN UNTIL PAYMENT IS RECEIVED. Each one having a box checked off for the eight dollar seasonal fee for Flush Sodded Graves as opposed to the planted grave (no replacement) option, and the hefty $250 Endowed Care Fee for Flush Sodded Graves. And she had a letter that informed her that the annual assessment of $315 did not include individual grass cutting and trimming of plots or graves; "We do cut the grass wherever it is feasible to come in with a large machine; however, where we have to hand trim or use hand mowers, we must make an annual charge." Signed Laurence G. Selinger, President. And a wad of the updated computerized Care Plan Forms with the embossed tacky logo of leafy trees and squarish monuments. A big message was printed out over the top of each: PLEASE NOTE: PLAN "A" PROTECTS YOU FROM INEVITABLE FUTURE PRICE INCREASES, AND ELIMINATES THE POSSIBILITY THAT THE GRAVE MAY SOMEDAY BE NEGLECTED. Plan "A" cost $350 and included cleaning and maintenance eight times throughout each growing season. With this plan no further payments would ever be necessary. Otherwise, it was $22 a year, subject to annual increases, and somewhere down the line someone might forget to pay and those dearly departed loved ones will be left in perpetual landscaping disgrace and abandonment. Plants were guaranteed for one year from date of planting unless permanent care was arranged. And on the contract from Jaffe Memorials — "Your Guarantee of Satisfaction" — on Grove Street in Newark read across the top: MANUFAC-

TURERS AND DISTRIBUTORS OF GRANITES FROM ALL QUARRIES. With the following disclaimer printed in small letters: Jaffe Memorials shall hold complete title to the complete goods herein mentioned until the full amount is paid. If for any reason, full amount has not been paid before erection, Jaffe Memorials are authorized to remove the goods from the Cemetery without any claim for damages by the Customer and the expense of said removal is to be paid by Customer. Performance of this contract is contingent on strikes, fires, accidents, and other causes beyond our control. Included was a personal note by Mrs. Lloyd Koch assuring Harriet that the stone would be sandblasted in printto match the other family stones and that the Hebrew name and the Star of David would be added and billed as per Harriet's request.

Harriet knew what to do as she whimpered in disbelief. Jacob would gain equal status with her parents and siblings. He had known about these plans for years and was wholly unphased. "I don't care where they put me as long as they loosen my belt and put in a bottle of seltzer water," he'd joke. "Whatever is easiest," was his only request. And the list in the file. Easy and orderly. He had come to like order more than anything, the calm of organization, the sanity of predictability. His desk reflected this. Paper clips and staples and postage stamps neatly segregated in compartments of his desk divider. The rubber bands never got mixed in with the thumb tacks. All the shoes in the house he had perpetually kept polished and lined up in the closet on old copies of the *Star-Ledger*, where his picture and death notice would appear two days after the funeral. The toaster he kept free of crumbs. The pencils on the old manual Singer sewing machine that had belonged to Rebecca Neiman and resembled the model that Emmanuel Simon had stocked in the store in Nowy Targ, were always sharp and there was never a shortage of scrap paper by the telephone. Every important telephone number was clearly written and updated on a card taped to the wall. Even poison control and the Decamp Bus Company Information Line. He sent birthday cards that arrived on the exact date if not a day early.

"He deserved to die in his sleep."

"Oh, Benj," Jane replied.

It wasn't just the dying now, it was the way that hurt so much, the cruel irony of having zig-zagged across a minefield of enemies and horrors and then having reached safety on the far side, being killed by the allies, "friendly fire," they called it. Benjamin sat still now, drumming his fingers in the clean glass ashtray of the hotel. Jane dressed quickly, not caring what she looked like, or caring slightly, but too embarrassed to recognize it. She stuffed the rest of her clothes into the Val Pack that hung on the back of the closet door. Harriet slowly worked on folding a silk blouse, centering her whole existence for a moment on each crease. Then she let the whole thing fall and whinnied like a colt or a seven year old who'd been slapped for crossing the road without permission. For Harriet there was only extremes: breakdown or block-out. There was no middle ground. Massive fantasy and fabricated half-truths or fatal doses of masochistic realism. No moderation. Her existence had been dependent on Jacob's need for order, passive but real, and she wielded it as a profession. She ran the carnival, insisted, stipulated, bossed, set down the rules, read the riot act, andhe followed, perverse and happy as a light-security inmate. His need to be controlled dove-tailed with hers to be depended on. His need to operate in a totally predictable and orderly universe synchronized with her need to impose one. Now, in the first minutes of the new order a wave of emotional chaos, far beyond Harriet's ability to conceive it, rushed over everything. She'd know how to bury him, how to continue up to there, but the thought of the afterlife, hers, was already haunting. The lie that she had hid from hadn't gone away, hadn't dried up over the years and croaked; it was out now and searching for a way to hide again. Unable to live without supervision, her needs were now going somehow un-met. "Mother had died, Papa had died, Jane had married, and now Jacob was gone." She would dwindle before long into that horrible drain of Alzheime's and leave this world babbling and disconnected, finding her place ultimately once again beside Jacob.

Benjamin picked up the fallen blouse and placed it on her suitcase. The baggage tickets attached to the handle saddened him. Pan Am to Sydney. The SS Shalom. Eastern to Arizona. Exodus, migration, inquisition. The room became a cage suddenly; there was nowhere left to go. He couldn't know if they were now in a hurry to get out or if time now didn't matter. What do you do when a loved one dies? Just stop and sit and talk? Harriet had kilowatts of nervous energy to generate, could have powered a food processor from chop to purée if there was a way to hook up an individual to an appliance. Jane moved in surges like the current of a small developing country, pouring overloads into the light bulbs and then stalling-out the tired refrigerators.

Finally, they went downstairs — Who has the key? — where many Shriners were up and ready. Their hats in place. Today was the day they were to visit the Houston Space Center, a source of national pride despite the wave of accidents and setbacks that had rocked Americans' confidence in Yankee technology. And tonight they'd be off to see Tony Orlando at the Civic Center. Tomorrow it was a Seminar on Motivation with Guest Speaker Evil Kanevil and a video hook-up with Steven Jobs. On the last day they'd induct forty Cambodian boat people into the brotherhood. The country was changing.

244

Harriet insisted on the shuttle bus. These small in-
stances of capriciousness were Harriet's way of maintaining a sense of identity. Benjamin wanted to walk but didn't
mention it other than making a face to his mother.

"Let her get her way," she whispered. "It doesn't
matter."

Their feet carried them automatically to the ICU
Waiting Room. The place suddenly lacked all sense. There
was no more waiting, no more hope, the game was over,
the bleachers emptying. There was Cavenaugh's nurse in
the corridor, they saw. They approached the woman, ignorant of the steel pin inher left hip and the loss of her son,
Marion, in the Tet Offensive, the letter signed by Johnson
hanging in her husband's trophy room. The woman asked
solemnly if she could speak to Mrs. Simon alone. Jane
wanted to protest but squashed it like all the rest of her
anger. She took Benjamin's arm and walked with him into
the bright and sterile chamber of molded plastic seats. Fanny
was already there, her hair pulled back, her make-up fresh,
her deodorant fighting and winning. "It was a new day;
God loves you," written all over her face. One look at Jane
and she knew; the pillions that held her spirit so high played
emotional alchemy, transformed to rubber and brought
down the entire administration of her world.

Harriet returned. She had consented to an autopsy,
scrawled her hysterical chicken scratch on a line on the
bottom of a page on a clipboard. "Don't touch the head,"
she had insisted, and they made a notation on the work
order. She had known to say that; it was family policy. You
don't defile the face. It was a fetish. She wasn't selfish and
earnestly believed in helping modern science but, stood
unbending here, "leave the head alone." She'd done some
real living of her own, and was no dope. Jane would have
never thought of mentioning the head, would have probably just said no to an autopsy. They'd cut into her father

enough already, seventeen days of hell. "Nazis," she'd think of them. "Bastards." She thought that but would have never ever shown such unjustified rage. Later, a psycho-therapist would postulate a theory about Jane's perverse search for renewed Nazi domination. For Harriet the autopsy was for the public good and the system needed such cooperation. She was a defender of the system, the moral fiber of the country, it was a good country, and it stood for good and right principles. The adage "What's good for General Motors is right for me," fit her to the T. Jane was less trusting, less American at heart, although appreciative of this country that had let her in, given her a new start, but less generous toward the whole. Her principles would start leaning a bit when she got pissed off at something, a bad crime, an unjust law, some outlandish foreign policy move, and might suddenly be in favor of capital punishment. For her, autopsies were butcheries; real damage could no longer be done. They sawed briskly. They knew by habit how the parts fit together and came apart, most of the time. But they didn't have to put everything back quite the same way in which they found it. The organs, they could shove into the cavity, like the way turkey giblets came bagged in frozen Butterballs each November.

The head would be untouched, but the stitches in the aorta would be examined. As would the mitral valve and the three by-passes. They'd be determined to be in A-1 order. Passed inspection. The copy of the autopsy came three days later along with a condolence note from Dr. Cavenaugh and acopy of his report to the attending physician at the Cora and Webb Mading Department of Surgery.

Provisional Anatomic Diagnoses
from Dept. of Pathology:

Primary: Atherosclerosis: of coronary arteries, grade 4 focal narrowing of left anterior descending and circumflex and grade 3 of right coronary artery; of aorta, grade 4 fibrous streaking with extensive ulceration. History of coronary artery bypass of LAD and obtuse marginal, 9-14, both grafts intact and patent; porcine mitral valve heterograft placement, 9-14, graft intact with small fibrinous thrombus adherent to atrial margin of valve annulus. Myocardial infarct, recent posterior transmural. Pulmonary thromboembolus, occluding right pulmonary artery. Bronchopneumonia, diffuse bilateral.

Accessory: Left ventricular hypertrophy, heart 780/322, left ventricle 20 mm. Nephrosclerosis, severe bilateral; right kidney 130 gm, left 120 gm. Renal retention cysts, multiple bilateral, to 1.8 cm.

The letter began:

Dear Mrs. Simon,

This note is to again express my sorrow in the loss of your fine husband. I would like to again assure you that his life was extremely limited without surgery and that we did everything we could to bring him through. He almost made it, being the fine fighter he was, but unfortunately both his diseases and his operation was just too much. Although this did not save him, I think it is better that we lose trying rather than to neglect a loved one. He was certainly aware of the problem, the risk involved and this is the route that he wanted to take.

The calls were all made to those who'd take over. That was their job. The family was now free to mourn in peace. Hank and Lily would be waiting again for the arrival of Jacob and his daughter, this time in a late model car with cruise control. In a back room in North Jersey Jacob would be wrapped-up in white cloth and arranged in the Orthodox pine box. He'd take nothing with him, no loosened belt and not a drop of seltzer. Not a good suit or pocket watch, Bible, family portrait, momento, ring. He'd just go down into the soon-to-be sod-lipped grave alone like so many before. The Jewish way. At least he had made it to a proper burial and for all intents and purposes everyone assumed that the stone would never be overturned nor the Hebrew letters rubbed out. If that wasn't true, it'd be others who'd have to worry about it. At least now there'd be peace. In any case, the Rabbi, in his London Fog, got fifty bucks for saying so. And Menorah Chapels at Millburn, Mount Lebanon, and Jaffe Memorials had all done their parts. It was all quite normal.

19

"You poor thing, Dzidzia," Fanny whispered to Jane. Jane cried torrentially but her output of tears was blocked somewhere as she squeezed Fanny's arms and back finding for the first time in this strange embrace with a Texas Christian housewife her long perished mother. Two and a half weeks earlier they'd been total strangers. Now she was her closest soul on earth.

"Faith child, have faith. He surely has a place in Heaven, a better place than this. He loved and was loved and that's what counts in the end."

Oh how Jane wanted to believe what Fanny was saying. At the end, it's only religion that matters. She inhaled the eggy freshness of Fanny's cream rinse. She'd shampooed nightly. Her arms felt strong and Jane pushed against the thick strands of muscle that were necessary for potting geraniums and hosing-down the driveway and lifting the waffle iron. Fanny knew that her own eye-make-up was smudging but she didn't care. "I can do my face again," she cried. She was a saint.

"I love you," Jane said, surprising herself. "You're so giving."

Benjamin looked on. He panned the faces that sat there in those chairs waiting with hope. The innocence, the belief,shoes tied, thermoses of iced coffee, knitting, things for the winter in Eire and Green Bay and Bogota and Oman, the weekly magazines, *People*, *Time*, *Money*. Icons for belief in the world as it was. He thought of his nurse friend. He didn't even know her full name. Barriers had been broken without the process of breaking them.

"And Bobby?" Jane asked.

"The same." She was embarrassed to mention his improvement in light of Jane's bad news. With her voice she guarded his condition as critical as possible. Sympathy came naturally to her. There was nothing to muster? She would have given up her entire, sacred knitting bag without a flinch, complete with the new cardigan she'd been slaving over for Bobby, or anything else she possessed, if she'd thought it would have brought a petal of consolation to Jane or Harriet. She knew better. She placed a fresh, rose hankie in Jane's clenched fist. And would never ask for it back. Jane would launder and iron it and stick it in a padded envelop with a short but sweet note on fine mauve writing paper and then not be able to find Fanny's address for more than three months before dropping it off at the post office.

At two she'd see her man Bobby and he'd beg for a cigarette, a drag even, and she'd hate herself for having to refuse. She wouldn't tell him about Jacob. No negative news for her Superstar. He was antsy and blue enough, foolishly denying that he was even sick. "What are they keeping me here for anyway?" She spritzed into her wide and lovely, lipstick-graced mouth a dose of Binaca. There was no need teasing him with the trace of tobacco on her breath.

"We'll be leaving in a day or so, Fanny, just as soon as the arrangements are all made. I have to get your address and I want to give you ours."

"Sure, child, and you reach out and pick up that little phone and call Fanny now and then, you hear." She referred to herself in the third person to add emphasis and sincerity.

"I will." But she never did. The bond was real here but with time and the shift of circumstances what one would actually do was kind of unpredictable.

"You too, Harriet," she called over Jane's shoulder, not wanting Harriet to feel neglected, especially just now.

"Fanny, you're an angel," she said, air whistling gently through the gap in her bottom teeth, not knowing just how much hearing that meant to Fanny. An angel.

"Never mind that, you call Fanny anytime your little heart desires, day or night." The word made Benjamin cringe. No one caught it.

Doctor Cavenaugh's name was said over the paging system. He was still alive, walking around, and they couldn't think of him as a friend anymore. He'd already cut into thirty some oddhearts since he'd touched Jacob's. Jacob's hadn't worked out but a lot of others had. That's how he kept going, working on the big picture. And he had won some major awards for his role. The taxi drivers all knew.

They parted and Jane's walk took on the rounded posture that her entire adolescent upbringing had battled against. All those scoldings, those inane sessions in the living room with Harriet and the Newark City Yellowpages balanced on her head had suddenly amounted to nothing. She was turning her back to all that, rebelling like a teenager, to the city, the day, the past, her parents, the facts, the 20th Century. She was an orphan.

She wanted to see the doctor, to make him explain. She told herself that she'd hear him out first. She'd not make his life any easier though. He'd earn his late-evening Manhattan. He'd say that the heart held-up; the liver and kidneys didn't, as if the battles were detached. Liver and

251

kidneys weren't his thing. That was Fraser, who, off until the next day at noon, had jetted down to the Caymans for a day of diving. Usually, the liver and kidneys just went back to work on their own. That Jacob's had been worn-out and tired to start with, chemically over-shocked, enzymes weakened, no one in Houston knew or thought to ask about. So that was why Jacob was always looking for the men's room, and kept fresh tap water in an Acme juice bottle in the fridge, why he needed fresh water running through him all day, everyday. Like a radiator in an otherwise decent automobile whose antifreeze had lost its force.

They walked towards the central lobby. They'd never return. Menorah had made the reservations with Delta. They'd be at the airport, hadn't missed a stiff yet. They'd made pick ups at all three New York Metropolitan airports, even the Wall Street Heliport, Teeterboro Commuter Port, and Grand Central Station. Once had a customer rail in on the Amtrak Montrealer from Plattsburgh. The older Hearse, not the new one that they paste waxed for the funeral itself, but the dented one that was too shabby and not good for attracting new clients, they'd send, unmarked, burning diesel across the Pulasky Skyway, over the Jersey swampland and dump sites, in the nasty traffic that coughed through the stagnant meadows at high speeds along the turnpike. They'd get there in the nick of time to meet that Delta flight, pull up on the tarmac and snag their boy.

Benjamin wondered if he was weird or sick or something to imagine the body in the cargo hold. Would there be a baggage ticket on the coffin? Were cadavers even sent in coffins? Did the hospital have a stock of them? How did the airlines ticket the dead? No smoking section, of course. Pushed up against the oversized bicycle cartons and ski bags and the airline approved cages for dogs? He felt ashamed, but he couldn't help it, it just came to mind. With Jacob lying flat in the belly of a Boeing wide body, streaming across the lowlands of the American South and then over Appalachia and the Poconos and the Borscht Belt of the Catskills and then onward into the dense gray maze of the carcinogenic Northeast and then down into the Garden State. Two guys with the old Hearse were parked with the service vehicle ready to chauffeur the cargo back to the Home on Rahway Avenue (next to the Shell station which used to be a City Service Station and now was used on Sundays for extra parking) and across from the VFW Lodge and the famous Pescador Restaurant, the one who'd serve booze to minors as long as they ate something, the one with the best Take-Out spinach lasagna between Rahway and the Holland Tunnel.

Three of them rode the elevator for the last time and crossed over to the private ward where they'd pick up the remains of Jacob's room. There were more cards that had piled up on the night table. Eventually, Harriet would answer them all. People had been nice enough to take the time to write. It was her civil obligation to reply correctly. The local lodge of the B'nai Brith had sent a group card signed by the Acting Secretary, Mel Himmelfarb. Jacob had held Mel's job, an orthodontist with a Lincoln Continental that had an oil leak, himself for eight years. When Jacob retired the Lodge awarded him a plaque, a gold-filled pin, and a ceremonial dinner. The guys in the hardware department of Channel Lumber, where Jacob worked part-time so not to go batty in his retirement, sent a Get Well Card from the Housewear Department. So did Harriet's cleaning girl, a 30 year old Portuguese immigrant from East Orange whose child had a learning disability and a very kind nature. Her card was the expensive Hallmark kind with a plastic cover and she closed the envelop with Easter Seals.

"I don't know if I want to see my nurse," Benjamin thought with a bit of nervousness as they approached Jacob's room. "Why not? That's silly," he reconsidered. And he braced himself for the eventuality.

She wasn't there. She wouldn't get on again until eleven that night. She knew already. And had left a brief but sweet letter and her address for Benjamin.

The diary was neatly in its place. So was the watch. They didn't steal in this hospital. In others they even took your overcoat while you were dreaming of the pilgrimage to heaven. The watch had stopped of course, days, weeks, earlier. Seventeen past two and twenty five seconds. AM or PM? No way of knowing. The time of his death, precisely, perhaps, symbolically in any case. A man's watch stops when the man does, Benjamin thought. A broken clock is right twice a day, someone should write a novel called that someday. "I'd read it."

As Jane prepared Jacob's modest suitcase, Benjamin reread the first page out loud. Tears rolled down her cheeks now asshe folded his pajamas into the bag. Harriet didn't even want to try; she waited in the corridor, reading the numbers on the door to keep busy.

I was born on October 26, 1904 in a small town near Zakopane in a beautiful valley named Podhale in the Tatra Mountains. My father Emmanuel and my mother Helena had a country store established by my grandfather Solomon in a village between Nowy Targ and Zakopane named Poronin.

My first years while attending school in Nowy Targ I lived with my Grandmother, who had a restaurant and a saloon. On the corner next to the saloon there was always an old lady selling fruit. When I stopped by on the way to school she'd give me a pear or an apple. Once she refused to give me anything so I pulled down one of her baskets of plums, turned it over in the middle of the street and stomped on the plums with my feet. I ran away. When I came back

from school my grandfather reprimanded me, but my grand-
mother protected me. I said I didn't do it, but they saw the
purple juice that had stained my shoes.

That was enough. Jane was almost finished. "He had
started with his own grandfather," Benjamin acknowledged.
And Jane thought just then that she'd go back; she'd return
to the place of her birth and find out for herself. She'd go
to hate and bless and mourn and know. She'd find those
that saved her and cry for her mother. Benjamin flipped to
the end of the diary. Amy's envelop was stuck in the last
page with Benjamin's name on it. He took it and folded it
gently into his pocket. The diary then too went into the
valise. Jane wanted everything in tact, in one bag. She didn't
want any loose ends, nothing extraneous to distract her.
Benjamin would get the diary and the watch and a pair of
black dress shoes that sat at the base of the naphthalene-
protected garment bag, polished. That was about all that he
wanted. There were uncles and cousins who'd eat well after the funeral and would do Harriet a favor by taking away
his suits. You see, they get the overcoat in the end anyway.

The view from the window had changed. Primarily
because it was now day. The neon slept in the anonymity
of daylight and the ordering of space in the human perspective was grossly altered. The Interstate still cut across
the city, East-West, and the Hilton sign stood above everything to the right, although it no longer shouted for attention. Arby's was open already, selling pressed roast beef
and holsters of fries that'd been par-cooked and flash frozen in Nebraska. It was a wonderful world. How things
had changed.

They turned and left, double checking as if it were a
motel room, not bothering to gather up the *Times* and the
Houston Post that Jacob had read on his last conscious night.
The last news he had had of the world included a curious

255

item at the bottom corner of the page of the *Post*, "Tractor trailer jackknives in Henderson, North Carolina spilling two tons of frozen chicken fryer parts on State Highway 24. Motorists traveling in the eastbound lanes were reported as having stopped their vehicles and filling up their trunks with the bruised poultry before State Troopers arrived on the scene."

He was gone. Removed from life as unremarkably as a flattened hedge hog on a back road. Nothing more. Neither pain nor pleasure. Nor memory. Neither Poland nor New Jersey nor the sensation of a drop of water. Nothing registering anymore. Not even the thought of nothing. Not even irony. Just...

They left, without speaking, innocent as unborn children, with everything still left to be done in the world, burdened only by memory and the pain it would continue to inflict.

In the elevator, Benjamin read that *Opa* too had died in the night.